Immortal Dominion

Age of Awakening
Book Two

Lynda Haviland

Immortal Diva Press

REVIEWS

BOOKS BY LYNDA HAVILAND

Age of Awakening Series

Immortal Dynasty
Immortal Dominion

Hidden Coast Romances

Borrowed & Blue
Mistletoe & Magic
Unveiled

The Last Ringmaster

The Last Ringmaster: Kindred

This book is dedicated to the many creative divas
in my life who motivate and inspire me every day.

A special thanks to the remarkable and fearless
women of the Fiction Chicks.

PROLOGUE

Sweat dripped down the side of Jayden's face, and she shivered as the last brittle images of her nightmare shattered away.

Hallucinations. That's what her fancy Miami doctor called them. Whatever they were, she'd had them for four years — since Grandmother died.

Reaching under her pillow, Jayden felt for the pill she'd hidden there. She pinched it between her fingers and carried it to her bathroom. This one would suffer the same fate as all the others she managed to avoid taking. She didn't blame the doctors. They meant well. But she knew better. These little pills brought *more* yellow demon eyes from the shadows. Not fewer.

She watched it swirl round and round, before the toilet sucked it away with the water. *Far away.*

On her nightstand, two iced sugar cookies sat in a sandwich bag. Looking out her bedroom window, she found the driveway empty. Daddy was still out on his date.

Jayden smiled though. There was only one proper way to celebrate her eleventh birthday.

Quickly, she tucked the baggie into the pocket of her robe, pushed the window up, and crawled out. Perched on the narrow sill, she took a moment to enjoy the balmy ocean breeze fanning across her face.

A short dormer peaked above her window and

then angled to the main section of the roof. Turning toward the siding, Jayden grabbed a loose section of the soffit and pulled her weight off her feet. She curled her bare toes around the window frame and pushed up until she could feel the barrel tile. She gripped the curved clay with her fingers and released the frame with her toes.

Jayden hung in the air, with the concrete driveway two stories below her. She enjoyed the sensation until the edges of tile started to cut into the skin of her inner elbows.

She swung her right leg up and over the edge of the roof, anchoring her toes under one of the curved tiles. She hauled her body onto the roof and crawled to main section. At the junction of two peaks, she settled in for her party of one.

Two. Grandmother was here in memory.

Jayden slid the baggie out of her pocket and withdrew the cookies. In the moonlight, the shiny blue icing almost glowed. She'd picked the color because it matched the shade of Grandmother's eyes. Jayden missed those beautiful eyes, which saw only the good things. And she missed the arms which used to wrap around her with squeeze hugs.

A tear slid along the side of Jayden's nose and over the edge of her lips.

Why did you have to go and die, Grandmother? You promised you'd never leave me.

She'd been Jayden's only joy in a home too perfect, too cold, too lonely. Every afternoon was filled with Grandmother's special tea and fantastical stories about the things she used to dig up when she worked in Egypt. Tales of ancient gods and great battles.

Jayden couldn't remember the stories anymore,

but she would never forget Grandmother's eyes.

Bright lights flashed across her face, momentarily blinding her. At the end of the driveway, Daddy stepped out of the car and stared at her. She didn't need to see his face clearly to know that he was angry.

A tall dark-haired woman stepped out of the opposite side of the car. "What is she doing up there, Jared?"

Daddy ignored the woman and reached back in for his new cellular phone. Jayden knew he was calling that fancy doctor again.

"Jared, why did she climb onto the roof?"

This time, he answered, his voice rough with emotion. "Because she can. She climbs everything: appliances, walls, houses."

"Isn't she afraid?" The woman's voice pitched high in disbelief.

Fear was not a word in Jayden's vocabulary. It was the one lesson from her father she'd never forgotten. *Control your fear.*

"Hello? Yes, it's Jared Hamilton."

She listened as her father's words drifted up and surrounded her. *Crazy little girl. Fix her.* And then came the words that chilled every cell in her body.

"Meet me at the hospital. We're checking her in tonight."

Jayden looked up into the deep blue midnight sky and sent a prayer to her grandmother. The only one who ever understood. If Jayden could, she would climb all the way to heaven just to be with her.

CHAPTER ONE

20 years later...

The Great Pyramid of Egypt.

A slow smile of satisfaction spread as Jayden drew a line through the words with her blue Sharpie. Above it, she'd already crossed out eight other jump sites, from Angel Falls, Venezuela to the KL Tower in Kuala Lumpur. After tonight, only the massive Troll Wall in Norway remained on her BASE jumping bucket list. To capture this moment on video, she proudly held the wrinkled notecard within the beam of light from her helmet cam.

She shivered as a cold October wind whipped tiny pellets of sand against her cheeks. After tucking the list back into her waist bag, she surveyed the night sky. Clouds scudded inland and cast the plateau into shadows. Moonlight would have been helpful since the climb up the darkened southwest corner of the pyramid sheltered her from the lights of Cairo.

Jayden readjusted the angle of the video lens upward for a better view of the limestone blocks. Only halfway on her ascent of the ancient monument and her calf muscles already shook with exhaustion. She watched her scrawny but nimble Egyptian guide move quickly and expertly up the corner of the pyramid in little more than a dusty robe and sandals. *I admit it. I'm slightly jealous.*

Her foot slipped on the next block, scraping her shin across the edge. Her skin burned, and even in the dark she could see a smear of blood, which dripped slowly down toward her own expensive climbing shoes.

Determined to act like a professional, she cinched the harness of her backpack a little tighter so its weight wouldn't throw her off balance. She'd climbed with packs before, but the custom designed wingsuit inside this one sat a little heavier on her back than she was used to.

Her guide had offered to help carry her pack, but she always carried her own gear. That was a rule she'd never break. However, she did give him enough *baksheesh* to bribe the guards into ignoring their illegal climb. She knew he'd kept a little extra for himself, and she had plenty more to help buy her way out of an arrest if the police caught her at the landing site.

Her cell phone vibrated against her hip. Pausing between steps, she ripped open the Velcro strapping which held it to her belt. As it buzzed again, the blue light of the digital screen gave a celestial glow to the limestone. She clicked to open the text message.

If you are done trying to kill yourself...come home. I found a new doctor with a new experimental treatment.

"So nice to hear from you, Daddy." Her sarcasm whisked away with the cold midnight wind. There was always another diagnosis, another drug — another *experimental* treatment. None of which would ever have a prayer of success as far as she was concerned. Nothing ever had.

Her father held a very different opinion on the matter. At least with texting Jayden wouldn't have to listen to a long lecture on how she should be taking her disease seriously.

Dusty prints blurred the screen as her fingers tapped a two-letter reply.

No.

There was no need to include an explanation. The great J. Jared Hamilton didn't do explanations. In his world, only solutions mattered, and Jayden was the perpetual problem he could never seem to solve.

She slapped the Velcro shut, but the cell phone buzzed again with the arrival of a new message. She almost ignored it, but curiosity won out.

Consultation scheduled for Tuesday. Don't show and I'll personally Baker Act you!

She jammed the phone back into its holder. So, she had five days to get back to Miami. Five days until her father was going to have her declared mentally ill and forced into another facility for treatment. He'd twist all of her recent accomplishments as proof of self-destructive behavior.

Damn it! She wasn't dying yet, but she might as well be. At the rate her neurons were wigging out, there'd soon be no more joy left in life. That's why she'd recorded every moment of her bucket list on video. Every climb. Every jump. She'd wanted visual memories to help her endure her future — when her body would fail to obey her.

But this was not a night to waste with pity. It was time to experience the very essence of life and freedom. Maybe she *was* a little bit suicidal. *They can play the video at my funeral.*

Nervous excitement shivered through every muscle and she savored every second of the feeling.

"Yalla, yalla! Shurta!" The guide had come back down a few steps, gesturing up and then down.

"Come! Police!"

A glance back down turned out to be a bad idea. Even in the darkness, the vertigo it caused made her grab the ancient stone for support. Egyptian police pulled into the Giza complex by the vanload. Tiny uniformed men waved guns and flashlights. She wondered if Egypt had a women-only prison.

"You're right. I'll hurry it up," she nodded in agreement. Far below, men scrambled up the same corner. Excitement spread like a wave through her mind, and Jayden smiled. The chase was on.

She re-tightened the straps of her fingerless leather gloves and launched herself upward. She ignored the sharp stone edges that slashed at her fingertips and the dust that jammed underneath her nails.

As Jayden arrived at the top of the pyramid, she found the platform to be about the size of the patio behind her condo. The lights of Cairo spread in a hazy glow off to the east, interrupted in the distance by a dark swath that could only be the Nile. She had a good twenty-minute lead on the police. While there was no time to enjoy the view, there was time for one important ceremony. She dropped her gear, removed her gloves, and withdrew a small red pouch from her waist bag.

She let her fingers trail across the smooth silky fabric. As she forced the bag open, the thin drawstring disappeared until only the little gold tassels remained at the corners. Holding the pouch over the edge of the Great Pyramid, Jayden tipped it over and watched as the gray ashes disappeared with the wind.

Bye, Grandmother. Jayden closed her eyes and whispered a prayer. She felt a wave of joy wash through her. It had taken twenty-four years, but she'd finally fulfilled her grandmother's wish.

Her guide sucked through two cigarettes in the time it took Jayden to slip into her specially made wingsuit. As she sealed the zippers along her arms and legs, she constantly checked the ribbed fabric under her arms.

BASE jumping from four hundred fifty feet up wasn't ideal, but it was the fifty-two degree slope of the pyramid that made this jump difficult. She had no room for free fall to gain speed. Thus, she would rely completely on the custom ribbing in the wing fabric to reach the ideal glide ratio immediately after launch. Otherwise, she would slam into the side of the pyramid.

She mentally travelled through her planned flight path. Launch to the southwest for about six hundred feet. Then, she needed a sharp angle to the southeast to align with the causeway for about thirteen hundred feet. Her landing zone was a cleared worksite about three hundred feet beyond the Sphinx temple enclosure.

She memorized the pattern of floodlights around the Giza complex and then checked on the progress of the Egyptian police. Two men were less than five minutes away from reaching the top, while the others waited patiently on the ground.

Jayden almost laughed at how well this was going. She was no ordinary pyramid climber. They were not expecting her to leap from the top and fly to the ground like a bat. Otherwise, they would have more police around to catch her at the possible landing spots.

It was time for her final checklist. Goggles? Check. Chutes ready? Check. Helmet cam on? Check.

Awesome idea? Priceless.

With one last look at the eerie glow of Cairo, she faced into the wind and prepared to make her leap of faith. But her vision stuttered like an old film and tunneled to pinholes. A fat tear slid down the side of her nose as she recognized the signs of a seizure.

"No!" She screamed her frustration into the wind. This was not the time for hallucinations of demons and darkness. Nor was it the time to lose control of her body. She'd only seized once before during a climb, but it was at night while she was resting in her bivy sack.

Not today. She refused to give in to it. Digging frantically into her waist bag, she withdrew one of her pills from the side pocket and swallowed it dry.

As the dizziness passed and her vision recovered, Jayden positioned herself facing the next pyramid to the southwest. In four strides, she launched herself into the darkness. She welcomed the cold, wet air as it pummeled against her. Adrenaline seared through every fiber of her body, burning away the shadows and awakening all of her senses. She filled her lungs with freedom.

She used the floodlights around the Giza complex as her guide. Dropping her left shoulder, she angled eastward to follow the ancient causeway away from the pyramids. Speeding toward the Sphinx, she had a good view of it. In the misty glow of the spotlights, it looked like a deformed cat.

Air pounded past her ears like the roar of an engine. But through it, she heard a staccato popping sound. She didn't need to look. She felt it. The tension in her wings shuddered as the special support rods fractured and snapped.

With less efficient control over her speed and

altitude, Jayden watched in horror as the ground approached too quickly. She no longer had enough height to properly use her canopy, but she desperately needed to slow down. Deploying her pilot chute, she listened as it released the fabric of the full canopy, which snapped and billowed from the rush of air. Just as her speed slowed, one of the cords became entangled around a wing, preventing her from controlling a landing.

Helplessly, Jayden braced her body for impact and careened into the rump of the Sphinx.

The instant pain of broken ribs knifed through her body, but adrenaline kept her focused on the fight for her life. She smoothed her fingertips across the stone, searching for anything to grasp onto. The weight of her gear tilted her over the edge and she slid down to the ground. Her ribs felt submerged in hot oil. Her breath came in short gasps.

She nearly fainted from the effort to stand up. Blinking back tears, she tossed her goggles aside and slowly managed to unzip the arms of her wingsuit. In great pain, she finally shrugged her upper body out of the whole mess. She welcomed the cool air on her bare arms.

The wheezing sound coming from her mouth meant big trouble. She needed a hospital. Fast. Where were those policemen when you really needed them?

She dusted herself off and limped along the great stone beast, using its side to hold herself upright. Still wrapped around her legs, the wingsuit and canopy dragged behind her like a lead ball. She bent over to try to untangle the hopeless mess, but something squeezed her lungs like they were in a vise. Just a few more feet and she'd be under a floodlight, where she could flag down a passerby on the walkway above.

The support rods stabbed into a small hollow beside the Sphinx. She tugged on the ropes to free them, but they wouldn't budge. She tried kicking them sideways to loosen them, but it only seemed to loosen more sand instead. The burgeoning hole swallowed the tangled ball of fabric and cords.

That was fine with her. If the Sphinx wanted her ruined gear, he could have it. Leaning over, she fumbled with the zippers along her legs. As more and more sand slipped into the hole, she felt the pull on her legs increase.

She realized what was happening and sat down to concentrate on getting her body free of the wingsuit. Somewhere down in the hole, the sand was quickly filling up her canopy, turning it into one damn huge anchor.

Tears stung her eyes as the last zipper filled with ripped fabric and froze halfway.

In one moment, she was sitting next to the Sphinx. In the next, she was in a free fall in pitch darkness. Like riding a wave of sand, she floated for a few seconds until she landed. But it wasn't the bottom. The ground angled sharply — deeper into the earth. In the inky blackness, she heard only the sound of sand and fabric sliding across stone.

Time ceased to have value. She couldn't tell how long she'd been there. Her body ached with many fractures and now her breath hitched with a little gurgle sound. She didn't fight the tears this time. They flowed freely with choking sobs.

Blood slipped across her tongue, hot and sticky. She unsnapped her helmet to free her jaw and rolled over to spit out the blood. As she lay on her side, pain speared through her lungs. She knew then that she had broken more than one rib.

Without immediate help, death was unavoidable. Her life didn't flash before her eyes, but she did try to envision her father standing beside her grave. Would he cry? Or would he be relieved not to deal with her issues anymore? He'd probably send her eulogy by text.

Cell phone. Sliding her hands around her body, she tried to find the waist bag with her phone strapped to it. But before she could find it, she heard her sand-filled canopy sliding again, pulling her along with it.

Without the helmet on, sand rubbed across her cheek like sandpaper. Her hair snagged on everything. Then the world tilted away again. Falling. Usually she enjoyed the free sensation.

Her blind free-fall ended with a sick thud. She heard her helmet crash a few inches away from where she had slammed into the floor. Blood dripped in warm puddles around her head. Her body felt blessedly numb. Incoherent thoughts and images crowded into her mind like a loud, vibrant collage. Then, darkness returned.

Deep in the silence, something moved. Something scratched across stone. But blood flooded through her ears and drowned out all other sounds. She listened to her own heartbeat —until its final thump.

* * *

Seth blinked a few times, adjusting his eyes to the darkness of the cave. Something had jarred him out of the deep sleep of hibernation. The oracle in the pool pulsed in a spastic pattern. Its pale blue glow illuminated the cave with an unusually excited display. He would have ignored it, but he spied a small pile of sand on the floor. The pile seemed to grow as more sand trickled down from the airshaft in the ceiling.

After a ritual stretch of each limb, he circled twice on his pallet and settled in to rejoin his slumber. Drawing in a deep breath, he inhaled the unmistakable scent of blood. He snuffed the air more deeply. His senses thirsted for more information.

He didn't have time to think any more about it. A low skidding sound reached his ears, growing louder by the second. His skin flinched with anticipation. Something was sliding down his airshaft.

More sand tumbled onto the pile, followed by a big colorful ball. On impact with the floor, the ball exploded into a wide mess of fabric, ropes and sand. He tucked his head under a wing to muffle the explosive sound, which was amplified by the stone walls. Ropes still dangled from the hole until another large mass of fabric landed on the floor with a heavy thump. The smell of fresh human blood flooded his nose.

He tried to force the scent out of his nostrils in a huff, blowing a trail of white fire upward. Too late. His lungs were so filled with the smell that he could taste it. He shook his head and gave in. After uncoiling his long body, he crawled over to investigate.

He resented the intrusion into his peace, but deeper instincts compelled him to investigate the human's condition. He nuzzled along the body and felt the curves of a female. His whiskers followed trickles of blood down the side of her face to the floor.

He watched her aura fade as her life force ebbed with each shallow breath.

Heedless of good sense, he drew his tongue across the warm pool. Her blood tasted sweet. He licked again, shivering as it tingled all the way down his parched throat. Hunger rumbled loudly in his stomach. Luckily for the woman, he did not eat humans.

It was apparent that she needed medical attention. He shifted to his human form and held his hands above her. Mentally reaching through the warm cloud of energy that enveloped her body, he assessed the damage inside her.

Slamming into the stone floor of the cave had left a large crack along the back of her skull. He sensed swelling and tension in her brain, a fatal combination. Her internal injuries seemed to be equally traumatic. Three ribs had speared into her lungs. Collapsed, they had no way to drain the fluids. She would drown slowly in her own blood.

As if in response to his assessment, her body stilled at the end of one last gurgle.

He willed his fangs to descend from their sheaths. Finding a vein in her forearm, he bit down as gently as he could. His fangs slid easily through her skin and injected a toxin, just enough to temporarily paralyze her and give him time to heal her. If she started to move too soon, she could do more damage or hinder his efforts.

Quickly, he moved through the ebony darkness to the niche behind his pallet. He slipped into a small adjoining cave through a hidden break in the side wall. Retrieving his sword from within, he rushed back over to the dying woman. He ripped away the sheath and held the blade horizontally over her body.

Too many years had passed since he'd spoken the language of his kind, yet the healing spell flowed easily from his lips.

The sword glowed with pure white energy as he summoned healing powers from the diamond in its hilt. Thin bolts of blue and green slid from inside the stone and entwined in a dance before fingering across the woman's body. Slowly, Seth's mind moved through her, mending fractures, repairing lungs, and resealing ripped skin.

As the glow from the sword faded, he set it aside. Leaning over her face, he pressed his lips against hers and blew. Her chest rose as air refilled her lungs. He waited patiently until finally she coughed and drew in a long breath all on her own.

He'd healed her physical wounds, but her body would need time to heal the trauma. He removed the bag from around her waist and the tangle of material from around her ankles. Stumbling back to his pallet, he stabbed his sword into the thickest part and collapsed beside it. The effort to heal another had drained his energies.

New sounds travelled down through the hole. Human men gathered far above on the surface. Humans occasionally grew curious enough about what was underneath the Sphinx that they would dig tunnels and pits in search of treasure. Seth had tapped into one of those old tunnels to allow some fresh air to find its way down to the low-lying cavern.

Grimacing at the unconscious woman on the floor, he cursed his luck that more than just air had found its way down into his solitude.

Fortunately, no more sounds came from above. It wouldn't be long before someone decided to descend into the hole, but he hoped he had time for now. He needed rest and time for his energies to replenish before he could close up the airshaft.

The distinct clack of teeth drew his attention back to the woman. Fever. Her body racked with it. She needed warmth in this damp place. In this empty cavern, he would be the only source of that.

Resigned, he moved to lay his own body next to hers and willed his temperature to rise. Instinctively, her body rolled toward the source of heat. His skin flinched at the cool touch of her palm on his stomach and the warmth of her breath on his chest. How long had it really been since he'd felt the touch of a woman?

Memories of another woman and another time flicked through his mind. Memories that he'd purposely buried thousands of years ago. Teased by fantasy and flesh, parts of his body thrummed to life. Instead of enjoying the sensation, he was irritated.

Soon, his muscles shivered from the effort to control his body heat and his lunatic erection. But the woman still shuddered feverishly. Stretching his limbs, he shifted back to his beastly form and curled his body in a circle around hers. At least in this form, he could warm her unconscious body while it fought through the chills and fever — without doing anything stupid.

He stayed wrapped around her through the many hours until her body stilled. The fever had finally broken.

Slowly, he backed off into the shadows to wait for her to awaken. Circling his pallet again, he settled in a good spot.

Sleep eluded him. Too many thoughts needed attention. When could he return her to the surface? Through the airshaft, he heard the activity of tourists.

He couldn't take her back up that way until nightfall.

He shouldn't have licked her blood. He remembered the sweet taste of it and how it tingled on his tongue. He prayed the Rage would not return. Exile was supposed to ensure that it didn't happen again.

He growled his frustration.

Why did he save her? He'd successfully avoided humans for a long time. Then, when one practically landed on top of him, he'd lapped up her blood and tasted her life force. He'd healed her. What had possessed him to do this? And now what the hell was he going to do with her when she woke up?

CHAPTER TWO

When Jayden awoke it was so dark and quiet, she couldn't tell if she'd actually opened her eyes or not. She blinked a few times and tried to focus on something. Anything.

"Am I dead?" She'd meant sarcasm, but her voice quaked. It also echoed around a room obviously larger than a coffin.

She tested her body, rolling over and sitting up on her knees. Without sight, she focused on her other senses. The air felt cool to her skin, raising goose bumps all along her arms. The air was also heavy with moisture. She could smell the scent of mold and something else. Something musky. Yet, beyond the sound of her breath and an unsteady dripping of water, nothing else stirred in the darkness.

She twisted her head around and finally spied a meager, misty glow emanating from a spot on the floor about ten yards behind her. From the way it waved and danced, it seemed like the source of the light was underwater.

"Water!" She licked dry lips as her throat clenched with dehydration. She scrambled over to the glowing pool. Her hands shook, but she didn't waste a second in scooping sloppy mouthfuls to her lips. The water was so cold she gasped for breath as she felt its chilly slide all the way down to her stomach.

Quenched, she stared into the pool and wondered how it cast its light. Only an oddly shaped aquamarine stone sat in the middle of it. But it wasn't the light that concerned her. It was the dark. Again she tried to look deeper into her surroundings. Her eyes failed to adjust to the blackness beyond a few feet from the pool.

She shivered from the cold and suddenly realized that she didn't feel any pain. Where had it gone? She searched her memory for a clue.

She remembered slamming into the Sphinx. Then, there'd been a hole with lots of sand. She remembered falling into it: lots of falling and rolling. She rubbed her chest where pain had knifed at her before. It was fine, no pain. That couldn't be right. She'd had enough injuries in her extreme lifestyle to know that she'd definitely broken a few ribs.

Not to mention the terrible headache that she should be feeling after that final landing in here. Yes, she did indeed remember that moment. She could never forget the sound of her own body as it slammed against stone or the warmth of her own blood as it dripped from her ear.

Jayden knew it had been real. Not a vision. Not a blackout. She'd fallen to her death. So was she dead? Or had she taken too much Sinemet again?

She didn't think being dead would involve serious thirst like she had a moment ago. And then another memory came to her. The memory of a sound. She'd heard something in here with her. Something with claws that clicked on the stone floor. Something that snorted with hot breath.

Slowly, she backed away from the glowing pool until she felt a rocky wall against her back. Anxiety prickled across every nerve. Adrenaline rushed through her muscles. She usually loved the feeling, but now it was like acid pouring through her body.

She blamed the darkness for her terror.

Her nightmares had always been set within a dark cave like this one. Would demons appear, glaring at her with bloodshot yellow eyes? Would she feel the cold prick of talons across her skin?

Nothing leaped out at her from the shadows. Yet the hair on her neck lifted in a shivering wave. Her only defense was silence. She didn't want to make another sound for fear of attracting the attention of whatever it was that had licked her.

* * *

Seth awoke to the faint scrape of rocks and a torrent of Arabic curses. Dawn apparently brought a fresh crew of humans to begin an exploration of the hole next to the Sphinx. It wouldn't be long before the men decided the hole was safe enough to crawl into. It was time to refill the tunnels he'd created to bring fresh air down to his cold, dark lair.

The tempo of the woman's breathing drew his attention, as it slowed and deepened. He'd never doubted his ability to heal her, but he wondered if he'd prevented a death that might have been her destiny. She'd slept through an entire day and night, which made it impossible for him to sneak her back up to the surface through the tunnel.

Intently, he watched her awaken and crawl to the oracle pool. He didn't stop her from drinking the water. It wouldn't hurt, and she couldn't contaminate the purifying waters. In fact, the aura around the oracle glowed with contentment.

He watched as the woman's body stiffened and she slowly backed into the wall. The scent of fear reached his nose, and he could just hear the quickened pace of her heartbeat. The jerky movements of her head meant that she was desperately trying to see.

A sliver of empathy grew within him, which only served to set off his ire. He no longer wanted to feel any empathy for humans. He wanted to avoid them. He wanted this one out of here. She was now the source of his frustration, and he decided to toy with her. Just a little.

He slowly uncurled from his pallet and spread his massive body across the floor, making sure his talons scraped and clacked on the stone. He shook his long neck and huffed into the air impatiently.

The woman flattened herself to the wall. She shivered, but no scream issued from her lips. Instead, he heard a tightly controlled voice. "Who are you?"

Three simple words. He heard a tremble of terror in her voice, and yet it carried a sense of determination with it. He realized that she hadn't really asked the question. She'd demanded it.

Impressed and irritated, he vented with a long, low growl. It vibrated in his throat and rumbled around the small cavern. As the woman tried harder to squeeze herself into the wall, his growl ebbed into a deep chuckle.

Her movement was so quick and unexpected, his scales raised defensively. But her destination was the oracle pool. Reaching in, the woman withdrew the oracle stone and held it aloft. As she waved it around, he realized that she used the oracle's light to try to see him.

He studied the woman more closely. How in the world was a mere human able to pick up the oracle stone? It should have burned her skin, but instead it pulsed with excited energy. It sat smugly on her palm and possibly even glowed a bit brighter.

He'd had enough of this game. If the human wanted to see what he looked like, that was fine with him. With a deep breath, he blew a flame onto several old torches on the walls. They sputtered and protested, but the petrified wood finally crackled with fire. In the flickering light, the human female would finally get to view her surroundings — and the beast that now stood a few meters from her.

Seth watched her blue eyes dilate rapidly, adjusting to the light. Her gaze darted everywhere along his body. She blinked in awe as he flexed and refolded his wings. He tilted his head, which brought her attention back to his face. As her eyes zeroed in on his fangs, blood drained from her face. Her skin turned as pale as the stone she held, and he realized she was about to faint.

He shifted quickly to his human form and reached out to catch her.

* * *

Control your fear. Her father's lesson echoed through her mind. Jayden's body tingled with sensory overload, and fear boiled through her blood. A scream lodged painfully in her throat. As she choked on small gasps of air, she never took her eyes off of the creature.

Thankfully, it wasn't a nightmarish demon standing before her. Instead, an incredibly beautiful dragon stood barely a few feet away, his hot breath fanning across her face. She blinked away a wave of lightheadedness which briefly blurred her vision. As magnificent as he was, she couldn't help but conjure an image of his long, sharp teeth piercing her skin.

Then, he changed into a man — a naked man — and reached toward her.

Hysteria burst through the knot in her throat in a fit of hiccups and laughter, but she batted his hands away. "Don't touch me!"

After several minutes of silent staring, curiosity shoved aside her fears. He made no move to attack her. The muscles of his face tensed into a scowl around dark eyes, and his long hair needed a good brushing. Tattoos wrapped around his arms from wrists to shoulders. In the dim torchlight, she couldn't make out their patterns.

He stood like a fighter — like one of those Ultimate Fighters. He would tower over his opponents. She was nearly six feet tall herself and he seemed to be at least a half a foot taller. *Obviously a necessary trait if you need to shift into a huge dragon.*

Her eyes instinctively travelled along every long, lean muscle. Jayden tried not to look at the particular one that hung proudly between his legs. Blood returned to her head, flushing hotly across her face. Somehow this nightmare had shifted into a fantasy, but she trusted neither.

She watched as black fabric slid from some invisible spool and gracefully wrapped into a perfect fit around his body. As the material relaxed its grip, it formed into a t-shirt, cargo pants, and military-style boots.

Cool air filled her mouth. She snapped her jaw shut as her body jolted with renewed hysteria. She'd definitely overdosed on the dopamine this time. This was one wild hallucination. She'd take this one over the usual demon nightmares any day of the week.

"What are you?" Maybe she'd fallen into another dimension. Maybe her father was right and she'd finally cracked.

No. Whatever it was, she knew it was real. This wasn't another drug-induced vision of yellow-eyed demons. Those were just nightmares. This seemed too real, but to prove it she slowly reached out and poked his arm.

She watched one of his dark eyebrows lift curiously.

The sound of small rocks landing on the stone floor drew the dragon man's attention away from her. He moved quickly toward a hole in the ceiling.

Was that the hole she'd fallen through? Twisting around, she could see only solid walls surrounding a cavern the size of a small house. In the light, she could now see a very large body of water taking up almost half of the cave. The water had to come from somewhere, but other than that there were no other obvious or usable exit paths.

He mumbled in a language that sounded far more guttural than any Arab dialect she'd ever heard. Wispy lights appeared above his palms. He threw them up into the shaft.

The earth rumbled and shifted slightly under her feet. His fingers pointed toward a nearby pile, and he shifted rock after rock without even touching them until they filled the shaft completely. A few final strange words mumbled from his lips and the sand smoothed across the ceiling. He left no trace at all that a hole had been there moments before.

"Hey!" Jayden moved toward him, not pleased to see her only exit disappear. Anger emboldened her to challenge him. "Why did you do that?"

"Peace and quiet." His deep voice was clipped with irritation.

"You speak English?" She should heed his rigid

body language, which warned her to keep distance between them. There was something very powerful about him — god-like. But he looked far too dark to be divine.

"I speak everything." There was something exotic in the way he rolled the *r* over his tongue.

"Great. So that way I can understand you when you decide to eat me." She scanned the cave for anything that might be useful. She noted a distinct lack of everything. Shouldn't a dragon's lair be filled with piles of human skeletons and golden treasure?

"I don't eat humans." He sounded sincere, but torchlight added a wicked glow to his shiny white teeth.

She shivered, remembering the sharp fangs on his beast form. "What happened?"

"*You* invaded my privacy." He radiated intensity, and her body trembled in response to it.

"I'm willing to give it back."

The muscles in his face relaxed and the scowl finally seemed to give up. "You fell. I healed you."

He healed me? With what? Those and many other questions queued up, ready to burst from her lips. She wanted to know how he changed his form. Or learn how and why a dragon lived under the great Sphinx of Egypt.

Instead, she took another look around the empty cavern. Her eyes paused briefly in the direction of the shredded pallet. It looked as inviting as a prison cell. Jayden wondered if it was at least more comfortable than the hospital bed that awaited her back home. "Why did you heal me?"

* * *

Frustration aside, Seth knew why he'd saved

her. Old habits. He'd exiled himself from physically interacting with humans, but he couldn't exile his oath to protect them. The bigger question at the moment was what the hell to do with her.

"Thank you." Her whisper barely echoed in the stillness.

He didn't want her gratitude. This was her fault. *She* fell into *his* cave. Yet the longer she stood there with her head cocked to one side and her eyes looking at him expectantly — his stomach knotted in a peculiar way.

"Since you healed me and you aren't going to eat me, now might be a good time to properly introduce yourself."

He resisted the urge to smirk at her audacity. Her aura glowed with the stubborn energy so indicative of humans. She was tall for a human woman, the top of her head just clearing his chin. Her eyes had darkened to a shade that reminded him of the Caspian Sea. How deeply could he dare to drift into them to read her soul?

"Okay, I'll start. I'm Jayden."

She was outwardly bold, but he noted that she kept fidgeting with the oracle, rolling it back and forth between her calloused palms. Maybe he should at least try to put her at ease until he decided what to do with her. "Pretty name. It means precious stone."

"Yeah, well maybe not so precious. I was supposed to be a Jared Jr. Too bad I came out a girl."

It was said in humor, but he heard the deep pain of truth lingering in her voice. She even looked away from him finally. A strong scent of coconut lotion hovered over her skin.

"I am Seth." He nodded toward her hand, the one that still held the oracle stone. "I would like that back now."

She opened her hand, but didn't hold it out to him. "What is it?"

"The Oracle of Siwah." He could tell that she had no idea of the significance of it. Nestled in her palm, the beautiful aquamarine stone glowed with an almost colorless pale blue aura. "It's an oracle of protection and purification."

Seth reached for the stone with his mind, gently removing it from her hand and floating it through the air toward the pool. As he placed it back into the water, its light dimmed away.

"What happened to the light?"

"I don't know." Deep down, a weird idea came to mind. The oracle might not want to go back. Maybe it wanted to stay with the woman. Or maybe Jayden did contaminate the water after all.

"What are you doing down here in this cold, dark cave?"

"Avoiding curious humans." He hadn't meant to sound quite so irritated.

"You have obviously been very successful at that — until me." She turned away from him and moved to the edge of the river. "This water — does it lead anywhere? Is it a way out?"

He could tell by her athletic build that she was tough, and her aura blazed with restless energy. As she moved to step into the shallows, he grabbed her shoulder to hold her back.

"Do not be deceived by the calmness on the surface. It may look glassy and still, but just underneath the pull is deadly. The current would rip you through many treacherous tunnels. You would drown long before you reached the Nile. Even I might not be fast enough to rescue you."

"Wow." She stared intently at the water before turning back toward him. "That sounded like a lecture."

"Then be a good student and stop talking so much."

"I'm sorry." Her apology sounded sincere. "I have this really bad habit of saying exactly what's on my mind. I blame it on a lonely childhood."

He could easily picture her as a lonely child, but in doing so his gut twisted into a knot of regret. His frustrated mood popped like a bubble. Even the beast inside him relaxed. She didn't have to be a threat to his solitude. All he needed was a plan to get her back to her own life. He couldn't go back in time and change the event of her fall, but he could erase her memory of it. He'd used memory spells a few times with fishermen who'd snagged the dragon in their nets.

After nightfall he could create a new airshaft. In the meantime, he needed a distraction.

He searched through the pile of cloth and ropes that had tumbled down along with her. He was surprised to find nothing feminine in her small bag. It held a tube of lotion, a flashlight, and a couple of small digital devices, all of which had taken quite a beating from the violent descent from the surface. He paused, puzzled by an odd suit with wings. "What is this?"

"My wingsuit."

"What do you do with this?"

"I BASE jump."

He lifted his brows, silently encouraging her to expand on her explanation. He didn't know exactly what a *base* jump was, but he had a pretty good idea. He envisioned a unit of paratroopers landing behind enemy lines, but she wasn't dressed like a soldier.

"It's like skydiving, only much lower to the ground. Instead of jumping out of an airplane, I jump off of things like buildings and cliffs."

"Why would you do that?"

"Why not?" Her eyes glittered and one corner of her lips lifted in a crooked smile.

The beast inside him stirred, excited by the challenge in her voice. It sensed a kindred spirit. It wanted out, to feel the freedom of the open sea. Seth felt a ripple of scales across his back, and it took a monumental effort to hold his beast inside.

He regained command of his body, but something else still bothered him. Egypt was a pretty flat country. "What the hell did you jump from?"

"The top of the Great Pyramid."

For a moment, Seth just stared at her. It was the craziest thing he had ever heard of. Well, maybe not so crazy. Humans loved to test the boundaries of physics. But this particular human was far more dangerous to him. Her fearless energy inspired his beast. Seth needed a distraction.

He found a camera device fixed to the top of her helmet. The lens looked like a shiny spider web. Pieces of the glass began to tumble onto his palm until nothing was left in the device but mangled parts. He tossed the helmet in her direction. "And you took pictures of yourself doing this stunt?"

As she inspected her helmet, her blond brows knitted together and her lips formed a tight line. "Absolutely."

Again, he felt a surge of anxiety as the beast paced inside him like a caged animal. Seth realized there was a very real danger in remaining in this particular woman's presence. She was a great threat to him — to his ability to control the water beast.

She'd ruined his solitude. She'd ruined his oracle. And now she was ruining his sense of control.

He quickly formulated a new plan, one that didn't involve waiting until nightfall. She needed to go back to her life right now. He wasn't worried about the camera, since it had obviously been destroyed during her fall. Erasing a few days of memory would take more energy than erasing a few moments, but he'd manage it.

There was only one way out for both of them. He would have to take her with him through the astral plane. Within seconds, he could drop her off in a nice shadowy spot in an alley across from the Giza complex. She could find her way home, and he could free the dragon to hunt in the deep waters of the Mediterranean Sea.

CHAPTER THREE

Jayden watched Seth move around the room in determined strides, collecting the oracle stone and a wicked-looking sword.

"We are leaving now." His voice deepened with the sound of conviction.

Sensing a need for urgency, she grabbed only her waist bag and helmet. But her eyes riveted on a leather sheath leaning against a mound of sand and chute material. Ages of polishing oils gave the dark brown leather a surface like liquid silk. Jayden couldn't contain the impulse to hold it. "I've never felt anything so soft in my life."

Seth didn't say anything, but the right corner of his lips lifted a bit, revealing a soft dimple in his cheek.

She still held the sheath in her hand when Seth slid the sword into it. Erotic tremors shimmied up her spine at the smooth sound of steel sliding across leather and the feel of the sheath swelling into a hard shaft within her grasp. Dark cave. Flickering torchlight. Inhumanly sexy guy. *Hot – damn!*

What happened to the air in the room? Where was it she wanted to go again? Her mind conjured a fantasy of white sands, waving palm trees and island music. She cleared her throat and blinked away the illusion.

She couldn't see any outward sign that Seth might have been just as affected by the moment. His dimple faded, and his lips thinned to a stern line. Maybe his eyes were darker, if that were even possible.

Reluctantly, she let go of the sheath. "Okay. How are we —"

He held the oracle stone toward her. "Here." He barked the word like a drill sergeant.

Not wanting to test his patience, Jayden strapped the bag to her waist, clipped the helmet to her bag, and held her hand out.

He dropped the stone into her palm and secured his weapon to his own waist. "Hold my hand." His voice seemed softer this time but still commanded obedience.

"Where are we going?"

"Across the street from the Sphinx enclosure. Give or take a few meters." The dimple was back, and just in time to make her wonder if she even wanted to go home. The only things she had to look forward to at home were more clueless doctors, painful treatments and cold hospital beds. If she had a choice, she'd choose the tropical fantasy in a heartbeat.

A swirl of dark air extinguished the torches. In the pitch darkness, she felt the ground melt away. Jayden savored the weightless sensation of floating in space. Cosmic winds whipped her hair into her eyes. Fascinated, she wanted to tell him to slow down.

A new wave of light blazed from the oracle stone and pulsed in a warm frenzy. Too quickly, solid ground formed beneath her feet and a salty ocean breeze pushed against her back. From Seth, she heard a sharp intake of breath and a string of unfamiliar words. *Curse words?*

"That was beautiful. Dark, but with little stars everywhere. Can we do that again?"

"You could see it?" Seth's dark eyebrows lifted again. "I didn't know humans could see the astral plane."

"I guess I'm not your typical human." She watched a group of seagulls weave through the air currents like gray knitting needles. "What's an astral plane?"

"It's a telepathic energy channel between dimensions. We use it to travel any distance very quickly. In a flash."

"Are you sure you *flashed* correctly? Because this," she pointed behind her, "creepy looking cliff doesn't look anything like Giza."

"I have never missed a location before."

The stone in her palm cooled as the strange light within it faded. It was only the size of a golf ball. Not very big at all. "Is this thing like a magic lamp? Does it grant three wishes?"

"No."

"Well, good. Because if it did, I'd have say it sucks at that. It got the island right, but totally missed the white sands and tropical palm trees."

The muscles in his face twisted into tense knots of confusion.

"Never mind." She wasn't about to clue him in on her recent erotic fantasy.

"Let's try this again." Seth took her free hand in his. After a few moments, he growled into the wind. He glared at the oracle, which briefly flickered spastically and then winked out altogether. "The oracle apparently wants to stay here."

He started to move away from the cliff and toward a tight cluster of pine trees.

"Are you serious? You let a stone decide where we go?" She called out to his back. At least now she could finally see the tattoos that covered his arms. A variety of blue designs swirled like water across his skin. Small symbols aligned vertically in between wave patterns along his biceps.

Jayden didn't get angry often, but she hated being ignored. She shouted her frustration into the wind and ran to catch up with him. He picked his way through the trees as if he was alone. "Hey, wait for me!"

Life was ridiculously repetitive when it came to the men in her world: her father, boyfriends, doctors. All of them liked to control her life without her input. She craved the day when she could be in charge of her own destiny. Maybe that day would come after the next procedure? Wasn't that worth one more shot at halting the progression of her body's decay?

She should at least try to convince Seth to take her back, but she couldn't seem to get the words from her brain to her mouth. It just wouldn't be like her to say no to a new adventure. As Grandmother used to say — *the Universe always has a plan*. So, why argue with the Universe?

But Seth's continued silence raked across her nerves like fingernails.

"Damn you!"

This time he did stop. He turned to glare at her. His irritation was very readable in eyes she now knew were a deep shade of green.

Why was he glaring at her? It was childish, but she felt a massive urge to lash out at him. "This is all *your* fault."

He looked stunned. "It's not *my* fault that your little stunt went wrong. *I* didn't invite you into my cave."

She marched right up to him, ignoring the

angry shadows that crept across his face. She harnessed her anger and glared right back at him. "I saw you close up that hole. It's not a coincidence. You made those tunnels. The law calls that negligence. It *is* your fault that I fell into your cave. So stop brooding and talk to me. Tell me what's going on."

Jayden struggled to keep her gaze fastened on his eyes and not on the muscles flexing underneath his t-shirt. She raised an eyebrow to emphasize that she still waited for him to say something.

He pointed toward the open space just beyond the tree line. A very-well-manicured lawn dipped and rose gracefully away from them like ocean swells. At the top of a small rise, a stone castle faced them like a well-preserved relic.

"Did I fall through a time warp? What year is this?"

He chuckled. "It's the same year in which you jumped off of the Great Pyramid."

"Then where are we?"

"An island near Greece. That is my brother's home."

"Why did you bring me here?"

"I think the oracle brought us here." Both of his dark eyebrows lifted, as if daring her to question his explanation.

"Oracle, my ass."

"Before you launch into another argument, maybe you should consider a hot shower and a soft bed."

She wanted to stay angry, but relief melted the tension in her muscles. "You had me at *hot shower*."

* * *

Jayden chewed on her lip. The thrill seeker in

her couldn't wait to get inside the castle and see where this adventure was taking her. She knew an opportunity when she landed on one. Her helmet cam was toast, but the memory card should have survived. Hopefully she could find a way to view what was on it.

As she stepped in through two massive oak doors, Jayden finally felt certain she was still in a modern time. The inside the castle was very un-castle-like. No eerie candles or moody pipe organ music. This was totally modern up to its digital sound system, cellular window shades, and mega-sized flat screen television sets.

The place was decorated more lushly than a luxury resort. Huge windows framed a breathtaking view of the Mediterranean.

After her last forty-eight hours, this all felt too normal. Except maybe for the prickly sensation of being watched that wriggled up and down her spine. For protection, she stuffed her hand into her jacket pocket where she could secretly rub the oracle with her thumb.

Seth escorted her up to another level and through a set of red double doors. She found herself in an office so richly appointed that Donald Trump would be envious. The room perfectly complemented the man sitting behind the computer at his desk. He rose as they entered.

She didn't know him, but she recognized his kind. He was like her father. He was a man of great wealth and power. She knew it not by the cut of his clothes but in the way he wore them. He wore his Armani as comfortably as most people wore their jeans. She recognized a casually dismissive stance belied by a gaze that sharply assessed every detail.

Raised by a father like J. Jared Hamilton, Jayden was extremely wary of men just like him. Type A personalities. A for achievers. A for always-right. A for assholes.

Regardless, she couldn't help but be riveted by the man who looked the exact opposite of Seth. He had the same height, but everything else differed completely. If Seth was a dark god, then here stood a blond god.

As Jayden drew closer, she could see that his eyes were much lighter than Seth's. At first they looked yellow, but as he smiled in greeting she could see enough brown in them to actually be inviting.

He approached her and introduced himself with a very gracious demeanor, which again starkly contrasted with Seth's wariness.

"Good afternoon, Miss..." He deliberately paused for her to respond.

"Jayden. Jayden Hamilton."

"Welcome, Miss Jayden." He took her hand in his, but looked very puzzled. "Forgive me if I looked a bit shocked. I have never seen my brother arrive with a girlfriend."

"Oh, we're not..." She pointed back and forth. "No."

"Well, then I am even more pleased to meet you. I am Ozimas Ilu'en. Call me Ozzi." He passed his gaze over her clothing. "Is that blood?" He leaned in far too closely, and she would swear that he inhaled her scent.

"She's fine now." The heat of Seth's body intensified as he moved to her side.

Ozzi's blond brows knitted together skeptically as he looked over her dirty and bloodied clothing. For once in her life, Jayden felt embarrassed for her appearance. She ran her fingertips across the back of her head, feeling the dried blood in her hair.

"It's a little early for you to drag yourself out of your cave, brother."

Jayden knew the statement was directed at Seth, but Ozzi kept his gaze on her.

"Do you turn into a dragon like your brother does?"

He couldn't have looked more shocked, but he recovered quickly. "Well, you may not be dating him, but you seem to know more about him than any other human has in a very long time."

"He doesn't say very much either."

Ozzi's whole body shook with his bold laughter. "Forgive my brother. One who sleeps in wet caves for years isn't much of a host. How in the world did you two meet?"

Turning to Seth, she realized that he was just as curious about her answer as Ozzi. "I fell down a hole and landed on top of him."

"Really?" Ozzi moved to the front of the desk and leaned casually against it. "Where was this hole?"

His focus on Jayden was anything but casual. He reminded her so much of her father. On the surface Ozzi was very engaging, but the slight lift of his upper lip revealed an underlying intensity. The powerful always maneuvered for control, and she was currently an unknown factor. He would be wary of the knowledge she possessed, and she decided to give him as little of it as possible.

Seth winked at her. "We're just here for a few necessities, like a shower, fresh clothes and some food. Then we'll be on our way."

"Why are you really here?" Ozzi nodded toward the helmet clipped to her waist bag. The broken camcorder waving boldly in his direction. "How much could you get these days with photographic evidence of a couple of dragons? Are you a fortune hunter, Miss Hamilton?"

"Absolutely not." She knew her answer was one hundred percent honest, but she squeezed the oracle in her pocket tightly.

"That was an awfully quick answer. How can I rely upon your word? I've just met you."

"She's no threat to us." Seth's voice lowered to a deep whisper, but she detected a hint of a warning embedded in his tone.

Ozzi chuckled, but once his amber eyes focused on hers, she couldn't look away. "Blind trust in a human is not a luxury I can afford."

Jayden heard the threat woven through his words.

"Relax. I just need to know who you are."

The words *who you are* repeated in an endless loop. His smooth voice coated her senses like a thick river of flowing caramel. She tried to shake away the sweet groggy feeling in her head.

"What are you doing?" Seth's voice drifted far away.

Far, far away. She giggled as images moved through her mind like a fairy tale movie. Then, her laughter choked into spasms of fear as the world in her head darkened to an all-too-familiar nightmare.

Demon yellow eyes taunted her as shadows wrapped around her like a cold blanket. Fingers covered in gray scales pointed toward her with thick black claws.

Bau! Bau! Bau! A chorus of chanting erupted around her from a sea of glowing eyes.

The nightmare demons had never spoken to her

before. Her mind struggled to make sense. She wanted to tell them to go away, but the words clogged in her throat. She tried to move away, but her feet seemed glued to the floor.

Suddenly, the world listed and warped. Before all thoughts faded from her consciousness, strong arms lifted her up, and she floated on a musky cloud.

"Jayden?"

Her name echoed until darkness silenced everything.

* * *

Seth released a slow, measured breath, thankful that he'd caught her before she smashed her head through the glass side table. After settling Jayden onto the sofa, he slammed his body into Ozzi's, pinning his brother to the wall. "What did you do?"

"How is she?"

"What the hell did you do to her?" Seth's anger triggered his beast who shifted the tattoo patterns into a dark red array of Nibirian threats. Even the beast demanded an answer.

"I didn't —"

"Cut the bullshit, Ozzi." Seth released him and backed away, lowering his anger to a simmer before the beast took over.

"You heard what I said. I needed to find out who she really is and why she's here." Ozzi resettled his tie and suit jacket. Drifting over to his armoire, he lifted the lid of a humidor.

Seth's nose easily picked up the smooth, earthy scent of Ozzi's favorite Havana Trinidad cigars. "You tried to read her mind?"

Ozzi selected one and clipped the end. "That's

not in my skill set. I was attempting to mesmerize her — make her tell me what I want to know — but something blocked me." His expression was so intensely confused that his brows nearly crossed. His face relaxed as he drew a flame into the fat cigar. Smoke rose in small plumes toward the ceiling. "What do you know about her?"

Seth's jaw ached from gnashing his teeth. He believed the oracle had protected Jayden from Ozzi's mental probing. But why had the oracle brought them here in the first place?

"Did you think you'd waltz in here and dump your problem on me?"

Another decade without having to deal with his manipulative little brother would have been just fine. "I promised to get her home. A shower and food seem to be an appropriate first stop." It wasn't the truth of how they'd come here, but it seemed a better strategy than to reveal the existence of the oracle to Ozzi.

Ozzi grinned, and smoke sifted in streams between his teeth. "Leave her with me. You can go crawling back to your hole." He moved back behind his desk dismissively.

Seth shook his head.

"What is it?" Ozzi stilled. "There's something you haven't told me."

"Her wounds were fatal. I healed her." The memory of her taste elicited a tingle across his tongue. "I tasted her blood."

Ozzi looked back at him very carefully. "You wanted more, didn't you?"

Seth remembered being fearful of just that, but now he realized nothing at all had happened. He hadn't been overcome with bloodlust. "No."

"It's an addiction. There is no cure for the Rage." Ozzi came back around quickly and put a hand on Seth's shoulder.

He felt the warmth of a calming spell spreading from Ozzi's hand. Seth smacked it away.

"I can only hold it at bay. Exile is the only way to ensure your stability. That, or death."

"Which would you prefer, Ozzi? Death?" It was no secret that his brother resented being the younger one.

"How could you question my loyalty to you? I saved you."

For Seth, that knowledge rankled most of all. To be grateful to the brother who'd once betrayed him.

"You are so predictable. You're thinking of *her* again. That was more than three thousand years ago. Get over it." Ozzi jammed the cigar into his mouth and drew violently. "You never believed me. I told you then, human women are trouble. We were a team, brother. The Lords of Command." He spread his arms wide. "We held dominion over everything. But you..."

The smallest sound of shifting weight from the sofa distracted Seth's attention. "She's awake."

"Seth, time has changed. Human women have not. I will prepare a dose for you, and then you should leave. The harvest moon is tomorrow night. The dark energies will be too powerful for you to keep the bloodlust at bay."

"I'm stronger now."

"The last time you were awake for a harvest moon, you massacred hundreds of humans."

Seth wrinkled his nose as if the smell of death still lingered after all these years. "It was a German battlefield."

"Spoken like an addict. Deny. Make excuses. Are you really willing to put more *precious* human lives at risk?"

CHAPTER FOUR

Addicted to what?

The sound of men arguing drew Jayden out of the dark netherworld of unconsciousness. Bloodlust. Massacre. Battlefield. Those heated words became colorful puzzle pieces, images scattered across the landscape of her mind. Ozzi's final question only made the puzzle more intriguing to work with.

As a warm hand lifted hers, she felt cold, damp plastic pressed against her palm.

"Drink."

She forced an eye open and found Seth leaning against the arm of the sofa. Had she noticed before how green his eyes were? They looked like emeralds studded in armor. In weaker lighting, they looked almost black, but now as sunlight flickered across them she caught a glimpse of sea green. She imagined a raging ocean lurked underneath, yet his face showed no visible sign of anger. In fact, he looked almost apologetic.

"Thank you." Slowly, she sat up and gulped down half of the water in the bottle. "I'm sorry."

"For what?"

"For having..." She wasn't ashamed, but she didn't feel like explaining her seizures. There were other perfectly valid reasons she could use to explain what happened. She yawned politely behind her hand. "For passing out. I didn't realize how exhausted I am."

"Come. I think you're due for a hot bath and a fancy bed."

With a huge sigh of relief, she stood and followed Seth out of the room. Before turning down the hall, she tried to look for Ozzi to thank him too, but he seemed to have vanished.

On the way up, she had a dozen questions zinging around her mind, but she settled on one she hoped he would answer. "What are you addicted to?"

She followed him into a room that could be described in one word. Blue. It was stylish in a retro way. She couldn't remember the last time she'd seen blue velvet, but here it was hung around the windows and draped across a huge bed.

"Blood." He briefly disappeared into the attached bathroom.

"Oh." The sound of metal skidding across a curtain rod brought goose bumps up along her arms. "Human blood?"

He shrugged. "It's a sickness that plagues my kind. A violent state of mind."

"What exactly *is* your kind?" She positioned herself between him and the doorway. He moved too fast, which agitated her thinking process.

He hesitated slightly. "Anunnaki."

"Sorry. Never heard of you."

"We've had other names. Literal translation would be *those who from the heavens came.*"

"Like angels?"

He shook his head and laughed. The crooked smile that broke across his face did something funny to her stomach. "I cannot picture Christian angels with the Blood Rage."

"Is there a cure?"

His expression sobered. "Once afflicted, the rage overtakes the mind, overriding all logical senses. Like a rabid animal."

"How did you get it?"

"Don't know." He moved around her and headed for the door to leave. "The symptoms are triggered by the smell of blood."

Bloodlust. Massacre. The puzzle pieces began to fit together, but she would need hundreds more to complete the picture of this man. "Then how come my blood didn't set you off? I left plenty of it on the floor of your cave."

Just outside the doorway, he turned back around. "How many more questions do you have rattling around in that brain?"

"Tons."

"Get some rest."

"Then what?" Jayden removed the bag and helmet from around her waist and tossed them onto the bed.

"My brother has *offered* to take care of you now."

Was Seth seriously considering that? Leaving her on this island with Ozzi? "What if I don't want his help?"

He didn't answer, but his body relaxed slightly and leaned into the doorjamb. She watched his dark green eyes narrow as he calculated his answer.

She decided not to wait for one. Action would be more effective in swaying his answer. Jayden moved to stand directly in front of him, ignoring the sudden lines of tension that hardened his face. She let out a breath she hadn't known she was holding. "Please. Don't go."

I need you. She couldn't say it out loud. He wouldn't understand. She watched the irises of his eyes dilate rapidly and his chest inflate with a quick intake of breath.

If he hadn't made that stupid hole to begin with, she'd probably be in an Egyptian hospital or prison. Falling through those tunnels had nearly killed her. He could have let her die, but he didn't. He could have left her in the cave, but he didn't. While she wasn't ready to fully trust him, she knew she needed him. She hated the idea of being left alone with Ozzi. Something about him felt as scary as her demon nightmares. Seth was her only known ally. Her lifeline. A good climber always kept a grip on her lifeline.

"Please don't leave me here with your brother. I hardly know him."

"You hardly know me." One dark brow lifted on the last word.

"Contrary to what your brother said, I don't feel my life is at risk being around you."

He flashed a wicked smile, his pearly fangs sliding down slowly from his upper jaw. "Maybe you should be scared."

Instead of fear, she felt herself sway under the impact of his full smile. Everything about this man was so dark. She couldn't remember what color he was in his dragon form. She bit her lower lip to keep herself from asking him.

Then, she saw something odd. It was as if she could almost see the energy around him, and it began to draw away from her. He'd begun to shift his weight away from the doorjamb. Away from her. Would he leave her here? She had one card she could play. Lifting up on her toes, Jayden pressed her lips to his.

It wasn't a Hollywood kiss, but it melted her

brain just the same. Although she initiated it, somehow the power shifted. His raw energy dominated. Her lips felt the pulse of blood through his. With each thump, her pulse answered in kind. She wanted to see his eyes, but her lids were too heavy to lift. She remained frozen in place, just breathing.

Gathering the wispy edges of her sanity, Jayden finally stepped away. Seth's eyes slowly opened. She'd never before seen eyes so dark the irises disappeared. She knew she should be terrified, but when had she ever chosen to do what she *should* do?

Instead, she tempted fate. "Please, don't leave me." Then she shut the door and collapsed against it, fanning her face. *Is it a stupid idea to tease you, Dragon Man?*

* * *

Seth was unsure of what had surprised him more. The hunger to taste more than her lips or the telepathic echo of her thoughts in his mind.

I need you. The sudden sound of her voice inside his head had nearly rocked him off his feet. It was not unusual for his kind, but humans did not know how to direct their thoughts to each other mentally.

Still leaning against the doorjamb, he could feel the warmth of her body up against the other side of the door. He felt her aura still crackling with curious energy. He heard her inside his head once again. She questioned the stupidity of teasing him. He was hearing her messages perfectly, but he wondered if she'd really meant to send them.

Jayden?

As he felt her energy move away from the door

and deeper into the room, he knew she could not hear his telepathic question. But how was he able to hear her? Could others hear her?

Moving away from her door, he briefly considered letting his brother take care of her from this point. Trouble followed this human woman like a shadow. His intuition was certain of it. But it just wasn't in him to leave. Not when matters were unsettled. He knew he could not abandon this woman. Seth would make that promise to her and keep it.

He entered the room directly across from hers and headed straight for the shower. He stood under the stream and felt the temperature quickly rise from ice cold to near scalding. The hot water loosened muscles that had cramped from sleeping in a cold, damp cavern. He wished the water could wash away much more than dust.

Like bitterness.

For thousands of years, he'd fought hundreds of battles beside his human allies. Even when many of his own kind enslaved humans, Seth championed their right to live free.

He'd even fallen in love with one. *Nefertiti.* He'd shut the name out of his mind for over three thousand years. He could barely picture her now, but this wasn't the time to bring her out of his memories. He shook his head and mentally locked them away again.

Once the Rage took him, he'd chosen the path of exile. He could no longer join human allies on the battlefield for he risked turning into a rabid beast. He'd tried to watch from the sidelines, just far enough upwind to avoid the scent of blood that would permeate the air. He was a warrior who could not join the fight. Bitterness drove him to the sea.

A vision of Jayden formed in his mind. For all of his effort to avoid humans, she'd broken through. Fallen through. For someone so smart, she was completely reckless. No doubt she was trouble — but she'd asked him to stay.

Seth preferred the solitude of the ocean. He never stayed on his brother's island very long. A few days at the most. Just long enough to get acquainted with life on the surface and to get a dose of the medicine that held the Rage at bay.

The oracle had definitely brought him here, and it didn't want him to leave either. Why? Jayden's curiosity must be seeping in, because for the first time in half a century, Seth felt a growing desire to find out what Ozzi had been up to. Maybe a quick peek around the island would give him some answers.

As quietly as possible, he removed a long stone from the wall behind the headboard of his bed. Carefully he laid the sword inside. As he replaced the stone, he erased all energy traces he might have left behind. A trick he'd learned as a child in order to keep his annoying little brother from getting his things. Otherwise, Ozzi would be able to see the energy trace like a dirty fingerprint.

The floorboards in the hallway creaked. Jayden had left her room, but her footsteps were going in the wrong direction.

* * *

Jayden avoided the allure of the incredibly soft-looking bed and headed straight for her waist bag. She was anxious to find out what worked and what didn't. The helmet cam was busted, but the SD card should hold the footage of her leap from the pyramid, at least up until she'd slammed into the Sphinx. Inside her bag, she had a backup camcorder. It was more of a spy cam. It didn't record onto a memory card, but when hooked to her iPhone it could display the view using a special app.

The big question that remained regarded her cell phone. It had also been clipped to her waist bag. The battery was dead and the screen had one shallow crack started down the middle. But it otherwise looked in good shape.

Digging deeper into her bag, she drew in a breath of excitement in finding the chargers for her cell and mini cam. Kneeling next to a plug, she hooked them up and waited. She smiled when she heard the chime that signaled emails in her inbox.

She had only one. It was from her father, confirming the details of her upcoming experimental procedure. Stem cells.

Jayden clicked *reply*, but her fingers stilled over the keypad.

What could she possibly tell her father? She'd basically died and come back to life. She'd held an oracle, travelled through some other dimension, and was currently on an island with two men that shape shifted into dragons.

Any one of those kind of messages would guarantee *another* trip to one of Miami's finest psychological facilities. Death held more appeal than a hospital bed with thick leather straps.

She backed out of the reply screen, turned the phone off, and headed for the bathroom.

An impressive bathtub beckoned, but she opted for a quick shower. No matter how much she fiddled with the knobs, she couldn't get a decent flow of hot water. Lukewarm would have to do. Apparently the modern upgrades to the castle didn't include the plumbing.

Stepping into a warm stream of clean water felt a little like heaven. She poured a handful of shampoo onto the top of her head. Slowly she worked it through her hair, washing away the dust and dried blood. Then she tackled the dirt lodged under her nails. One grain at a time, the sands from the Great Pyramid slipped through the drain. Good riddance.

Splaying her hands to inspect her efforts, Jayden nearly fell over. Below her, the shower floor glowed. As she ran her hands through the spray of water, she watched a prism of light sparkle around her legs. The stunning display disappeared as she shut off the water.

Wrapping her body in a fluffy blue towel, she stepped out and groaned at the sight of her clothes. They sat in a miserable heap of fabric, dirt and blood. She refused to put them back on, yet she had nothing else with her. After applying a new layer of sunscreen to her skin, she launched on a mission to find something to wear. She tore through the guest room, hoping that a previous guest had left something behind.

She was excited to find the closet full of women's clothing, but the joy fizzled quickly. Sequins? No. Gold beading? No. Leather corsets and garters? *Hell, no!* This was a selection fit for a hooker. Definitely not the kind of impression Jayden wanted to give.

Fortunately, the hooker apparently liked to work out. Folded in a dresser drawer, she found a pair of black jogging pants. Her favorite kind: non-spandex. They fit perfectly, hugging her butt and flaring very slightly at the ankles. In another drawer, she found a white tank top and a gray hoodie, which she zipped up high enough to hide her lack of a bra.

Not that she really needed to worry in that department. She'd long ago stopped praying that Mother Nature would send a little more cleavage her way. Not even an epic pushup bra would have a chance of giving her curves. On the bright side, she'd always appreciated being able to hug a cliff a little closer when climbing mountains.

Jayden remembered one more item she needed to keep with her. She fished through the pile of bloody, discarded clothes and removed the oracle from the ruined jacket. The stone sat innocently on her palm, looking like nothing more than an uncut aquamarine. She was nuts to think that it had any real magic within it, but she tucked it into the pocket of her hoodie anyway.

The oracle reminded her of Seth. Curiosity seeped through her system. What *had* she captured on video that night and how could she review the footage? An image of Ozzi's computer came to mind.

* * *

Jayden stepped into the hallway and stood confused for a moment. At least a dozen doors lined up identically in either direction. Which way had they come up?

She also had no idea which room Seth was in, but she wasn't going to knock on every door to find out. It was probably better that he *not* know what she was up to. He'd almost certainly try to talk her out of it.

Inside the soft pocket of her hoodie, she

squeezed the oracle for support. No enlightening messages entered her mind. Left seemed as good a direction as the other.

The corridor stretched much longer than she remembered. She finally found a staircase. Unlike before, these steps were not lushly carpeted. The rubber soles of her sneakers squeaked against the polished marble. The staircase descended further than one floor, but as long as it went down she could find her way.

The last step brought her into a dark, empty room instead of the hallway she'd expected. She felt around the wall, searching for a light switch. Finding none, she walked toward an amber glow up ahead. As she moved through a series of connected spaces with highly arched doorways, she felt like she was walking through empty museum galleries. In the dark, they showcased nothing more than dust and shadows.

She found the source of light in a great hall. Two black chandeliers hung from a vaulted ceiling like gothic spiders. The bulbs were barely lit, and she could hear the faint hum of electricity as it passed through them with weakened power.

Bloody battlefield images framed the massive room in a colorful but gruesome display of stained glass. It felt like a grand ballroom. The sound of running water drew her to a platform at the far end of the room. A short waterfall tumbled into an irregularly shaped pool about the size of a hot tub. A short wall with glossy onyx tiles surrounded the pool, low enough to sit on.

Kneeling, Jayden reached over to feel the waterfall. Freezing water hit her palms and sprayed across her sleeves. Below her hand, a prism of light flickered across the surface of the pool.

Shaking the water from her sleeves, she approached the only other object on the platform. An altar covered in the same black stone faced the center of the room.

"He must have some great parties in here." Her voice echoed around the hollow room. Isn't that what rich Europeans like Ozzi did for fun? Hold huge parties with their famous friends. She wondered what it would be like to experience a party like that.

"I'd like to think so."

Startled, Jayden nearly fell off the platform as she spun around to find Ozzi standing so close. As before, his entire body showed elegant culture and style. Not a hair out of place. Not a wrinkle on his gray suit. He held his right hand pressed flat against his chest, and a flash of reflected light drew her attention to the dark stone set inside a gold ring.

The contrast between Ozzi's white-blond hair and the black watery backdrop behind him made him glow like a beacon. She avoided looking into his amber eyes and instead watched the lift of a blond brow. "I'm sorry. I wasn't snooping. I got lost and came down the wrong staircase."

"I know." His voice was as smooth as cream and held no note of distrust.

"It's a beautiful room. Ballroom?" She met his gaze with a weak smile.

"Thank you." His smile revealed a perfect set of white teeth.

Thankfully no fangs in sight yet. She'd irritated Seth with her infinite questions. Best not to irritate Ozzi, especially before she found a way to sneak onto his computer. Or — maybe she wouldn't need to sneak after all.

"You clean up nicely, Miss Hamilton." He nodded towards her clothes. "I see you found something that fit."

Humor flickered in his eyes. Could he have been thinking about some of the other items hanging in the guest closet?

"Thank you."

Ozzi stepped down from the platform first and held his hand out to assist her. He seemed ever the gentleman, but something inside her didn't buy it. Her father could put on a similar act.

She accepted his help. "What do you use the altar for?"

"Altar?" Both of his brows lifted this time. "That's a display table."

"Well, paint that thing white and it would look like the altar at the church I went to as a kid." His laughter spurred her on. "You must have some wild parties in here."

"You have no idea." His voice had deepened, but his eyes still held a flicker of humor.

Now was as good a time as any to get down to business. "I noticed your computer earlier. Would you mind if I used it to send my father an email? I need him to postpone my doctor's appointment."

"Doctor's appointment? I hope it's nothing serious."

"No. Just some new doctor my father has summoned to Miami." She cleared her throat in a manner that hopefully meant *end of discussion.*

Thankfully, Ozzi didn't probe the subject any further. "Of course you can use my computer. This way, please."

Ozzi led her to a staircase hidden behind the black curtains beside the dais. Back in his office, a tray of fruit and sandwiches awaited her on his desk. Her stomach rumbled with extreme interest.

"Make yourself at home here." He held his personal chair out for her. "Please do not go wandering *again*. I have some business to attend to, but I'll be back shortly."

"Okay. Thanks." She already had a sandwich halfway to her mouth.

"When I get back, I will take you on a tour of my island."

She tried to smile at him over her shoulder, but he'd already vanished.

CHAPTER FIVE

Seth followed Jayden down to the darkened lower level. He'd never been in this part of Ozzi's home before. He'd never even been curious enough about his brother to snoop around.

He wondered how she could walk so calmly through these connected rooms, until he remembered that her human sight was impaired by the lack of light. She *couldn't* see the demons chained in the corners.

For undead humans, they didn't smell right. The aroma was too organic. He paused beside one to inspect it more closely. Shockingly, it didn't look anything like an undead human. It was a demon, but it looked like an overgrown lizard. The smell of death was long gone. Its curled body lay dry and stiffened.

Stepping away, he meant to follow Jayden into the main hall, but Ozzi's sudden appearance prompted Seth to tuck into a shadowed corner and eavesdrop on their conversation. Thankfully, they didn't linger. After the two left, Seth abandoned his hiding spot to inspect the water fountain and the altar.

Display table, my ass. It was a sacrificial altar. The big question was, what the hell was Ozzi sacrificing? Only the followers of Apophis practiced rituals of sacrifice. Ozzi wasn't the follower type.

Holding his palms faced down above the altar, Seth evaluated the energy surrounding the table. The black onyx tiles held a strange combination of energies: pain and pleasure. Sex rituals. Seth rolled his eyes. Now *that* sounded very much like Ozzi.

Seth scanned the large, empty room. He wondered who the voyeurs of these rituals were. Sex rites had been banned in ancient times, but nobody was left to enforce the ban. Their queen — and her entire royal bloodline — had died long ago, leaving the remaining Anunnaki basically leaderless nomads.

Although many of his kind abandoned their post on the Earth, Seth had stayed. He'd stopped Apophis and imprisoned him in the Underworld. The risk of the dark lord making an escape was miniscule, but the very knowledge that a prophecy existed regarding an escape had prompted Seth to remain. On the rare chance that it did happen, the human race would be powerless to protect themselves. It was not right that his kind had created the problem in the first place, but then to just pick up and leave was unconscionable.

But none of that answered the question. Demons and rituals. What the hell was Ozzi up to?

Seth wasn't going to find any more answers in this empty hall. He needed to catch up with Ozzi and Jayden. Using the astral plane, he moved to a spot near the office and hesitated just outside the room. He stood far enough away not to be seen, but close enough to hear Ozzi excuse himself and flash away.

Seth had to act quickly to follow his brother through the astral plane. Picking up on the energy trail, he flashed away in pursuit and found himself in Jayden's bedroom. Confused, he wondered if he'd followed the wrong trail. A slight sound came from the bathroom, and then Seth felt Ozzi's energy take off yet again. Seth followed once more. This time, he emerged on the same cliff where he and Jayden had arrived earlier.

Winds blew steadily from the sea, bringing the scent of salt and freedom. The ocean called to the water beast inside him. He ignored the call and searched around for a sign of Ozzi. Just southwest of his position, he caught a glimpse of blond hair in between the crumbling walls of an old building. Long ago, the ancient stone structure had been a monastery. Time and wicked elements had tortured and dismembered the abandoned holy place.

As he picked his way through the rubble, he slowed when he lost sight of Ozzi. Seth wandered in the last known direction and found a hole in the stone floor with a very narrow staircase along one wall. The mid-afternoon sun made it impossible for him to see down into the darkness. He reached out with his senses, but something blocked his mental probe.

Whatever it was, it didn't feel like a spell. Ozzi himself had to arrive at location above ground. Even he could not use astral energy to pass through it. So, was it meant to keep something out, or something in?

The steps of the staircase weren't wide enough for him to go in facing forward. Inching sideways, he felt his way down to the next level. Slowly, his eyes adjusted to the gloom. He stood in a corridor, which led in two directions. A tiny swirl of dust gave him the clue of which way to go.

The corridor sloped and curved for several hundred meters until it ended at an oak door, which stood ajar. Stepping through it, Seth breathed in clean, cool, conditioned air. This hallway was as modern and sterile as a hospital.

Voices echoed down the hall. He inched closer to the first door. The space was dark and empty, but light shone from a room beyond it. Seth slipped into a spot in the shadows where he could see what was going on in the far room without being seen.

"There's been a development." Ozzi was addressing someone in a white lab coat. "My brother has arrived with a woman — a human woman. I'm sure he'll be gone soon, but *she* will be our guest."

"But the Gathering is tomorrow. It's the fall harvest. Will she be a distraction?"

Seth could not see the man's face, but there was no mistaking the quick, raspy voice of Ozzi's eternal sidekick.

"Indar, she may turn out to be a feature. Here." Ozzi held out Jayden's shirt. "We will learn all we need to know about her from her own blood. Test it like the others. It can't be a coincidence that she's here."

"What do we know about her?" Indar held a large journal in his lap. Laying it aside, he took the shirt and cut out a small piece with a significant amount of dried blood.

"Her name is Jayden Hamilton and she's from Miami." Ozzi settled in front of a large computer screen. "We also know that she has some kind of medical condition."

While Indar spent a few minutes preparing some mixture with a piece of Jayden's shirt, Ozzi's fingers stumbled across a keyboard. His nails tapped a slow staccato beat that wore on Seth's patience.

"I found it. Her medical history is all here."

Indar paused his task and leaned over Ozzi's shoulder to view the screen. "She's had numerous broken bones and contusions through her life. Is she abused?"

"No, she doesn't have the weakened aura of a

victim. She's too curious. Restless even. She carried a very expensive-looking helmet. So I gathered she's into outdoor sports. That could easily explain her history of injuries."

Indar whistled and tapped a single key several times. "Well, look at that. She has quite a mental history too. She's been under psychiatric care since she was seven. Seizures. Hallucinations. They've tentatively diagnosed her with early onset Parkinson's?"

"Human doctors are idiots. Look at what they prescribed for her. That dosage would induce hallucinations and suicidal tendencies in a grown man, let alone a girl." Ozzi backed away from the computer. "She may be adventurous, but it's her curiosity that concerns me. Why is she really here?"

"Ozzi, look at this entry. The doctors all noted that she was convinced she saw demons during her blackouts. Yellow-eyed demons."

Ozzi shrugged. "Humans see all kinds of things during hallucinations. Sometimes they think they even see dragons."

Seth could easily tell where his brother's thinking was going. There was little fear of exposure from a woman who had a documented history of mental illness and visions of demons.

"They do, indeed. Ozzi, I need to talk to you about the last litter. The mother is dying."

"She can be replaced."

"That's not the issue. I found something in her blood. A mutated virus, I think."

"You *think*? I don't keep you around because you think. I keep you around because you know. Check it again. The answer is always in the blood. Blood never lies."

Seth agreed. Blood contained the truth of all living things. It also held more power than any other known substance. It held dominion over all beings. It had carried the line of succession in all ancient cultures. Kings could not have inherited their birthrights without the proper bloodline. Unfortunately for men, women held the keys to its secrets and power.

"What about the litter?"

"It has not shown up in their blood."

"Excellent, but keep checking. One more thing — you had leftover inventory from the shipment you just sent to Lilith's party in Boston. Use it to prepare a dose for my brother. Let's not keep Seth waiting."

* * *

Jayden drummed her fingers on the desk, impatiently waiting for the video files to load into the laptop's media player. Finally she was rewarded with a dark video of her climb up the Great Pyramid of Egypt. With the night vision cam, her jump had recorded the landscape with hues of gray and green. The final moments on screen showed her staggering around the paws of the Sphinx until she'd slipped into the sandy hole.

She removed the memory card and opened up the Internet browser, running dozens of searches on Ozzi and Seth. She found surprisingly little on Mr. Ozimas Ilu'en, but he was connected to a large number of international corporations: mostly fertility and blood research firms.

From behind her, a faint scratching noise distracted her from the computer screen. Leaning back, she waited to hear it again. She heard nothing but the whir of the laptop fan.

She returned to the computer to search for useful information on Seth. He hadn't told her his full name, and researching his first name produced mostly descriptions of the ancient Egyptian god. His legends showed a god of chaos and violence, and yet he also protected the sun god from the cosmic overlord Apophis.

Her finger paused on the screen over the paragraph about Seth's brother Osiris. Ozzi and Seth. Could that be a coincidence. Could *her* Seth be an Egyptian god?

She heard it again. *Scratch, scratch.*

Tired of the Internet, she decided to snoop around the office. The desk held no new information about Ozzi. At least, not in the drawers that weren't locked. She opted out of the idea of prying them open. Splintered wood would be impossible to explain.

In his armoire, she found Ozzi's stash of cigars. The strong woodsy aroma brought an image of her father to mind. He appreciated a fine cigar, but liquor was his true crutch. There was no business problem he couldn't solve over a sweet cognac or a spicy wine. She shut the door of the armoire and her memories.

Scratch, scratch.

There it was again. Scratching, and then chattering like a squirrel. She had to find out what it was. Moving around the room slowly, she finally spied a woven basket tucked on a bookshelf. The lid was secured shut with a pencil.

Tiny little breathing sounds came from the basket. Whatever was inside hissed and scratched like a small animal. Could something in a small basket be trouble? It couldn't be too terrible if it could be so easily secured by a pencil. *Just a peek.*

But the creature inside was far too quick for just a peek. As soon as she released the lid, the creature butted its head against it and pushed his way out of the basket. It took flight immediately, circling the room three times before crashing into the side of the armoire. On the ground, the strange little thing wobbled a moment before hopping up on the desk. Blinking a few times, it fastened round, yellow eyes on Jayden.

She moved closer. He looked like a fat, wrinkled, miniature dragon, no larger than a squirrel. It was unlike anything she'd ever seen.

"You are so ugly, you're cute."

It responded to her voice with a crooked smile, which revealed tiny, sharp teeth. Lifting a hind leg, it scratched at a spot just under its wing. His tail, which stretched almost twice the length of his body, whipped back and forth across the leather desk cover.

As Jayden sat down in Ozzi's desk chair, the creature hopped into her lap. She stayed very still while the creature sniffed her hand, licked it a few times, and then rubbed along her arms and thighs. *He's snuggling.*

She relaxed and slowly felt along his spine and tail. He responded by arching his back and curling around her neck. She couldn't help but giggle at the sensation of his tiny scales sliding across her skin.

Sensing another presence in the room, she looked up to find Ozzi standing a few feet away. He scowled at them. She couldn't think of anything that would gloss over the obvious. She'd been caught snooping. She cuddled with the evidence.

"Sorry, I kept hearing a scratching sound. I couldn't ignore it."

"How very fearless of you." Ozzi reached toward the creature but it hissed, revealing small but sharp-edged fangs.

The little creature seemed agitated by the sudden appearance of its master, but it was obviously emboldened from his position behind her head. It paced anxiously from shoulder to shoulder. Ozzi's eyes changed very briefly, his irises narrowing to glowing ellipses. The creature shivered under her hair.

"Leave him alone."

"Excuse me?" Ozzi's eyes widened as if he couldn't believe she'd just interfered.

"I said to leave him alone. It's my fault he's out. Look at him. He's so small. What harm could he be?"

"Careful, Miss Jayden. Wicked creatures come in all sizes."

Seth materialized in the room behind Ozzi. His expression was a mixture of surprise and something else she couldn't read. "What is that?"

"He's nothing. He's an annoying little runt." Ozzi's voice hitched up.

Jayden suppressed an urge to smile at Seth. His hair looked clean, curving around his ears and neck in brown waves. But more importantly, he was still here on the island. That's what mattered most right now. "Does he have a name?"

Ozzi made a face that clearly meant that she was nuts. "He's a runt. He doesn't get a name."

Holding the little demon-like creature on her arm, she gave it a thorough look in the eyes. "You remind me of a gremlin, but I hated that movie."

Seth approached and gently offered the back of his hand for the creature to smell. Sensing safety, it dashed up Seth's arm to perch triumphantly on his shoulder. "In our language, the word for dragon is *ushum*."

Ozzi shook his head, irritated. "He doesn't get a name."

Jayden ignored him. "We'll call him Ushum. It sounds very dragon-like. See, look how proud he is of it."

Ushum held his chest out, his scales raised in flamboyant display. But he kept a wary yellow eye directed toward Ozzi.

"Please put him back in the basket before he gets into my humidor again."

It was Seth's turn to look disgusted. "You put a demon in time-out?"

"He's lucky I didn't fry his little ass on the spot."

There was that odd dark look on Seth's face again. She couldn't decipher it at all.

"Now that's a phrase I haven't heard in very long time. Lilith used to say it just like that. How is our stepsister doing these days?"

Jayden felt like she just witnessed the opening move of a chess match. Seth set his piece. Ozzi's body tensed so slightly she almost missed it. Now she understood Seth's poker face. He was laying a trap. But why?

"She's fine. She's having a party tonight. Maybe you should drop in."

"Funny. The last time I saw good old Lilith was when I imprisoned her in a block of diorite and sunk her deep into the sea floor. Any idea how she got out?"

"None, but that explains why your name's not on the invitation."

"That would explain it. So, when's *your* next

mega party, brother?"

"I'm sure you won't be around for it."

"Ozzi, I've decided to stick around for a while. You won't mind putting me up for a few days."

"It's not safe for you to be here during the harvest moon."

"Why? Are you serving blood in the cocktails?" Seth raised a very challenging eyebrow.

Jayden felt Ozzi's eyes fall on her. She shivered slightly at the depth of his inspection. His lips quirked upward and renewed confidence relaxed his body. She felt the game shift.

"Once an addict, always an addict."

"I can control it."

Ozzi shook his head. "That's exactly what an addict would say."

Jayden understood what Ozzi was doing. He wanted her to see Seth for what he was — an addict. He might be, but she also understood what it felt like to be alone and have such a strange problem to deal with.

"Avoidance and drugs. That's your prescription, Dr. Oz? Well, I'm tired of those methods. I've been in the dark for far too long. Exile is over."

Ozzi remained quiet, analyzing his brother's face.

Seth moved a step closer to his brother, cornering him between the desk and the wall. "It's just a party. Right?"

Jayden felt tension infusing the room with heat. The game had clearly never shifted in Ozzi's favor. The trap had been a few turns longer than she expected. Seth's eyes never wavered from his prey. Ozzi looked more puzzled than ever. He couldn't see the next move.

"You'll be very busy with your party. Someone needs to look out for Jayden. We wouldn't want any of your rich, horny party guests to get the wrong idea about what's on *display*. Would we?" Seth made it sound like the most natural question in the world, but Jayden felt the undercurrent. That was his checkmate question, and she couldn't contain the sigh of relief that expelled from her lungs. *You're staying!*

His lips curved up slightly as Seth swung his eyes toward her. She kept silent, but hoped he could read the expression of thanks on her face.

Ozzi's face broke into a wide, wicked smile. He nodded toward his brother. She was confused. Had he just laid down his king? Had he surrendered?

"Come, Miss Jayden." He stepped deftly around Seth and held out his hand toward her. "I owe you a *private* tour of my island."

"But what about —"

"Oh, don't worry about Seth. He's a big boy. He already knows his way around."

* * *

As Ozzi's palm slid across hers, Jayden felt the ground begin to melt away from underneath her. Just as the darkness closed around them, she felt Ushum land on her shoulder. She cringed as the cosmic winds carried a mournful tune this time. Thankfully, solid ground appeared under her feet, and she felt her full weight sink back into her sneakers.

Ushum hissed at Ozzi before tucking himself safely into her hoodie. She shivered at the sensation on her neck as he twirled the ends of her hair.

She avoided the aggravated glare she felt

coming from Ozzi. A swift sea breeze whipped around them. She recognized the cliff where she'd arrived with Seth earlier.

"So, what was all of that back there?"

Ozzi's body relaxed and he drew her over a little closer to the edge. "Sibling rivalry."

Nervously, she turned her back to the sea. "Like Cain and Abel. I'm just not sure who's who."

"Honey, we pre-date those guys."

Questions crowded into her mind like the waves crowded the rocks below. They whipped up and crashed around in a frantic order.

"How old are you two?"

"I think an easier question is when did we arrive."

"That's easier?" She had to look in his eyes now. Seth had also referred to their arrival on Earth. She'd let it go then, but she couldn't let it go now.

"Well, let's just say that if we hadn't arrived, it would have taken a lot longer for humans to develop a civilized society." His words and his tone clearly reflected an air of superiority.

"I'm not sure I like the way you said that. You make it sound like we should be beholden to you."

"Not all species were created equal."

"What brought you here?"

"The same reasons that Columbus sought the New World. Resources. Expansion. Conquest." The last word he stretched out longer, like savoring a memory. He was more than brutally honest. He was a snob. An alien snob.

He inhaled the salty air, his chest expanding with a cleansing breath. "Come, carefully. From here you can see the whole island."

The view was truly stunning. The island curled

in roughly the shape of a crescent moon. Other islands dotted the sea, some near and some so far they fell away with the curve of the Earth. The islands clustered around the azure sea like scattered jewelry, forming a beautiful archipelago.

"Where are we?"

Seagulls and falcons screeched into the wind, darting through gusts and swooping around the dark cliffs like tiny daredevils. Jayden smiled at their antics. She knew the feeling. Adrenaline seeped into her veins, begging her to drop a line and join them.

"Greece. We're a part of the Cyclades prefecture." He started to put an arm around her shoulders, but Ushum growled an objection. Scowling, Ozzi settled for pointing at various landmarks around his island.

She followed his line of sight to the east. Above the pine forest, she could see his castle on the far rise. It sat nestled in between cliffs and a vineyard. Pasture land swept away from it in rolling waves, dotted with a large herd of cattle. Below them along the south shoreline of the island, a long dock stabbed into the middle of a small harbor.

As a cluster of high clouds drifted off to sea, the late afternoon sun glared across something on the western side of the island. Not too far from where she stood, through a thin crop of trees, she could see white, sun-bleached stone.

"What's that over there?"

"My monastery."

"You have a monastery?"

"Well, I *had* one. When I moved in, the Byzantine monks decided to move out."

"I don't suppose a dragon and monks could live peacefully side by side?"

"They were afraid of becoming my next meal." His grin was so wicked it could easily have come straight off of the Cheshire cat himself.

"Can we go see it?"

"No." His answer was quick, but his smile remained. "The area is too dangerous. The monks loved to dig underground tunnels. It's all slowly caving in."

Caves. That was like dangling a nut in front of a squirrel. More adrenaline leaked into her body. The word also reminded her of Seth. He was definitely the most interesting thing she'd ever found in a cave.

"Why is the harvest moon a bad time for Seth?"

The smile drifted away from Ozzi's face like the clouds had drifted away from the island. He remained silent, thoughtfully tapping his fingers against his lips. The movement reflected sunlight off of the stone in his ring, which now seemed to be a lighter opalescent brown. She grew restless under his intense stare. Long shadows from the pine trees skulked toward their toes.

"Jayden, you are quite fearless. You jump into things headfirst, without thinking."

She felt the heat of a blush on her cheeks. "I've never been the look-before-you-leap type. If you're going to jump off of a mountain, what would you be looking for? You just jump."

"There must have been a lot of injuries in your kind of lifestyle. Dangerous."

They were inches away from the edge of the cliff. She could no longer read the expressions on his face. The adrenaline high curdled into the sharp sting of alarm. Was he threatening her or warning her?

Ushum must have felt her anxiety. Little arms snaked around her neck as his head nestled under her ear. His chatter calmed her nerves.

"Comes with the territory."

"How about — mental illness?"

"Excuse me?" Jayden quickly put several yards between her and Ozzi and the wicked drop off.

"You are prone to seizures and you take hallucinogenic drugs. That's insane, if you ask me."

"Why are you digging into my history?" It was a stupid but instinctive question. She'd been doing the same thing, trying to find out more about him. He just had better access to information than she did.

"Self preservation, Jayden." Ozzi closed the distance. "The daughter of the biggest media mogul in the United States suddenly shows up on my island? I have to assume that you're working on a story. Coincidence does not exist in my world."

"I'm *not* insane and I do *not* work for my father." Tears formed hot pools along her lower lashes.

"Then why are *you* on *my* island? How did you convince Seth to bring you here?"

"I didn't." Jayden put her hand in her pocket and squeezed the oracle for strength. It warmed her palm. Instinct whispered through her mind to protect it. She would not show Ozzi the stone. "I'm not here to expose you. I'm just trying to live every moment — until my body no longer allows me to."

He drew his hand across his forehead. After a deep breath, he resettled his gaze on her, but he'd softened his expression. "Maybe I can help you."

"Why would I want *your* help?" She looked at the old monastery and felt just like it, like her life was crumbling into uselessness.

"Because human doctors are not as smart as they think they are." He physically turned her away from the ruins and his smile reappeared. Mr.

Charming seemed to be back. "Come. Let's have dinner. The view of the sunset from my balcony will be a much better memory than an old pile of stone."

She accepted his hand, but before the landscape disappeared, she stole one more glance at the monastery. Jayden bit her lip to hide her adventurous thoughts. Her skin tingled with excitement. *Caves...*

CHAPTER SIX

Ten o'clock. Jayden looked away from her watch in disgust. The memory of that spectacular sunset replayed in her mind endlessly, interfering with her ability to fall asleep.

Ozzi was right about one thing. The view from his balcony was stunning. The moon loomed so large, Jayden felt she could almost have reached out and caressed it. Only one day away from a full October moon. The barest sliver had been missing from the side of it.

She'd watched it dip slowly toward the edge of the horizon. Within seconds, the heavenly sphere slipped quietly beyond the curve. Like a backdraft, the sky had blazed with a kaleidoscope of colors from purple to blood red before settling into a deep cosmic blue.

One thing still bothered her. Seth hadn't joined them for dinner. Had he not been invited? Or had he changed his mind and left her in Ozzi's care after all?

Checking her watch again, Jayden glared at the black digital numbers taunting her. Ten-thirty.

Giving in, she switched on the lamp and reached for her waist bag. Ushum's curious hands slipped in between hers as she rummaged through her things. To buy herself some space, she handed him her fingerless leather gloves and pulled apart the Velcro strapping. As she'd hoped, the noise excited him and he scampered to the end of the bed with his new treasure.

Pulling out the mini-cam, she checked it to make sure it was working properly. She turned on her cell phone, setting it to vibrate. She plugged the mini-cam into the iPhone and waited for the application to begin. Within seconds, the screen of her cell became the viewfinder of her camera. The self-adjusting lens zoomed in on Ushum, and she laughed as she watched him close and open the Velcro repeatedly.

"Cool. We're good to go."

Except that she wasn't sure where on her body she could hook the camera. With the cell phone strapped to her waist bag, she had enough cord length to feed under her shirt and hook it over the top of the zipper. This would keep her arms and hands free to climb around crumbling stone walls.

"Come on, Ushum." Sensing her excitement, he dropped the gloves and scrambled up her arm.

After pulling on her sneakers, Jayden closed her eyes and released a long breath. She mentally visualized the path she would take to get to the monastery. Maybe other people thought she was impulsive, but she knew what she was capable of. She trusted in her gear and her instincts.

As she moved quietly through the halls, euphoria spread through the cells and fibers of her body. Was there anything more exciting than being on the verge of discovery? This was an adventure she'd relive for years to come.

Once outside, Jayden enjoyed the freedom of moving more quickly, jogging across the lawn toward the line of pine trees. The light of the moon guided her way. She swiveled through the trees like a test car avoiding the cones. She paced her breathing to maintain energy.

Breaking through the final tree line, Jayden stopped to catch her breath and soak in the view. The white stones of the monastery glowed pale in the moonlight. There was nothing left to give shelter to the elements, just a wide expanse of rubble. But to Jayden, it was a midnight obstacle course.

Ushum, however, was not impressed. As he crawled out of her hoodie, he screeched and chattered frantically. Flapping his wings and clutching her sleeve, he tugged her back in the direction of the trees.

"No." She patiently pulled his fierce little grip off of her jacket. "I'm not ready to go back. I want to explore this."

As she moved over and around crumbled walls, Ushum tucked himself under her hair. She could feel the wrinkles on his body shivering. He'd ceased his screeching, but his chattering continued at the level of a whisper.

His behavior began to creep into her excitement. Shock pierced through her chest like a knife when she stumbled over a clay pot. She'd been able to break her fall with her hands, but Ushum tumbled from her shoulders.

As Jayden brushed the dust from her hands, she looked around for the nervous little creature. "Ushum? Where are you?"

Ahead of her, a black circle interrupted the whiteness of the floor. She heard a flutter of wings coming from it. His head appeared in the circle as he lifted himself out of a dark hole.

Moonlight didn't penetrate it. Pulling out a small flashlight, she aimed the weak yellow beam down into the darkness. A narrow staircase hugged a curved wall. Euphoria spread through her body again. What had the monks left behind?

Ignoring Ushum's whimpers, she steadily descended the time-worn steps and came to a bare hallway. She chose to go in the direction sloping downward. Using her hand on the wall to guide and balance herself, she followed the hall until it ended at a door. It stood ajar, and bright light spilled around it.

She stepped through and immediately shivered from the chill. She stood in a very modern and very sterile looking hallway. It reminded her of a psychiatric ward where her father had once left her.

Ushum trembled so violently that she pulled him from behind her neck and cradled him. Neither direction called to her. Only silence greeted her. She chose to go left, but halted a few steps later. Her sneakers squeaked loudly against the polished floor. Continuing on tiptoe seemed to go a little more quietly. Very hard to do in climbing shoes, but she managed.

The hallway continued for at least a dozen yards before she came across an open door. She paused beside it and slowly peered around the doorjamb. The room seemed empty. As she started to tiptoe past the opening, she felt a hand close over her mouth. An arm wrapped around her waist and hauled her into the room.

Fear shuddered along the same pathways forged earlier by adrenaline. Anger galvanized her muscles into action. Releasing Ushum, she arched her back and tried to kick out.

"Jayden, shh." Seth's voice whispered into her ear.

Relief washed away the fear instantly. As her body relaxed, Seth released her. In one swift moment of retribution, she stomped on his foot. Turning defiantly, she watched as pain hardened the muscles in his face.

"What the hell was that for?" Even through the pain, he kept his voice at a whisper.

"For scaring the hell outta me — and Ushum."

Ushum stared at the both of them with a don't-blame-me look on his wrinkled little face.

"What are you doing here?"

"I was exploring the monastery ruins."

"At night?" His tone clearly said that he thought she was totally nuts.

"Okay. Truth is, I wanted to see what Ozzi didn't want me to see."

"Well, you saw. Now you turn around and go back." She felt Seth's hands on her back, propelling her towards the door.

But she wasn't ready to leave yet. "Why weren't you at dinner?" *I was afraid you'd left.* She felt his hands move up and curl around her shoulders. She swayed, leaning back into his chest. "I'm glad you're still here."

An irritating sound distracted her from enjoying the warmth of Seth's body against hers. A low buzz wobbled in cycles like the sound of an unbalanced dryer. Flicking on the light switch, she found that it came from a machine which covered the far wall from corner to corner. Round floor-to-ceiling tanks flanked the machine like bookends.

The left tank was filled with a red liquid and bits of organic tissue floating throughout. Jayden had spent enough time in hospitals to recognize what the thick mixture was. "I know that's blood, but what is that?"

She pointed to the tank on the other side of the

machine. It was filled with an opaque liquid that had a slight golden iridescence to it.

Seth didn't answer her right away. He inspected the machine, and then opened every cabinet in the room until he found what he was searching for. From inside a plastic bin, he withdrew a small white disk and handed it to her. "It's manna."

With her finger, she traced the edges of the ankh symbol embossed in the center of it.

"Ozzi manufactures a supplement for the Anunnaki. It's called manna."

"A supplement?"

"You're athletic. Think of it as creatine. It boosts our astral energies."

"So it goes from that silky liquid to this dry wafer?" She didn't think that it looked particularly appetizing in either form.

"Ozzi has apparently made use of modern technology to synthesize it into a more condensed form. In the old world, it was a drink, and contrary to popular legends it did not taste like nectar."

"So it's like Red Bull for aliens." She loved how his dark eyebrows would slam together when she said something he didn't understand.

She wanted to ask more about how and why manna was produced from blood, but Ushum suddenly whimpered and scrambled to the doorway. Standing tall on his hind legs, he peered down the hall intently. His ears pricked forward, flicking and angling anxiously. Then, he launched his body into the air and flew off.

They followed him down the corridor to a large room filled with machines and tubes. Ushum sat on top of one machine, rubbing against the glass. He sounded like he was crying.

Jayden tried to reach for him but paused when she saw what was in the tube. Floating in light green liquid was a horribly mutated human baby. Jayden's lips curled as she held back the bile rising up her throat. Or maybe it was a demon child. Looking from tube to tube, her stomach lurched at the sight of such abominations.

"Seth, oh my god. What are these?"

Some had human-like forms with reptilian skin or missing limbs. Others looked like small demon creatures with human flesh or malformed appendages. Some held no features at all, as if they were caught between transformation cycles. They all seemed to be dead, suspended in time. To be — studied?

The tube Ushum hugged held a creature that looked an awful lot like him but without wings or scales. With exposed flesh, its outer coat had never formed.

A tank on the far wall was filled with dozens of creatures that looked like lampreys. These were very much alive, and their cup-like mouths sucked at the glass walls, showing round rows of sharp cutting teeth.

Seth remained quiet, but the tension on his face and the shock in his eyes told her what she needed to know. He had known nothing about this.

Ushum chattered nervously and took off again, disappearing through a doorway at the back of the room. They tried to keep up as he flew down a long unlit passageway, passing more than a dozen unmarked doors.

Skittering to a stop on the floor in front the very last one, Ushum nuzzled his nose under the door. He sniffed the air flowing through. Chattering excitedly, he flicked his tail in all directions.

Slowly, Seth turned the handle and pushed. Soundlessly, the door swayed inward. Inside, a long fluorescent bulb illuminated the room. In the middle, a hospital bed sat surrounded by beeping machines and a stand holding an IV bag. Thin tubes twisted away from the bag, bringing fluids to someone lying under the sheets.

It was a human woman.

Ushum approached her cautiously. Chattering in a low tone, he sniffed her and seemed to find something about her that calmed him.

Jayden stroked Ushum's back gently. "I wish I knew what he was saying."

"It's actually a *Nibirian* dialect. A very primitive one."

"You can understand him?"

Seth nodded. "He says that she is his mother."

The harsh lighting did nothing to soften the woman's abused features. She looked like she should be young and vibrant, but her skin held the gray cast of death. Her eyes were sunk deep into her face, ringed by red bruising.

As Ushum tried to snuggle under her limp hand, her lids flickered open. Jayden held back a gasp. The woman's blue eyes stared, but with a hollow detachment. Until her eyes fell on Ushum.

The scream she vented pierced through Jayden's heart and galvanized her into action. She removed Ushum to a safe distance away from the woman's flailing arms and returned to the bed quickly.

"Shhh. It's okay." Jayden held the woman's shoulders. A metallic sound clinked across the metal side rails. Someone had chained the woman to the bed. Just above the wrist cuff, Jayden noticed an angry red welt with dozens of tiny punctures encircling a round wound. "We're not going to hurt you."

Wild blue eyes finally settled on Jayden. The screams weakened to a whimper.

"Jayden, you need to leave. Right now." Seth's voice sounded strained and thin, as if he was holding back a great weight.

She wasn't going anywhere. "Can you help her?"

He expelled a short sigh. "Not without my sword, but I can find out what's wrong." He held his hands over the woman's head and moved slowly down her body.

"W-what are you doing?" The woman's voice sounded dry and cracked, and she tried to lean away from Seth.

"Shhh. He's trying to help you."

The woman grasped Jayden's jacket frantically. "No. Please. K-kill me."

The request stunned Jayden, and broke her heart. She knew exactly how it felt to be strapped to a cold, stiff bed. But how could anyone seek death? What had this woman so terrified and abused that she asked for death? She looked at Seth for answers.

He shook his head. "She's dying."

Ushum chattered from the corner, hopping up and down. The tone of his chatter had lowered to a mumble. Seth spoke to him in his own language. Ushum seemed to answer.

"He is certain. She is his birth mother."

"That's impossible!" But somehow it wasn't. Jayden replayed images in her mind: the dead creatures in the tubes, the live creatures in the tanks, and Ushum. It all added up to one sick experiment. Her gut wanted her to pull out memories of her nightmares. Demons battling each other like a pack of rabid wolves. Those thoughts couldn't possibly help her now. She shoved them away.

"Kill me." The woman tugged at Jayden's hoodie again, nearly unhooking the mini camcorder from the zipper.

Jayden had forgotten all about it. She quickly secured it and leaned in closer. "Who are you? What's your name?"

Seth unhooked a clipboard from the end of the bed and scanned through the pages.

"We have to save her." Jayden felt the woman's desperation.

"That would be most unwise." A new raspy voice came from the doorway. Its source was a tall, thin man with a short military-style crew cut. "You should not be in here."

Seth's eyes darkened and narrowed. "Hello, Horus."

"Who is he?" In his white lab coat, he looked like any other doctor, and Jayden had seen plenty of those in her life. But something in his eyes sent a shudder of unease up her spine. He looked at her like she was a lab rat that he couldn't wait to begin testing on.

"He's Ozzi's stooge. Lacky. Enforcer. Take your pick. But always in Ozzi's shadow. Right, Horus?"

"Don't call me that." The pale man stepped into the room, but he kept a wide space between himself and Seth. "I am Dr. Indar Hor'az, and you must be Jayden Hamilton. What is a media mogul's daughter doing on our island?"

Jayden felt like he was sneering at her, but his

bird-like face held an ineffectual smile. "How do you know me?"

He cackled and a sneer slipped into his tone. "I know more about you than any of your stupid human doctors ever have. Did you like your walk with Ozzi this afternoon?"

She disliked this man — with every cell in her body.

From the corner of the room, Ushum shrieked and hissed in the doctor's direction. He was repeating something that sounded menacing. *"Bau. Bau. Bau."*

Where have I heard that before?

The woman resumed her plea to be killed, grasping at Jayden's arms and rolling away from the doctor. But the doctor would not be ignored. Screams filled the air as the patient bucked and strained, fighting with what little strength she had left.

"We need to leave. Now." Jayden felt Seth's hand enclose around hers. Briefly, she soaked in a wave of emotion she could only describe as comfort.

She didn't want to go. She wanted to stay and fight, but again she felt an infusion of energy from Seth pushing through her body and spurring her flight reflex. It was time to go. She wanted to save this woman, but she also knew that she was capturing all of this on video. If anyone knew, they would never let her leave this island alive.

* * *

The most important thing on Seth's agenda was getting Jayden the hell out of there. The more the woman in the bed had pleaded for death, the more Jayden's skin had paled. A tight line of determination on her lips spelled trouble. If she fainted, he could easily carry her, but it would slow them down.

Her impulsivity had recklessly brought her to explore the ruins at night. She was damned lucky she hadn't fallen down that stairwell. She could have broken her neck, and he wouldn't have been there. He felt his own blood pulsing in a vein above his eye.

If that weren't enough aggravation, she kept sending him mental messages. They entered his mind so unexpectedly that they diverted his thoughts in all the wrong directions. When he wanted to be angry, her voice would be there. *I need you. Stay. Don't leave.*

Thankfully, she didn't know he could hear her mind speaking to him. Because then he'd have to acknowledge how the sound of her voice soothed the beast inside him.

Pulling her closer, he led the way through the maze of corridors and through the lab. In the main hallway, he aimed past the large door leading to the stairwell. Instead, he needed to get what he had come here for.

"Aren't we leaving?"

Before Jayden's surprising arrival, he'd spent several hours spying on Indar. Everything he did, he recorded in that fat brown journal. Seth wanted that book, and he wasn't going to leave without it.

"Wait here." He knew right where it would be — propped open on the lab table. Snatching it up, he returned to the hallway. Ushum's yellow eyes stared at him from the shadows under Jayden's hair. "Let's go."

They dashed through the door and up the staircase. Seth took a little more time, having to navigate the narrow stairs sideways. Once they crossed through the line of pine trees, he grabbed Jayden and her strange new pet and flashed all of them to his room.

Having seen Ozzi in her room earlier, he didn't trust going there. He probably couldn't trust going anywhere on this island, but he at least needed to retrieve his sword.

Jayden slowly lowered herself onto the bed. "What are we going to do?"

"Try to take you someplace safe."

"I'm not leaving."

"I brought you here." Guilt stabbed through him like a liquid fire. He felt pain in parts of his body that he hadn't felt in a long time. He realized that he had exiled far more than his physical being. He'd exiled his soul.

He watched her rise and approach him. Fearlessly. She pulled the oracle out of her pocket. "No, this did. I believe that now. It flickered in my hands when we were in the astral plane. It shifted our course. I *am* supposed to be here."

"No."

"Yes, I am. Seth, I'm terrified by what I've seen. If I were to describe to you the visions I've had since I was seven, maybe you'd understand. I would black out and find myself in a strange world. Dark and cold. I was a spectator watching gladiators fight in some underworld arena. Only the warriors were creatures with long fangs and yellow eyes."

"Did they scare you?"

"Yes, and I was all alone. Nobody ever believed me. Not even my father."

"Just because you had visions of demons doesn't mean you belong *here*."

"I'm not leaving without helping that woman."

"We have to go now, or we won't have a head start on Ozzi."

"I'm staying."

"The hell you are." He watched her aura grow brighter with her passionate defense.

"Stop. I can't tell you why I'm not terrified enough to want to run." She threw her hands in the air. Her blue eyes dared him to object. "I can't even explain to you why I've never shied away from hanging over a cliff or jumping out of a perfectly good airplane or speeding through the air with little more than a small chute to slow me down. I've just always been an adrenaline junkie. I'm not insane. I've never feared or wanted death. I crave freedom and life."

"Which is exactly what I want for you. To live."

"I can't leave that woman strapped to that godforsaken bed." Her voice cracked from emotion, and then she whispered, "I just can't do that."

In that moment, he felt he understood her in a way no one else ever could. She would always choose freedom. He couldn't picture her chained to a hospital bed. Caged like a sideshow freak. The fire in her ignited something deep in him. The water beast yearned to come out and fight.

Seth knew he wasn't going to change her mind. Even more disturbing was the realization that he didn't want to. Pulling her close, he wrapped his arms around her and prayed to whatever god was listening that he could keep her safe. "I know, and I won't leave you. I promise."

He felt her fingers digging into his back. Her slim body heaved with several deep, calming breaths. Her hair was clean and smooth against his neck. He could smell the coconut scent of her lotion. As she lifted her face toward his, he didn't think. He tasted.

Seth tasted the salt on her lips from the tears

she'd struggled so hard to hide. Through her lips, he felt her heartbeat quicken, challenging his to keep pace. Fingering through her hair, he cupped her head and explored more deeply. She offered no resistance, but asserted herself in other areas. Her palms slid down, pulling him tight against her.

At first, he thought he felt her heartbeat racing. But the vibration came in short pulses and from lower down her body. Pulling away, he lifted her jacket and found a wire leading up from her waist. It was connected to one of those hand-held phones that humans seemed so dependent on.

Lifting it out of its holder, he saw a live image of himself on the screen. Following the wire up through her shirt, he found a flat round disk hung over the top of her zipper. "What the hell is this?"

Her face still held a flush of passion, but her eyes cleared and raised a cold wall of defense.

"I'm sorry. I can explain."

CHAPTER SEVEN

Jayden reached for Seth, but he twisted away from her hand. "I put it on to capture my exploration of the ruins on video. I had no idea that I'd be recording — whatever the hell that was. I didn't mean to record you. I honestly forgot I had it on."

She read the tension in his face easily. He remained unconvinced by her explanation. His eyes swept over her whole body as if trying to find more evidence of deception.

"Seth, it's what I am. I do extreme stunts and I keep a video diary of them." She sat back down on the bed and coiled the wire around the cell phone. The battery symbol blinked rapidly, as if gasping for breath. Its life sucked dry by the video application. "Sometimes I post them online for my blog followers to see."

"Doesn't that just encourage those followers to do these dangerous things?"

She shook her head. "I think most people live vicariously through others. Soon, I'll be just like them."

"You refer to your disease. I overheard Ozzi reading your medical history."

She nodded and dug into her waist bag. Withdrawing the wrinkled note card, she handed it to him. "That's my final list of places to climb and jump from."

As he scanned the list, his brows met in a deep

frown. "The Trollveggen? You *are* trying to kill yourself."

"No, I'm not. I'm just — living. And videotaping it so in the future I can remember how good it all was before I ended up stuck in a bed."

As she watched the muscles around his face soften, Jayden felt her body relax a bit.

Seth picked up the journal and sat down next to her. "Time to focus on the present. What are Indar and Ozzi up to?"

The journal seemed well used. Many pages held creases in the top corner from being turned down. Strange pictographic symbols covered the paper, occasionally interrupted with quick slashes and dots. "What is that?"

"It's *Nibiri*, the language of the Anunnaki."

"So, Indar is like you?" Her question elicited only a quick chuckle.

Seth seemed to be scanning each page intently but quickly. He finally paused when he reached a blank page. "The most recent entries are about you. They analyzed your blood."

"What does it say about me?"

"Indar uses a lot of scientific notations that I don't know how to interpret, but I see a pattern in the numbers between you and the others."

"What others? Like the woman we saw?"

He nodded. "It seems that she — and many others — have been chosen to be birth mothers because of something in their blood."

"Birth mothers..." The words trailed deep into her mind, melting into a dark fear. "Birth of what?"

"*Viperidae damienos*. Ozzi's new demon species." Seth's fingers trailed along a specific passage on the opening page. "Jayden, whatever it is they look for in the blood, you have it. A lot of it. Far more than the others."

She couldn't shut away the memories of the woman in the bed. The dark, red-rimmed eyes. Skin the pallor of death. Soul-deep screams of terror. Jayden shivered. "So my body is sick enough to stop me from climbing mountains but healthy enough to give birth to a...to a demon child?"

"A damien child." Seth cleared his throat. "Well, not just one. Litters of them."

"Keep reading." She heard the demand in her own voice, yet it came out barely above a whisper.

"I don't think that's a good id —"

"Keep reading!" She felt like she was watching one of those stupid horror films. Like she knew what was coming would be gruesome but she couldn't seem to close her eyes.

"The birth women carry about five eggs inside their womb for three months, until they mutate to their larvae stage. On spawning day, they are separated from the mother as soon as they are born."

"Why separate them?" Her stomach churned and she gasped for air.

"Remember the tank?"

The teeth. The lamprey-like creatures had plenty of them. She shuddered, remembering the wicked little suction mouths ringed with rows of sharp teeth.

"If the litter attaches to the mother, they will drain her blood, killing her."

Jayden looked at the smooth skin of her own arm, but pictured the unusual wound on the woman's arm. Jayden's stomach boiled and she barely made it to Seth's bathroom. Everything in her stomach lurched up her throat until nothing was left.

All the way to the last dry heave, Seth

continued to hold her hair away from her face and wipe her lips with a cool cloth.

"Jayden, the woman is dying. You can't risk your life to save hers."

"I have to." She rinsed her mouth in the sink. "If what you read is true, there may be more like her down there right now. Strapped to beds. Waiting to die."

She looked into his eyes and hoped he understood. Hoped he would help her. *I have to try.*

He nodded, as if he understood her unspoken plea. "My brother is playing god. He doesn't do things without a clear purpose. I need to know what that purpose is, so I can stop him."

She followed him back into the bedroom. He pointed his hand toward the wall behind the bed and waved it in the air in the shape of a long rectangle. Then he pulled his hands toward himself and a section of stone came forward. As the block of stone hovered in the air, Seth reached into the exposed hole and withdrew his sword.

"What else can you do?"

"What do you mean?" He placed the journal into the hole and reinserted the wall over it, smoothing away the cracks until it looked untouched.

"Magic. You can heal others, travel telepathically, change your form, and move physical things with your mind. What else can you do?"

"It isn't really magic, Jayden. We are energy benders. Everything in the Universe is a form of energy. My kind is just more in tune with it than your kind."

"What about the magic in this?" Jayden pulled the oracle out of her pocket.

"Some items have a special relationship with

energy. Like a chemical bond."

"And that means you know how to make that special energy work." The beautiful aquamarine felt cool to the touch, and no wispy lights swirled within it. "I don't, so maybe you should hold onto it."

Seth took her fingers and gently closed them around the stone. "Trust it. Keep it safe."

"Maybe this thing will let us flash off this damned island after we save the birth women."

"I like the way you think, my dear." Seth was trying to give her his most encouraging smile, but she could still see a heavy sadness in his eyes.

* * *

As Indar entered Ozzi's private rooms, his nose filled with the smell of sex and chlorine. The midnight moon cast plenty of shadows from which he could watch while waiting for the perfect moment to interrupt.

Three of Ozzi's favorite damien whores attended him in the sunken bath. One nibbled his ear, flicking it with a forked tongue. Another one licked rings around his nipples. A third lover hovered underwater caressing her master's proud member.

Panels of red silk trailed from the tub to the large bed, where the sex play had obviously begun. The pillows lay limp and trampled, and the sheets barely hung onto the mattress. Gold ropes, which usually held the silk drapes to the canopy, now looked knotted into handcuffs.

Although the alphas were the prize of each damien litter, Ozzi had discovered a unique value in the submissive omegas. Indar mentally tucked away the jealous, vindictive ideas that flew across his mind.

Now was not the time, but an image of strangling one of the damien whores with the gold rope spread a wave of desire through his blood. Indar felt a single drop of hot semen bead at the head of his cock.

Ozzi's breath panted and moaned just louder than the hum of the underwater jets.

Silently, Indar waited for just the right moment to interrupt. The situation at hand required Ozzi to be alert — not sluggish. As the heavy breathing rapidly increased to a near peak of ecstasy, Indar moved closer to the tub and bowed his head.

He bowed not out of deference, but to hide his smirk. "Lord Ozzi. We have an urgent situation."

Ozzi managed to grumble in between heavy breaths. "Go away."

"It requires *immediate* action."

Indar enjoyed Ozzi's string of profanity as he ground his cock deeper into the underwater damien's mouth before giving up and allowing her to resurface. Then Indar watched his lord step angrily out of the water, his member still swollen with need and bouncing with each violent step.

"This had better be urgent indeed, or I will slit your throat, Indar."

It was never an idle threat. He'd felt the slice of Ozzi's dagger many times. Their kind healed very fast. But a cut to the right vein would send a hot, slick coat of blood across Indar's skin before it could reseal itself.

The damien whores slithered past Indar and back into their dark corner, meekly allowing their master to re-cuff them to the walls.

"You know what I love about damien?" Ozzi stood silhouetted by the moonlight, which gave his naked body a silvery glow. "They don't speak. They don't annoy. They just take care of business. But you — you have a bad habit of annoying me. So, out with it. Now!"

"I have the results of the tests on Jayden's blood."

A huge grin spread across Ozzi's face. "You would not have interrupted unless the news was in our favor."

"By my calculations, she is the grandchild of an Anunnaki. That's the highest percentage we've ever come across. But..."

"But?"

"In her, the cells are latent."

"Meaning..."

"Meaning we would need to wake them up. Unlike the other humans, the Anunnaki cells have not merged with hers, and yet they've been totally disruptive to her nervous system."

"Skip the biology lesson. What you're saying is that she could be our most productive birth mother." Ozzi lifted a half-filled glass of wine from the bedside table and sipped thoughtfully. "I wonder how we never picked up on her before. There is no medical data on this planet that I don't own, or own the process of retrieving it. Are you slipping?"

"No, my lord, I am not slipping. I will look into why our sources didn't provide this sooner."

"You have more?"

"Oh yes. The bad news."

"Don't toy with me, Indar."

"Seth has been watching us. He's found the lab."

"Seth will not be an issue."

"He's taken my journal."

"That may be disturbing to you, but what would he do with the information? All he will find is your notes on the damien species. Do you think he really cares? He's sick. Or he thinks he's sick. He is no longer the warrior defender of the human race that he once was."

"Jayden was with him."

"Ah, definitely more interesting." Ozzi took another deeper sip. "But her fate is in our hands now anyway. I don't see this as bad news."

"Your brother will try to stop us. He will interfere with our plans."

"Yes. It is time. Time to end him. Put him out of his misery." Ozzi tossed the wine glass into the empty fireplace. Glass shards and red wine splattered across the blackened stone. "You know what to prepare. It's time for the Rage to return."

Indar grinned at a vision of Seth writhing in a pool of his own blood. "We should act quickly before he takes her off the island."

"Then, as you said — time for immediate action." Ozzi flashed on a new dark gray suit. "Let's go properly welcome our new birth mother."

* * *

Seth still wasn't happy with the idea of taking Jayden back to the lab, but as long she stayed within his sight, he would find a way to get her off this island. "Stick to the plan, Jayden."

She obviously didn't like being directed. Her pretty blue eyes rolled in an exaggerated arc. "Yes, I know. Get the woman. Get back above ground. Never leave your side."

"That's the one." He took her hand in his and had a strange impulse to kiss her again. The feeling lingered in his mind like smoke. Smoke meant fire.

He compromised, drawing her into a quick hug and kissing her forehead. "And then we hope the oracle lets us get you two the hell out of here."

Ushum took his cue and tucked his body into the hood under Jayden's hair. His tail curved around her throat like a necklace.

Seth mentally reached out to the astral plane and found the dark path to the edge of the ruins. As they arrived, the moon was already past its zenith, but it still gave a full measure of light to the area. Taking in a deep breath, he let the salty ocean air energize every astral cell in his body. He knew the beast inside also felt the power surge as the tattoos on his arms rippled with anticipation.

He needed to be sharp. This was Ozzi's territory, and there was no doubt in his mind that they could be walking into a trap. Jayden was determined to save one poor soul. But after that, would the oracle finally let them flash away? As oracles went, this one was usually very responsive. Yet they could also be very stubborn until their wishes were met. So what did this one want?

"Why can't we enter into the lab through the astral plane?"

"A wall of energy surrounds the ruins. It seems to be a natural barrier, not a magical one. Once we cross through it, my powers are limited."

"Ozzi's too?"

"Yes, his too." He heard her expel a lungful of air and tension. "That doesn't mean this will be a walk in the park."

"No, but it feels better anyway."

Quickly, they descended the staircase and made their way through the maze of corridors. In the hallway where they'd found the woman before, the silence felt like an itchy blanket. When they reached her room, Jayden broke into a choking sob.

Dead. The woman's skin had faded to a pale bluish gray, and her eyes stared sightlessly at the ceiling. The weak aura of life she'd had before was now gone. In its void curled a black swirl of dark energy. It had not been a natural death.

Ignoring the plan, Jayden whipped out of the room without him.

Halfway down the hallway, a strange woman in a medical uniform stepped from one of the rooms and blocked their retreat. An opaque pattern of scales covered the skin along her arms and her fingernails sported wicked little claws. Her eyes were hazel, but the irises formed black, vertical ellipses.

She was unlike any demon he'd ever encountered. She had a life force all her own, evident in the aura of energy pulsing around her. She must be one of Ozzi's new species.

She reached toward Jayden's face, trailing a sharp nail along the jawline. And damn it, Jayden just stood there and let her.

"Seth, is she a damien?"

He advanced quickly toward them, closing his fingers around the hilt of his sword. His steps slowed as he realized that faces peered out of every dark doorway. A variety of green and yellow eyes fixed on him. Assessing.

The *she* in question smiled, revealing a perfect set of human teeth — except for the two narrow fangs from her upper jaw. She yanked her hand back when Ushum leaned over Jayden's shoulder and bared his own sharp little teeth.

The silence ended with the long, metallic sound of Seth's sword as it slid out of its sheath. He held the weapon low but pointed in the damien woman's direction.

Before he could decide how to proceed, every pair of eyes turned away from him and toward the double doors that led into the hallway.

Small, feminine voices began to chant a single word. "*Bau. Bau. Bau.*"

In his language, it meant *doctor*. The tone in their chant meant *hatred.*

The next voice wasn't female and it wasn't coming from the front of the hallway. It came from behind him.

"Hello, *brother.*"

* * *

Jayden watched Ozzi saunter casually out of the dead woman's room. If evil could be elegant, Ozzi was the very image of the term. He looked immaculate in his fashionable gray suit. His blond hair glowed against the dark silk. His gaze zeroed in on her, but the gloating smile was all for Seth.

"Well, Jayden, dear. You *are* full of secrets." His lips pursed and he blew an air kiss in her direction.

"And you're full of shit. What you're doing to these women is wrong."

"They serve a higher purpose — as will you." His amber eyes glittered with anticipation.

"You have to get through me first." Seth leveled the tip of his sword toward Ozzi's neck.

Ozzi's expression darkened but the grin remained. "You were supposed to die on that German battlefield. It's time you had your final sad episode of the Rage."

Before Jayden could scream out a warning,

Indar stepped out of a room to their right, and plunged a thick needle deep into Seth's neck. Bright golden liquid emptied quickly into Seth's body. He stumbled slightly, leaning a hand against the wall for support.

"Seth?"

He didn't answer her. Or maybe he couldn't. Waves of tremors shimmered through his muscles. After several minutes, he seemed to compose himself.

Looking past Seth's shoulder, Jayden watched Ozzi's face brighten with a satisfied gleam. He laughed, every note sharp with the sound of victory. Then, he turned and ran away from them.

Seth sprinted into action, chasing his brother.

"Hold on," Jayden ordered. Ushum seemed to understand and tucked deeper into her hoodie as she tried to run fast enough to keep Seth in sight. She felt Indar close behind her.

After several long corridors, Jayden followed them into a large, empty room. Seth stood in the center, panting heavily as if he was in great pain. His sword lay useless on the floor. His eyes were closed and when he opened them, she nearly screamed. Blood filled them so completely that the irises had disappeared.

Ozzi paced around his brother. "Bloodlust rules his brain now. His beast craves blood."

"Your blood, I'm sure." Jayden couldn't resist the taunt.

Indar arrived and doubled over, huffing from the exertion.

A deep gurgling scream plastered everyone to the nearest wall. All eyes fell on Seth as his body contorted in weird poses. He roared as he began to shift into his dragon form.

Jayden remembered his transformation back in his cave — from beast to man. He'd changed his shape so seamlessly, like a swift melding of muscle and bone. This transformation held no sense of beauty to it. The room filled with the sound of joints cracking and Seth screaming. His skin stretched until it turned bright red and threatened to rip apart.

He settled into his dragon form, but the great beast panted heavily. Dark sea-green scales lifted across the center of his arched back like an animal wanting to be left alone. His wings slumped to the floor as if he had no strength to lift them. She could tell he needed time to recover, but the beast didn't remain. The human in him screamed in agony as he transformed back.

His body continued to shift painfully back and forth for several long minutes. Finally, Seth collapsed on the pile of his ripped, useless clothing. His muscles continued to spasm. His human skin turned red and bruised from so many forced transformations.

Ozzi's triumphant laughter echoed around the room. "It's like old times, isn't it?"

"F-fuck you." Seth's voice quaked from exhaustion.

"Fifty years ago, we tried to kill you with a toxic dose of mannah. But our failure then pushed us to perfect it." Ozzi stepped near Seth, but stayed just beyond arms reach. "All these years you came to me for doses to keep the Rage at bay. It never was a medicine. We were testing for the addictive and lethal levels of mannah."

"You experimented on me?"

Ozzi kneeled down to gain eye contact with Seth. "And I've made lots of money doing it." He smiled cruelly. "Lilith even came up with the idea to turn it into a perfume to sell to humans. Brilliant plan. Perfume has a wider audience and draws no legal attention."

Jayden's heart pounded fiercely as Ozzi picked up Seth's sword and waved the tip around his face. Seth pressed his palms to his head, and his knuckles turned white from the strain.

She dropped to her knees, feeling the weight of his suffering. This was her fault. She'd asked him — no, pleaded with him — to help her save the woman. She'd led him right into a trap. Had she led him to his death? *Please, Seth. Fight!*

He finally looked in her direction. She couldn't read his face. He leveled such a blank stare at her that she suddenly felt alone. Even more alone than when Grandmother died. Jayden shook her head, refusing to accept what was coming.

Then Indar's hands closed around her arms, yanking her up. "Let go of me." She tried to pull away from his grip. Ushum came to her aid and lunged for Indar's eyes. He struggled with Ushum, but kept one hand firmly wrapped around Jayden's arm.

"My dear brother, you've always been a guinea pig. The great warrior — the great Prince of Eridu — reduced to a lab rodent. Absolutely priceless." The last word slithered from Ozzi's lips and his eyes closed like he savored every moment.

Seth's voice choked, sounding distant. "But why? There is no kingdom to rule. There is no throne to inherit on my death here."

"Indeed." Ozzi's voice cracked like a whip. "History would have gone a lot differently if I had succeeded in killing you the first time — three thousand years ago. But at least I had the satisfaction of killing your woman."

Seth remained limp, but his face took on such powerful darkness that even the room seemed a shade gloomier than before.

"Nefertiti." The word was barely whispered through Seth's lips.

Instead of giving him power, his anger seemed to diminish him. Weak and suffering, he sank even closer to the floor.

Ozzi danced within Seth's eyesight. "Yes, the brave Nefertiti. So defiant to the end — right up until the moment I sliced her beautiful throat." Ozzi laughed wickedly into Seth's shocked face. "You always thought my betrayal was in not protecting your lover while you were gone. It was far deeper than that. It was so easy to convince our queen that your loyalties had shifted and that your human lover was to blame. Queen Tia eagerly approved my suggestion of eliminating your temptations."

Seth's form shifted again back and forth, from human to dragon and back again. Each time, a bitter growl vibrated from deep within.

Ozzi pushed a button and a section of the wall slid up like a garage door. Fresh air breezed into the room. Below the new opening, waves crashed violently against the cliff side. The sound echoed through the room ominously.

"Only one thing would have made that moment sweeter." Ozzi continued his mental torture. "If only I'd been the one to kill your unborn son too. But he'd already made his unfortunate delivery into the world."

"You sick bastard!" Jayden screamed at Ozzi. But another look into Seth's eyes silenced her. Enough blood had receded from the beautiful green of his eyes to reveal his utter despair.

"I have a son?" He seemed to blink through another wave of pain.

"Had. He is long dead. Just not by my hand."

"Stop listening to this, Seth." Hot tears burned a path down her cheeks. "He's trying to torture you before..." She couldn't continue. She couldn't bring herself to say it out loud, as if keeping it inside would prevent it from happening.

But inside she screamed. *Fight, damn it! You promised you wouldn't leave me!*

Seth struggled to his feet, his eyes fixed on his sword. As he stumbled in Ozzi's direction, he began mumbling something in that old language he'd used back in the cavern.

Jayden smiled, gaining emotional strength from Seth's renewed determination. Her smile died when Ozzi lifted the sword and drove it straight through the center of Seth's chest. Air and life seeped from his body as he collapsed back down to his knees. His eyes closed and his head slumped forward.

Letting go of the sword, Ozzi pushed Seth's lifeless body through the opening.

CHAPTER EIGHT

Anguish. That was the sound Jayden heard screaming through her own lips. She felt her soul ripping from her chest and flying through the air toward the opening. Anchored by her body, her spirit hung over the edge, watching helplessly as Seth's body slammed against the cliff and tumbled limply into the crashing waves. Her out-of-body spirit came crashing back, the force knocking her against Indar.

As Jayden ran out of breath, her scream subsided. Guilt prompted her to reach inside her pocket and clutch the oracle. Could she have used it to save Seth? *No.*

She'd sworn to keep it safe. Revealing its presence to Ozzi would have broken that promise. But that didn't make her feel any better. Despair threatened to make her vulnerable.

If she waited a moment longer, the opportunity to flee would disappear. Seth would still want her to fight to stay alive.

As Ushum was taking another slash at Indar's head, Jayden did what her father had taught her when she was a teenager — grab, squeeze and yank hard. What she found in her hand was so incredibly small that she needed to alter her attack. Stamping hard on the tips of his toes, Jayden felt Indar's grip loosen enough for her to make a quick dash out of the room.

"Get her!" Ozzi still stood at the opening,

gloating over his victory.

Jayden kept enough distance between herself and Indar. She ran down many corridors, but never seemed to find the one that led to the staircase.

Ushum held onto her hair. His squeaky little voice chanted. *"Bau. Bau. Bau."*

From deep in the rooms lining the corridors, voices joined the chorus.

"Bau. Bau. Bau."

Her goal of saving the woman had failed. How was she going to save herself and Ushum? *The boat.*

She remembered seeing a boat at the end of the dock in the harbor. She'd seen it when Ozzi was showing off his island. If she could get back to the surface, the boat was their best chance to get away. She couldn't flash off the island without Seth, and she had no idea how to use the oracle on her own.

Once Ozzi went back above ground, he'd be able to flash to anywhere she was. She shut down that line of thinking. It would only add to her feeling that escape was useless. She refused to allow hope to disappear.

Hope rewarded her. A new idea formed in her head. If she stayed down here where their immortal powers were vastly limited, she could trap them and free the women. If she could find the lab room, she might have time to fashion a weapon from broken glass.

She ran in the direction she prayed was right, slamming doors to slow Indar's pursuit.

Rounding a corner, she recognized the lab and ducked inside. She locked the door and scanned the room for potential weapons. She tried to tip over the tubes, but they were bolted to the floor. As Indar pounded on the door, she grabbed a scalpel from the table and slipped through another door in the back.

Jayden found herself in a long room that felt like a tomb, with bare stone walls and a single bulb hanging by its wires. A shiny metal grate took up most of the space on the floor with a few feet of clearance all around it.

Ushum peeked out of the hoodie and screeched.

Beneath the grate, she could just barely make out the shape of a metal staircase descending into the dark. She had no time to evaluate her next move.

Indar opened the door behind her, triumphantly waving a set of keys in the air.

As she turned to face him, she spied a round silver button on the wall. She was trapped in here, unless that button opened up the grate.

Indar looked very pleased with himself.

"Stay away from me." She purposely nodded toward his privates. "You small-balled freak."

His expression reddened with anger. He lunged for her, but she forced him back when the scalpel drew blood from his hand.

"Silly girl." He tried to affect an evil laugh, but it came out more like a fake cackle. "You are trouble. But soon I will have you strapped on my table, begging to die."

"Come get me, you freak!"

He didn't like that word. It brought a shadow of hatred to his eyes.

Waving the scalpel in his face, she forced him to step back through the doorway. "Give up. You're trapped, Jayden."

She glanced at the button again.

He seemed to figure out what she was looking at. "Don't open that!"

As he took a step forward, she slashed at his

arm again and pushed the button.

"Bitch!" Fresh blood seeped from the new slice across his skin.

From behind her, Jayden could hear the sound of metal sliding across metal as the grate slowly opened. Now she had a choice. It could be a quick way to freedom — or death. In this place, one never knew.

Ushum screeched in her ear and tugged at her hair. He made his choice perfectly clear, pointing toward Indar.

Moving slowly, Jayden backed toward the opening and descended one step at a time. She kept the scalpel between herself and Indar. He followed her, but made no move to come through the grate.

After a dozen steps, she felt solid stone under her feet.

Indar's angry and shocked face briefly appeared in the opening above. The grate moved across and closed, settling into a locked position with an abrupt clank. Her choices were gone now. She was locked in.

* * *

Indar slid the key back into his pocket. He couldn't help but feel a small measure of excitement over the turn of events. He'd hated Ozzi's brother since they were all young. Seth always seemed to interfere at the wrong time, sometimes ruining well-laid plans. This time, he finally got what he deserved, and Indar had enjoyed being front-and-center for it.

He was slightly less entertained by Jayden's situation. He admired her for her quick action under pressure, but he hated her. She'd touched him — humiliated him. For that offense, he deeply wanted to torture her and bring her to madness. He had a special gift for that — inducing madness.

Ozzi's footsteps echoed more closely from the corridor. Quickly, Indar wiped away the smile on his face and replaced it with a more worried expression.

"I haven't felt this great in centuries." Ozzi's triumphant smile weakened slightly. "What? Where is she?"

"I finally cornered her, but she opened the nest and ran right in."

"You were supposed to catch her, not chase her into the nest."

"I tried to stop her."

"You didn't try hard enough." Ozzi's eyes turned black with new rage.

Indar waved his bloody wounds for Ozzi to see.

"Scratches. We need to get her out of there."

"You know I can't go in there without gassing the whole nest. They're too dangerous."

Furious, Ozzi flicked his fingers in the air. One by one, the nails turned black and narrowed into sharp talons. Before Indar could move, he felt four nails digging into the wound Jayden had made. As Ozzi tore the flesh open, blood dripped onto the floor.

The initial pain brought tears to Indar's eyes.

"Do not fail me again."

Swallowing hard, Indar accepted his punishment and swore he'd kill Jayden. It was her fault. She made him look bad. "The cameras. We can watch her on the monitors. Figure something out."

Ozzi withdrew his nails. Turning on his heel, he left the room.

Indar let the wicked smile return as the pain morphed into pleasure and his whole body shuddered.

* * *

"Well, what a pleasure." Jayden tucked the scalpel into her waist bag and tugged the frantic Ushum into her arms. "Another dark hallway."

Not a hallway really. More like the dead end of a naturally formed tunnel. Not so natural were the lights embedded in the ceiling and encased with barbed wire. She wondered why would someone need to protect lighting. Or mabye a better question was what did they need to protect the lighting from?

Cooing and stroking Ushum's back, Jayden walked slowly through the tunnels, which slanted downward. Indar and Ozzi obviously weren't following her anymore. At least, not yet. That gave her time to find a way out, to find some kind of freedom.

Freedom to do what? Go back to Miami and suffer through a slow, painful death? No. That sounded too much like swapping one prison for another.

She could continue traveling the world, but that only delayed the inevitable. Avoidance wouldn't solve anything for her. Wasn't that the lesson she should learn from Seth? She swiped away the tears that welled up at his memory. He'd given up long ago, avoiding life with his self-imposed prison.

Ushum whimpered as if he knew who she was thinking about.

She kissed top of his head and encouraged him to resettle into her hoodie. "I miss him too." But dwelling on Seth's memory now wasn't going to help her down here. She buried her feelings to examine later.

Smoothing her hands across the tunnel walls, she absorbed the cool sensation of the stone. An indented impression in the lower half of the wall seemed similar to the indentations she'd seen while hiking through a lava bed park in California. Hopefully these lava tubes were just as extinct. The good news, they led somewhere. The bad news, it could be right into a trap or worse.

Finally, she reached the end of the tunnel and stood at an entrance to a huge room with a ceiling at least four stories high. Recessed spotlights dotted the room from behind protective glass. The arched openings of many tunnels lined up along the walls like theater boxes. Fear stabbed at every nerve as she viewed her nightmares come to life.

A silent scream lodged at the base of her throat. She reached for the wall for support, gulping for oxygen. She could hear the rasp as she hyperventilated.

She looked around the room again and the nightmarish hallucinations she'd suffered since she was seven flashed mercilessly across her mind. Could they have been visions? Possibly some form of premonition? Her whole body trembled as she stood at the edge of an underworld arena. If her nightmares were real, then any moment now, dozens of yellow-eyed demons would descend on her.

Her silent scream broke free.

The sound of soul-deep fear ricocheted between the stone walls. Dark shapes slithered from tunnels and shadowed corners. They crawled down to the floor and gathered in the center.

Ushum whimpered softly in her ear, and Jayden broke free of her horrified trance. Turning back, she started to run, but several creatures blocked her path and moved slowly towards her. Where had they come from? She hadn't passed them in the tunnel. She would have seen them.

Two creatures approached on the ground and one on the ceiling. Like wicked shepherds, they were herding her deeper into the cave. As she backed slowly into the middle of the room, Ushum moved to her shoulder. He chattered and postured, flicking his tail in a frantic pattern.

They were completely surrounded now. The sea of angry yellow eyes around her was exactly the scene from her hallucinations. The detail was too fine to be ignored or discarded as coincidence. Somehow, she'd been here in her nightmares. Now she knew that they weren't nightmares at all.

The oracle stone in her pocket warmed. She reached in and rolled it tight between her fingers like a large worry bead. *Is this why you brought me here — to fulfill my visions?*

* * *

Jayden tried to keep in mind what Seth had said. The oracle's power would protect her. At this moment, she highly doubted it was working. She gripped the stone a little too hard, allowing herself a small measure of anger toward it for bringing her into the hands of these demons.

Not demons, she had to remind herself. These were creatures created by Ozzi and his mad doctor. These were damiens — made of flesh, blood and teeth. And unlike her nightmares, she could see and smell every detail. They smelled of musk and earth.

Ushum chattered loudly, adding in screeches

that sounded like warnings.

The largest of the creatures moved closer, hissing at the smaller ones who retreated a few steps. As he reached for Ushum, her protective mode kicked in.

"Don't touch him." Jayden batted the creature's arm away.

Angrily, it bared sharp teeth slick with drool and licked the air as if it could already taste her flesh. Its elliptical irises expanded and contracted wildly with excitement. It leaned in close over her hair. At the end of a short nose, the nostrils flared wide and inhaled her scent.

She decided this one was a male. Looming a good foot taller than her, he seemed to be the largest. He stood like a human, but the shape and musculature of his hind legs resembled a lizard. Gray scales covered the skin across his back and all the way to the tip of a long, thick tail, which he used to swipe several large damien away.

The shape of his head showed a human genealogy, except for a slight protrusion of the jaws. She could see a full set of sharp cutting teeth with two snake-like fangs descending from the top row. As he hissed a warning to others, a thick forked tongue licked his thin lips from between the two fangs.

He reached for her face with a human-like finger. The skin on his arms was dark green and very smooth. He trailed the tip of a black claw across the curve of her jaw and down her throat, pausing at the base of her neck. Her blood pulsed in a stressful pace just under his fingertip.

She watched the swell of his vertical irises and knew he could feel the rush of her blood beneath the skin. She felt like prey being closely examined by a predator. Had he figured out the optimum kill spot?

Grabbing her arm, he dragged her into the center of the arena.

Her stomach churned after an unwelcome vision of damien tugging off bits of her flesh while she was still alive. Jayden refused to go down without a fight. Reaching into her waist bag, she slipped the scalpel into her palm.

The large damien hissed in her direction. Slowly, he circled her in a pattern of lunges and retreats as if toying with her. Or was he waiting for her to do something? Even Ushum seemed to be waiting for something. He sat completely still on her shoulder, his eyes cast down to the floor.

Jayden would not meet whatever fate awaited her with her eyes cast down. She'd meet it head on like she always did.

As the damien completed a second circle, he glared at her. Being uncooperative was apparently getting under his skin. She understood that feeling. She didn't like being patient either. Doing her best to mimic him, she bared her teeth, lunged one step forward, and growled out something that hopefully sounded like a warning.

At first the tactic seemed to be the right move. The damien took a step back and eyed her more warily this time. But on his next lunge, he came closer and swiped a hand full of claws toward her neck.

She moved on instinct, ducking under his reach and swinging her own hand across his bicep. In its wake, a thin red line of blood formed across the thick skin of his arm.

The damien hesitated, taking another long look at her. His eyes paused over her hands and short, useless fingernails as if searching for an explanation.

She kept the scalpel hidden in her palm. Her mystery weapon just might keep her alive long enough. *Long enough for what? A rescue?* She shut down that line of questioning when a tear formed a hot puddle in the corner of her eye, compromising her vision.

Distracted, Jayden missed the slight change in the damien's posturing. He'd slanted toward the ground, bringing his legs underneath his body. Every muscle in his leg coiled and released as his body launched through the air toward her.

Jayden tensed her body for the impact. Instead, another damien intercepted her attacker in mid-leap. They rolled across the stone floor in a violent blur of gray and brown. As they untangled themselves and squared off, the damien crowd moved back to give them more space.

The new damien was slightly smaller, but his arms and legs were thicker. His skin was different than any of the others. While they were a dark gray, he was dark brown. A whitish gray border around his lips indicated age. Older and wiser. Was he the alpha of this damien pack?

The alpha roared and postured until her attacker backed down and skulked away. But not before sending a look her way that conveyed a sense that this wasn't over.

Smaller creatures approached and grabbed Jayden's arms, pulling her toward the side of the arena. They pushed her to sit near a short waterfall into a pool about twice the size of the one from Ozzi's ballroom. As she sat down on a small rock, another damien held her in place.

Ushum chattered in a low, grumbling voice, but

the creatures seemed to ignore him now.

Blood pulsed rapidly through her body, making her nerves hum with the desire to flee. She knew what was coming. Hallucinations or nightmares, they featured the same bloody battle, which usually ended with a wicked set of claws inches away from her face.

As if on cue with her visions, the attacking damien re-entered the arena and lunged for the alpha. Panting with deeper breaths, the alpha swayed heavily when slammed by the body of the other damien.

Jayden shivered with each sound. Claws scratched across the stone floor as they lunged for each other. Tails thumped like massive clubs, cracking scales and bruising flesh. Teeth clacked together as they fought for a dominating position.

The alpha had the smaller damien subdued beneath him, until the young one found his footing and flipped his elder into the ground. Spinning on his feet, the victor lunged in Jayden's direction.

Screaming, she tried to twist away from the damien that held her on the rock. Sharp nails dug into her shoulders to hold her in place. She could hear Ushum whimpering helplessly behind her ear.

Did she really have to sit here and watch destiny leaping toward her face with bloodthirsty yellow eyes and sharp black claws? *Hell, no.*

Her arms were captive but her legs were free. With a hefty kick, she brought her sneaker right up under the approaching damien's jaw. The crack echoed through the cavern.

His momentum halted, he crouched low and flexed his bruised jaw. Blood drooled from between his fangs. Opening his mouth, he lunged toward her again.

Jayden prepared herself for the coming horror. For the feeling of sharp fangs plunging into her skin. But the damien wasn't approaching her anymore. He was slipping backward.

She had distracted him just long enough for the alpha to recover and attack. He'd grabbed the young damien by the tail. Growling from the effort, the alpha swung his opponent in a wide circle. He used the momentum to sling the body into the wall.

Bones snapped. Blood splattered across the stone. The young damien landed in a stunned heap on the floor. His chest heaved in an effort to breathe.

The alpha stood defiantly in the middle of the ring. Silently, his eyes traveled around the room, pausing at each young damien. He curled his lips and clacked his teeth as if daring anyone else to confront him.

Jayden sighed with relief as none accepted the challenge.

* * *

"Incredible." Indar sat back away from the monitor, but he did not find Ozzi to be equally amazed.

"Get her out of there."

Indar pointed to the screen. "But we've never seen this before. This is amazing. They are battling for her."

"Yes, it was very clear that young damien was drooling over a fresh meal." Ozzi tapped his still-extended talons against each other. "She is too important, and I don't have time for you to play scientist."

"But I *am* a man of science."

"Indeed." The word dripped sarcastically from Ozzi's lips.

Indar wasn't about to give up. Watching Jayden's distress excited him. It felt like foreplay. His skin tingled as blood hummed through his body. He wanted to extend her time in the nest for a while longer. "We've never had a birth mother interact with the alphas. I can't miss this opportunity to observe and document their behavior."

Ozzi's nails continued to tap. "A human womb with the power of a direct Anunnaki bloodline — we can't afford to lose her."

"I agree, but I don't believe they'll harm her now."

"How can you be so sure of that?"

"Because Jayden didn't act submissive. She fought back. She acted like an alpha."

Ozzi shook his head slowly. "Get her out of there. Now!"

"You know I can't go into the nest without gassing them all. The timer has already been set for eight o'clock." Indar giggled inwardly thinking about how much fun he could have toying with Jayden and the damien for the next six hours. He resented Ozzi's interference in his plans.

"I don't care how you do it, but get her out of there alive." Rising to leave, Ozzi retracted his talons and smoothed away the wrinkles from his suit jacket. "Don't disturb me again until morning."

"As you wish." Indar grinned at the screen. He had no intention of causing her a quick death. She deserved to live a nice long life of torture and madness.

The old alpha seemed very protective of Jayden, but his days were numbered. In a nest full of alphas, battles for supremacy were a frequent event. Odds would soon swing to a younger specimen.

Indar rebelled at the idea of keeping Jayden *safe*. Alive? Yes. Bloody, broken and begging for mercy? Gods, yes!

He could hear her voice in his head calling him a freak.

He wasn't satisfied with the calm that followed the alpha's victory. Indar wanted more excitement for Jayden to witness. More blood. He petted the screen around her head.

Pressing a button on the console, he released live food into the arena and waited to enjoy the bloodbath.

CHAPTER NINE

Jayden jumped when a loud bang echoed from an alcove above the waterfall. Ushum squealed with terror and ducked into the hoodie. The damien — including the one that had held her down — gathered in a distinct semicircular pattern around the pool. The largest stood in front.

At first she wondered what they were waiting for. As saliva drooled from many lips, she realized they were waiting for food. *The strongest feed first!*

It was unsettling to realize that she sat front and center for a feeding frenzy. She loved the Discovery Channel, but this was a little too up-close-and-personal. Very slowly, she inched as far away from the waterfall as she could get.

A few moments after the bang came a long sound like sliding sands. Finally, several small, malformed damien landed in the pool. Instantly, they postured defensively — submissively. It didn't seem to matter. In fact, their weakness seemed to trigger the opposite action, like a match to gasoline.

It was like watching that nature show with the orcas tossing a helpless seal pup around. Playing with it — before devouring it.

Jayden covered her nose as the pungent smell of urine and fear permeated the stagnant room. She turned away from the pool as it filled with thick, red blood. The feeding ended too soon. There was not enough to go around. From the depths of the horde, she could hear damien fighting with each other.

A sea of yellow eyes zeroed in on her.

She must look delicious. She didn't *feel* delicious. Even Ushum had silenced, as if hypnotized by the fear.

But the alpha stepped in front of her, squaring off with the others. Where had he come from? She'd lost track during the frenzy.

She expected a mass attack. Instead, the creatures retreated, slowly disappearing into the many tunnels that feed into the cave. Clearly they could gang up on the alpha and defeat him. But they didn't.

The alpha urged Jayden to her feet and motioned for her to follow him. She didn't know what he intended to do with her, but he'd protected her from being eaten twice. She would rather take her chances with one damien than a whole mob of them. More than happy to leave the arena, she followed him closely.

Just before they entered one of the tunnels, Jayden stopped and stared at a black orb fixed to the wall. A few scratches marred the dark glass. She was certain it was a camera cover.

It made sense. From the journal, Seth had read about the progress Indar was making with the experimentations. What they'd seen in the labs were the failures. These tunnels contained their successes. Even the damien woman from the hallway wouldn't quite fit in down here. She was almost too human. Maybe that was why she and the others like her were in the rooms with the birth women. They must serve some purpose in that area.

But here, these incredibly-formed creatures seemed trapped. Trapped in this underground world.

For what purpose? That's what Seth had wanted to find out.

She thought of the timely arrival of live food, and she knew who watched her every move on some screen. Before she moved away from the camera, she flicked her middle finger in its direction and slowly mouthed, "*Freak!*"

She jogged to catch up with the alpha. He moved with a purpose, but paused in front of every opening along the way. The lighting system only traveled along the tunnel itself, but it cast enough light into the openings for Jayden to see into them a bit. They were small caves, and groups of damien seemed to live in them. Like family units.

She wondered if this tunnel was the alpha's family. He looked into each cave briefly but intently, as if taking note of all of his charges. Very paternal.

From each cave, two would approach. Of each pair, one looked slightly more feminine. They were equally fierce in their posturing, especially towards Jayden, but their features seemed slightly softer and a shade lighter. As the damien greeted the alpha, Jayden knew they studied her. Their nostrils flared as they gathered her scent, and their eyes dilated as they looked her up and down.

Strangely, she felt safe walking through these tunnels with the alpha. He allowed none of the others to harm her. One female dared to lunge at Jayden. The alpha responded by burying his teeth into the female's neck. He held on until she understood the warning and backed down.

Ushum obviously felt safer too. He chattered and mumbled to the others. Some ignored him. Some hissed at the stunted damien, but he hissed back, baring his little teeth and stretching his chest out. The height from Jayden's shoulder gave him more courage than sense.

He'd left her hoodie and half walked, half flew beside the alpha's legs. He looked very much like the damien only in miniature and with little wings. They were not big enough for him to be terribly good at flying. He didn't get much lift beyond a few feet. Maybe his wings were meant for opportunity rather than for endurance.

She caught the alpha watching Ushum with curiosity. They seemed to carry on a conversation. The alpha listened to Ushum like someone paying attention to a valuable source of information. Jayden wished she could understand what they said.

They came to a small room that appeared to be the junction of three tunnels. It also appeared to be the end of the lighting system. A slight movement of cool air passed across her skin, revealing a layer of hot sweat. It felt like a sauna in this part, which might be why the man-made lighting ended here. Too much corrosion with moisture.

The alpha led her into the far tunnel which continued on a steeper slope downward. Jayden made it through the final dark section with one hand on his arm and the other trailing along the wall. In the pitch black, a recognizable sound reached her ears — water. It sounded like they were now at sea level. Waves crashed against the walls outside in a muted symphony.

He brought her into a cave that looked a lot like the one under the Sphinx that she'd fallen into. Seth's cave. She knew he wasn't here, but she couldn't stop herself from looking for him or his shredded pallet.

The source of light in the cave came from the water itself. It glowed with eerie blue luminescence.

She moved toward the tidal pool and marveled at how crystal clear it was and how nearly still it was at the surface. A variety of glowing corals, urchins and shrimp inhabited the pool like a miniature city. They were safe from predators in this tucked-away cave.

After each crashing wave she heard outside, small ripples radiated along the water's surface. Somehow the tides swept water in and out of this cave. So if water could get in, she might have a way out.

She moved to the water's edge, but the alpha pulled her away. She could hear Seth's voice in her mind again, warning her to beware of waters that seemed too still. Undercurrents could kill her. But so could Ozzi and Indar. She'd rather take her chances with the water.

She wondered why the damien had brought her here. Was he showing her something pretty? If so, there was even more human in him than she thought.

Something new moved along the bottom of the tidal pool. A long, narrow shadow sliced through the water as its body undulated from side to side. One by one, a dozen damien rose from the water and passed through the cave. They held fish and sea snakes in their hands. The last one paused to offer one of his fish to the alpha.

Jayden would bet anything that Indar and Ozzi had no idea that their tightly-controlled stock of damien had found a way to leave their prison. But why didn't they escape? They fished and returned. Were they adapting for survival on their own? When they were ready, would they swim off into the night?

* * *

The marine glow began to fade. Jayden felt the

alpha's hand on her arm, tugging her sleeve. She followed him to an alcove where a pallet of dried seaweed covered the floor. She expected it to crunch under her weight, but instead it felt as soft as a down comforter. Even Ushum left her shoulder to dig into a warm spot next to her hip.

The alpha left and returned a few moments later with a large clamshell filled with fresh water. She smiled, accepted the offer, and shared it with Ushum. She shivered as the ice cold water chilled her body. A memory hovered tauntingly. How long had it been since she'd awakened in Seth's cave? Was that just yesterday?

Exhaustion poured from her lungs as she exhaled. Sleep was the last thing on her mind as the prismatic lights from the pool ebbed away. Complete darkness enveloped the cave, bringing with it an uneasy calm.

In the absence of light, her mind conjured images to fill the void. She saw Seth — in his cave, on the cliff, in the bedroom doorway. Even as a memory, his energy felt overpowering. She shivered, but not from fear. She ached to touch his face. She lifted her hand and tried to twirl his hair around her fingers.

Suddenly, his image lurched as the tip of a sword came through his chest. Seth's blood coated the tip. His brows knitted together and his green eyes darkened with an accusing glare. Guilt slipped over her like a leather sheath.

Jayden's body jerked awake.

How long had she slept? She wiped tears from her cheeks and tried to gather information with her other senses. She couldn't see the alpha, but he was near. His breath inhaled and exhaled in a raspy, even tempo, indicating that he was in a deep sleep.

Removing the oracle from her pocket, she cupped it gently and waited for it to swirl with light. Nothing. She shook it, and still nothing happened. Water. She remembered that it seemed to like water.

Tucking it back into her pocket, she crawled very slowly in the direction of the tidal pool. When she felt her hand dip into the cold water, she removed the oracle again and held it in the pool. As she swirled it around, tiny lights trailed behind it. Back and forth, she waved the stone around, creating more colorful sparkles. Finally, the oracle shimmered with misty light.

The stone only cast light a few feet, but it was enough for her to make some progress. Staying here was not an option. With the tidal glow gone, it would be too dangerous to try to swim her way out.

Think, Jayden. She was trained to inventory her surroundings. Remembering details could be the difference between life and death for a climber. What important detail lay hidden in her mind? She chewed her lower lip as she mentally reviewed the layout of the tunnels.

Tunnels. Ancient lava tubes. Where there was lava, there was gas. Gases always found a way out, sometimes violently pushing through layers of rock to escape.

Escape. Venting holes. *Air!*

That was it. She'd felt a very subtle wisp of air just before turning down that final tunnel to this cave.

Leaving the safety of the cave without the alpha was probably not the wisest choice, but she wasn't going to wake him for an escort. Gently, she lifted Ushum into her arms and moved away from the alcove. The oracle cast a fuzzy blue glow along the wall, which Jayden followed out of the cave and up the long inclined tunnel.

As the floor leveled out, she found herself in the junction. From down one of the tunnels she could hear more deep breathing. She shivered, thinking about the fangs on some of the female damien.

Instead of proceeding into one of the tunnels, she stayed in the junction. Moving around the room in a slow circle, she paused every few feet and waited. Finally, she felt it. The slightest movement of air ruffled along her skin. In the eerie glow of the oracle, she watched goose bumps rise and fall in a wave across her forearm.

Quickly now, she swung the oracle above her head for light. The vent would be high on the walls or possibly in the ceiling. She prayed it would be large enough for her to climb through it. She scanned every shadow and dip in the stone. She closely inspected a loose pile of gravel. Dusty slivers of obsidian poked from the pile and pointed in a telltale direction. Up.

There it was — hidden in the shadows near the ceiling. The hole wide enough for her to crawl into. But it was too high up and the walls held nothing she could grip. She tried jumping, but it was another foot higher than her reach.

Ushum whispered softly in her ear. It sounded like encouragement. Holding his body as high as she could, Ushum hopped toward the opening, using his wings to get up the final few inches. He disappeared into the hole for several minutes. When he returned, Jayden could tell by the flick of his tail that he'd found a way out.

But from the shadows of the tunnel, the alpha damien stepped forward.

Jayden nearly cried, exhausted and frustrated. She expected him to grab her and take her back.

Instead, he lifted her up by her waist and held her in reach of the hole.

What is he up to? She hadn't given it much thought before. He had kept her safe from the other damien, and now he was helping her escape the tunnels. She wanted to know why. But she didn't speak damien and this wasn't the best time to explore his motivations anyway. It was time to leave.

Before she climbed into the hole, she looked down and thanked him. His lips curved into a twisted expression that she hoped was a smile.

The hole was large enough to crawl through, and Ushum led the way, chattering excitedly. She had to shush him several times, fearing that he could wake the other damien. They crawled for what felt like twenty meters or so. The air became fresher, saltier. The sound of waves crashing inspired a bittersweet memory.

The hole opened onto a ledge barely wide enough for her shoes and about the length of her body. The full moon sat very near to the western horizon. Daybreak was probably a few hours away. Thankfully, the moonlight still shone bright enough to see clearly that they were about three stories up. Close enough to climb down but high enough to die if she fell into the rocks.

Focusing on deep breaths, Jayden cleared her mind of distractions. Then she unzipped her waist bag and withdrew her small flashlight to scan the rock around the ledge. Here she would not use her fingerless gloves. Without any gear, she would need every millimeter of skin on her fingers and hands to feel for the imperfections along the wall. By habit, she stood and looked over the edge, scanning for just the right path along the stone.

The first half would be easy. It was the bottom section, closest to the water, that would be treacherous. There the force of water had pounded the stone into a smooth surface. Not a climber's friend. But she'd figure that out when she got there.

She tucked Ushum into her hoodie and slid her body backwards over the ledge. Holding the edge with her fingers, she felt along the wall with her shoe until it wedged in a space. Slow and steady, she descended the wall from crack to crevice.

As she neared the smooth section at the bottom, she found fewer edges to connect with. Now, she had a choice to make. Choice number one: push away from the wall and hope that she and Ushum could clear the wicked rocks below. Not a very attractive option.

Choice number two: climb sideways and hope she could find a path down or a less rocky landing. A slightly more attractive choice, except that her fingers were cramping up.

A pebble bounced off her shoulder, drawing her attention up the cliff. The alpha stood on the ledge looking down the wall intently. Then, he leaned into the cliff and crawled face down toward her.

"Oh, I so want some of your DNA." Climbing skills aside, she exhaled with relief. Choice number three had arrived.

The alpha moved next to Jayden and wrapped an arm around her waist. She let go of the wall and felt gravity pull her toward the rocks. With the added weight, he slid a few feet. Slowly, he moved to their right, south toward a section where the wall curved away. As they rounded the corner, the number of rocks diminished until a stretch of sand glowed pale in the moonlight.

As her feet crunched on sand, she almost giggled. "Thank you."

Again, his face contorted into something that resembled a smile. Hard to tell with the fangs. He sniffed the air and a low grumble echoed around a small inlet. Something here made him wary.

Jayden respected that instinct. Ozzi and Indar could be anywhere.

Now that she had her bearings straight, thanks to the moon, she knew they were on the south side of the island. The harbor was on this side, and in the harbor was the boat. She would worry about where to go once she reached it.

Traveling along the base of the cliff seemed to be the best option. The shoreline would be easier, but it was also more likely that she'd be seen. A sharp outcropping of rock forced them into the water to get around it. As they waded into the surf, she peered carefully around the formation to see what was on the other side.

She found another inlet, slightly larger, with a smooth stretch of beach and tropical vegetation. But beyond it, she thought she could just make out the curved shape of the harbor.

The sand near the vegetation was softer, making it mushy to walk across and slowing them down.

Ushum suddenly stilled. His ears pricked so far forward he nearly leaned off of her shoulder. He finally flew down and scurried over to a deep set of lines in the sand leading away from the water.

The alpha growled a warning, which was amplified by the cliffs surrounding the inlet.

Jayden took a closer look at the lines. They were heavy drag marks, and they led into the vegetation.

Through a gap in the large leaves, moonlight glimmered off of something long, wet, and covered in scales. Her heart thumped madly against her ribs. *Could it be...*

Jayden didn't stop to think about traps or tricks of the light. She focused only on one word repeating through her mind. *Please?*

Ducking under the leaves, Jayden crawled along the body until she reached the dragon's face. Breath wheezed softly through his nose. "He's alive!" Gently, she cradled Seth's head on her lap and then struggled to breathe between choking sobs.

* * *

"Help me." Jayden pleaded with the alpha. The sword still impaled Seth through the center of his chest. Blood pooled into the sand below it. "We have to get it out."

She would need fresh water to clean the wound. She cupped her hands in front of her mouth and made a motion as if she was drinking water. The alpha nodded, gathered several fat leaves and disappeared.

Ushum whimpered softly and snuggled next to Seth's head, petting his cheek.

Jayden wrapped her hands firmly around the hilt of the sword. She typically wasn't a wimp around wounds, but the one who was wounded meant so much. She hesitated, uncertainty filling a chasm of doubt. Filling and emptying her lungs a few times calmed her nerves and gave her strength. She flexed every muscle in her arms and yanked the sword cleanly out of his body.

Something rumbled in the dragon's throat like a

groan. But Jayden's spirits shouted, thrilled to hear more sounds of life.

The alpha returned. He carried a bowl woven from the leaves and filled with saltwater. Carefully, he drizzled some of it over the wound on the dragon's chest.

The dragon's skin flinched from the contact.

Seth had told her that the sword had healing powers. He'd used it to heal her. She held the sword out but nothing happened. She turned it around, pointing the jeweled hilt toward him. Still nothing happened.

Frustration crowded her mind. She paced beside his long body, trying to focus.

The oracle's power was used for protection and purification. She decided that healing was a form of purification. Maybe she could use it. She pulled the stone out of her pocket and cradled it above Seth's body.

It really wasn't much different than any other aquamarine stone. No special markings. Yet she knew it held special power. She'd felt it, but right now it wasn't helping. *Water!*

Signaling the alpha for the leaf bowl, she nestled it into the sand next to Seth's body and placed the oracle into the remaining water. Still, it did not glow.

She balled her fists and yelled at the oracle and the sword. "Why won't you help me? How do I do this?" She cursed her inability to activate the power she knew existed in both items.

Ushum and the alpha both backed a little farther away.

Finally, she knelt in the sand and prayed her instincts would lead her in the right direction.

Hopefully the powers that be would understand her message even if they didn't understand the words. Couldn't they read her heart? Couldn't her love just be enough?

Holding the sword over Seth body, she begged both items to help. "Please, heal Seth."

The oracle seemed as lifeless as the sword. She tried swishing the water around and was rewarded with little lights. As she removed her hand, the lights disappeared. She circled her fingers through the water again, a glittering trail of light curled around the stone.

Sheer determination helped her hold the heavy sword over Seth with one hand, while she held the oracle under the water with the other.

"Please, heal him. I don't know the right words, but please... Please, I beg you to heal him. I love this man." She poured every ounce of passion she possessed into her plea and she tried to visualize Seth without the wound.

The diamond in the hilt of the sword blazed with a pale flame, and a fluorescent blue bolt of energy fingered across Seth's body. A stream of similar light lifted from the oracle and twirled in a graceful arc to join with the other above the sword.

"Please..." Jayden felt her teeth gnashing together from the force of the energy arching around her.

In one brilliant burst, the entire stream of light melded into a large orb and slammed into Seth's wound.

Darkness settled back into the inlet.

Jayden stabbed the sword into the sand and leaned against it for support. All she could do now was wait, and patience was not a word in her personal vocabulary.

CHAPTER TEN

Images break through the red darkness, spinning through Seth's mind like a bloodied carousel.

Proud, fearless Jayden. Her voice screams in his head, ordering him to fight.

Where is his sword?

Ozzi holds it, but there is something Ozzi doesn't know about the sword. Must create a distraction — give Jayden time to escape. Escape what? Why won't his memory cooperate?

Breathe. Ribs feel so tight. Coldness slides through his chest as the sword slices through bone and flesh. His body collapses.

Salt air fills his senses. The ocean calls him to come home. Falling through space and time, interrupted by a pounding against his body. Blessed ocean waters wrap their loving arms around him. They pull him toward the sea, down. The sandy bottom scratches his skin.

Nefertiti is here. Her dark hair flows between his fingers. She whispers in his ear but he can't hear the words. He feels a kiss on his cheek and then she's gone.

Peace. He's denied it for centuries but now his heart overflows with it.

So many battles. So much blood.

The sweetness of her blood. She'd tasted of sweet wine — and coconut.

Coconut lotion. What did it remind him of? A promise.

What was the promise? What was wrong with his

memory?

Slowly, Seth peeled his eyelids open. He inhaled a deep, shuddering breath, filling his lungs with the reassuring scent of salty ocean, sand and Jayden. But another scent triggered his defenses, raising his scales and extending his talons to their fullest.

Seth lifted his beastly body on all fours and vented his lungs in a fiery huff. On wobbly legs, he surrounded Jayden's body protectively and bared his fangs at the demon.

The demon's yellow eyes widened briefly with shock and he took a large step back. He didn't posture submissively, but neither did he cower. He stood taller.

Jayden stepped between them, pressing a calming hand on Seth's neck. "He's okay. He won't hurt me."

Every memory came back to Seth's mind in a rush. Ozzi playing god. Indar's new demon species. *Jayden's in their journal. They want her for something that's buried in her blood.*

"He helped me get out of the tunnels. If it wasn't for him, I wouldn't have found you."

Seth shifted into his human form, grimacing from the effort and leaning heavily against the cliff wall. He inspected the smooth new skin on his chest before flashing on a new shirt and pair of cargo pants.

His voice sounded like he'd swallowed a bucket of gravel. "And if you hadn't found me, you wouldn't have been able to heal me."

"Yes." Jayden rushed into his arms. "I saw you die. He stabbed you in the heart. How is it possible you survived that?"

He hugged her tight, burying his nose in her hair and inhaling her scent. "My sword is bonded to me. It cannot be used to kill me." He kept a wary eye on the large damien observing them. "The only way to save you was to convince Ozzi of my death. But that poison..."

"Shh. I know." She pulled him in for a kiss and her lips tasted of salty tears.

He wanted to deepen the kiss, but he felt Ushum tugging on a pant leg. Seth lowered his arm and Ushum scrabbled up to pace on Seth's shoulders. His chatter had a definite scolding tone to it.

Seth smiled. "I missed you, too." It seemed just days ago that he'd wanted only to be left alone, to hide from the world. In such a short time, his life had flipped around. Maybe Jayden's lust for life was rubbing off on him.

The tension subsided and Seth moved the group to a warmer spot at the base of the wall under a thicker canopy of leaves. Now that they were above ground, he could use his powers again. He cleared a spot in the sand and used his energy to create a small fireball, which hovered a few inches above the ground. It was just enough to light and warm their little haven under the trees.

The damien approached the fire with naked curiosity. He poked it with a claw, only to whisk it back with a very real burn on his finger.

"I'm sorry." Jayden's eyes filled with regret as she pushed a basket against Seth's chest. "You should keep this. The oracle doesn't seem to work very well for me. It only works in water."

He watched her demonstrate her technique. The shimmering trail of sparkles from her fingertips finally shed light on the mystery of the oracle.

Suppressing a grin, he took the basket and her hand. "My dear Jayden. The oracle works just fine. You are bonded with it."

"No, I'm not."

He wouldn't let her remove her hand and instead swirled her fingers until the glow returned. He lifted her hand out and the waters darkened.

"Those energy orbs are yours."

She looked like she was adding things up in that beautiful mind of hers. She licked her lips and — gods help him — his thoughts sank into erotic territory. He pictured her tongue licking a path across his skin. His body trembled slightly before he zipped up that line of thinking.

"The first time I saw them, I was in the shower. The second time, I was at the waterfall in the ballroom. The oracle wasn't in the water either time." She splayed her hands in front of her. "How? I don't feel any different."

"I think the oracle has been waiting for you. When you first held it in the cave, it accepted you and gave you some of its energy. You are bonded with it. The power is in the oracle, but *you* are its key."

The damien spoke suddenly, his voice strong but his language primitive. Seth listened intently and patiently.

"What did he say?"

"He said that you are shorter than he had envisioned." He couldn't help smirking at the idea. Although she was shorter than the damien, Jayden was tall for a human woman.

"Envisioned? What does he mean by that?"

"As the seer of his pack, he's seen you in night visions. He called you the *raba nagira*, the great herald of the uprising. He's been waiting for you. He said that it's his duty to protect you from the others."

"Other damien?"

"No, he meant from Ozzi and Indar."

"*Bau gula!*" The damien spit into the sand.

"I've heard that." Jayden's hand landed on Seth's thigh, and more of his thoughts plunged into the gutter. He fought the impulse to press her palm a little higher up. "Ushum said that over and over. *Bau.* What does it mean?"

"It's a very ancient word for doctor. It's not a nice term." Seth laughed out loud. It felt so good to laugh. "He specifically referred to Indar as *bau gula*, which is the feminine context."

"Indar is a female?" Jayden's eyebrows lifted high.

"Indar is the only one of our race known to be — I believe the Anglo word for it is androgynous. He is both, yet neither."

"Well, that explains a lot."

He pointed to his own chest. "Seth." Then to her. "Jayden."

The damien nodded and pointed to himself. "Zarick."

"He has to get back. The sun will be up soon, and in a few hours they will come to collect the alphas selected for tonight's Offering."

Seth asked several probing questions which the damien answered.

Seth expelled a long sigh. "I never knew."

"You never knew what?"

"The Offering is Ozzi's donation of damien to Apophis' army."

"Apophis? He's another Egyptian god, right? Why does he want an army?"

"He is evil in physical form, and I trapped him

in the Underworld thousands of years ago. But there is a prophecy that says Apophis will escape his prison and slaughter the human race with his dark army." The ball of energy reacted to Seth's rise in tension, flaring brighter and spitting out a stream of tiny orbs like embers. "I *must* attend the ceremony tonight. I have to see how Apophis accepts his offering — see if it jeopardizes the bonds that hold him in the Underworld."

Seth translated more of Zarick's unrefined descriptions. "Twice a year, alphas are collected and sent to the Underworld, but Ozzi keeps the largest and strongest for himself."

"Your brother apparently has some plans of his own."

"And you are featured in that plan."

"Is it my connection to the oracle?"

"No. It has something to do with your blood."

Zarick spoke once more, acknowledging that Jayden was safe in Seth's care.

Seth gave the damien a message he could take back to his pack. "I will be there tonight. Let your pack know that I am a friend and will defend your uprising."

The old alpha nodded respectfully to all and left.

Seth quickly spoke to Ushum, who promptly petted Jayden's face and dashed off to join Zarick. Ushum would be Seth's eyes and ears to the damien uprising. It would be bloody and violent, and he wanted to make damned sure that Jayden wasn't anywhere near it.

"Seth?" She had that tell-me-everything look in her eyes again.

"He said that he came to protect you. Because

when Ozzi and Indar go in to collect the alphas, they will find you gone, and they will hunt you down."

"Why?" Jayden leapt to her feet and shook her fists toward the cliff. Frustration hardened her features. "Why is he doing this?"

His gut twisted with each accusing note in her voice. "I don't know why. I — "

"Stop him!" Her voice cracked, and she seemed startled by the anger in her own voice. She lowered her gaze and whispered, "I don't want to be hunted."

Seth gathered a wave of calming energy and mentally pushed it toward Jayden. Slowly, her agitation subsided. He held a hand out and she accepted it, sitting back down beside him.

"Ozzi said that your kind came here as explorers and conquerors. Where are they? Could they help us?"

He shook his head. "Very few Anunnaki remain here. They are leaderless and scattered throughout the world."

"No. You're not leaderless. I heard what Ozzi called you. You are a prince. Doesn't that make you a leader?"

"We have a matrilinear line of succession. The right to rule would have passed down from Queen Tia to her daughter Inanna, and then to Inanna's daughter Shaila. But the royal bloodline was broken thousands of years ago during the Uprising."

"Well, I was suggesting that you lead, not rule."

He smiled and trailed a finger across the stubborn lines across her face. "You are right. I *can* lead them. But until the oracle allows us to leave the island, I have no way of reaching any of them in time."

He refrained from telling her that he had no

idea who and where any living Anunnaki might be — another drawback from locking himself away in isolation for so long. She didn't need to feel any more alone or helpless.

Jayden leaned into him. He felt the warmth of her arms around his waist and the press of her face into his chest. He wondered if she could hear his heartbeat. Did it make her feel less alone? Could she hear how it beat faster now?

Seth drew in a deep breath, inhaling the heady blend of ocean breezes and Jayden.

* * *

Jayden squeezed her arms tighter around Seth. He was alive. Joy coated the guilt, making it easier for Jayden to allow herself to admit it. *I love you.*

She'd never had a man in her life that she could depend on. She knew very little about this one. But she knew he had honor. He'd died for her.

She watched his chest rise and fall, proof that he was alive. Her body felt too heavy with emotion to move. As she tilted her head to look up at him, his lips hovered just above hers. She licked her own, suddenly starving for a taste of him.

The inlet surrounded Jayden with an erotic symphony. Gentle waves stroked the sands. The ocean breeze fingered through the woven canopy of tropical leaves. Firelight licked across her skin.

Seth cradled her face with his hands and pressed his lips against hers. Lightly at first, and then hungrily. Jayden reveled in every sensation. His teeth nibbled her lower lip. His tongue stroked hers. Deep. Possessive. She felt the blood pulsing feverishly through his lips.

Jayden's emotions tumbled over a cliff and she desperately needed an anchor. She slid her hands up his arms, hooking them over his shoulders.

She wanted to cry when he broke away.

"I'm like the oracle. I've been waiting for you for a long time." He opened his palm, and power spread from it in a pale blue glow. The world around them swirled in a slow dance. Leaves slid to the ground at her feet forming a soft mattress. Clothing unwrapped from their bodies and disappeared. Sparks burst from the fireball and floated in the air like shimmering dust. "No more waiting."

As he laid her down, she welcomed the press of his body on hers. This was nothing like her hectic, extreme life. This was slow, surreal and beautiful.

She felt his admiration along every inch of her body. The soft caress of his lips against her throat. The searing trail of his tongue around her nipples. The tender pull of her flesh as he sucked every silky drop her body could give him.

But she wanted more. She pulled him back up her body and wrapped her legs around his hips, silently demanding all of him.

Breath left her body completely as he plunged himself deep within her. She dug her nails in, needing a lifeline to keep from falling over the edge. Slowly, she felt her body adjust, relaxing and then begging for more.

* * *

Seth waited patiently for Jayden's body to accept him. His muscles shuddered from the effort to hold his body in check. It was damn hard when she panted and moaned so invitingly in his ear.

Lovely, fearless Jayden. She'd said she loved him. Not aloud, but whispered in his mind. He hadn't felt a woman's love in a very long time. It humbled him, made him want to live up to her. She deserved his patience.

Finally, he felt her body relax. As he moved within her, she grabbed his face and kissed him. She slid her tongue between his lips and paced her movements with his. She tasted so sweet.

He drove in, and her body opened. He withdrew, and her muscles gripped him fiercely. He buried deeper. She moaned, driving him toward madness. Beautiful madness.

But he commanded his body to wait for her moment. It was coming. Her skin sizzled with heat. Her aura glowed with passion. Her pulse raced.

"Oh." She nearly crawled on him in her effort to reach her peak. "Seth."

"Cum for me." He whispered in her ear, nibbling a spot on the edge of her earlobe. She wriggled in response, sending a wave of pressure all the way to his cock. "Yes, that's it. Cum for me."

Little noises in her throat rose into a scream of passion. Her body spasmed around him, sucking and releasing until her orgasm wrapped him in a hot glove.

Just as his body shook with the force of his own orgasm, astral lights appeared and circled around them. Weaving and dancing, they joined into an orb of energy and merged into Jayden's aura.

Like an aftershock, Jayden's body tightened and shuddered around his, milking every last drop of passion left in him.

The flame of the fireball ebbed to a vague wisp, leaving them cold in the dark moments before dawn's arrival. Seth wrapped them in a blanket of tropical leaves. Drawing Jayden's body across his, he willed his body temperature to rise. Exhausted and warm, he waited to hear her deep, even breathing before allowing his own mind to slip into the welcome embrace of sleep.

* * *

Seth awoke to find the noontime sun finally peeking over the edge of the cliffs surrounding them. Rays of light filtered through the tropical canopy and crawled across Jayden's face.

Sleep had given his body more time to heal, but fighting off the effects of the poison had left his energy depleted. He would not be able to fight Ozzi — and he was certain that tonight would come to that — without replenishing his energy. He needed to feed.

But that meant leaving Jayden alone. Her warm, naked body curled around his was far more inviting than a swim through cold waters. His stomach didn't agree, rumbling a loud protest.

"What happened?"

Seth kissed her sleepy eyelids. "I'm hungry." Desire surged through his blood at the double meaning.

Her body shook with laughter. "No, I mean before, at the end of our..."

He kissed her lips this time. "We awakened your astral spirit, which merged with you because you must be part Anunnaki. Blood holds many secrets but always the truth."

Suddenly, his mind cleared of everything but the journal. Symbols and phrases swirled and rearranged until a logical, understandable pattern emerged.

"Gods in hell, no!" Seth sat up and stared at her. "That's why he wants you."

"Because I have some DNA in common with you guys?"

"Only a human with at least a quarter Anunnaki bloodline can receive an astral spirit. Any weaker than that and the elements are too diluted to conduct the astral energy."

"I really hate it when you guys infer that humans are a weaker species."

"Jayden, they found the Anunnaki cells in your blood. They are tracking the percentages. The fact that you have more is important to Ozzi. I have to find out why."

Jayden found her clothes and pulled them on. "But we already figured that out. I'm their next birth mother."

"I think you might be their *ultimate* birth mother. With more elemental power in your blood, who knows what you are capable of producing for them?"

"My body is dying, Seth. They won't get much out of me."

He shook his head. "Jayden, I probably cured you with the healing spell after your fall. If not, then I most certainly cured you when we made love. Only an Anunnaki can introduce you to your astral spirit. Receiving it for the first time is called the Awakening. Your astral spirit would heal you of any human issues affecting your body."

He watched as joy bloomed across her features and then wilted into pain. Her eyes widened. "I will not be chained to a bed like she was. I..."

"Shh, I will —"

"Get me off this island. Now." Jayden avoided his outstretched hand and paced the area like it was a prison cell. "That cannot happen to me. I won't be strapped to a bed, inseminated with those things with those teeth." She shuddered.

He desperately wanted to wipe the terror from her eyes, but emotions lodged at the base of his throat, choking his words down to a whisper. "I will not let that happen to you."

"Then take me away from here. I'm bonded with the oracle now. I can control where we go, right?"

He hoped she was right. "You would be safe back in my cave. I can put wards up, which would deny his entry if Ozzi figured out the location."

He could tell by her hesitation that she feared exchanging one prison for another. It irked him slightly that she would view it that way, but under the circumstances her concern was valid.

She finally nodded in agreement.

He lifted his hand to cup her face. When she didn't push him away this time, he pulled her in and whispered into her hair. "I promised that I wouldn't leave you. I am still bound by that promise."

She stiffened in his arms. "Give me a minute, please."

Had she changed her mind? He sensed that she needed space and he let her go. She left the shadows to tiptoe across the hot sand toward the shoreline.

He had barely scooped up their things when Jayden's screams pierced through his heart.

His first instinct was to launch out onto the beach and fight. But as he watched Jayden struggle against Ozzi, Seth remained in the black shadows, keeping his existence unknown to his brother.

Rage seeped through every vein in Seth's body, but he was just not strong enough to fight Ozzi yet. Seth needed time to heal and to plan. He knew what was happening on the island tonight. He knew exactly where Jayden would be. Unfortunately, it would be right in the middle of a damned damien rebellion.

His lips curled and he barely stopped his beast from taking control.

Seth? Her voice pleaded in his head before Ozzi and Jayden flashed away. All that remained was the sound of water lapping against the shore.

Guilt stabbed through his mind. Harsh memories jumped in for good measure. Had Nefertiti called for him — screamed for him? He hadn't been there for her when she'd needed him most. Had she died not knowing how much he despaired of her loss? And what of his son — born and died without his father there to protect him?

He couldn't let that happen again. He wouldn't let Jayden die not knowing that he loved her. He'd held that back, too proud to be that vulnerable again. The despair was no less this time around. Holding back was stupid. He knew that now.

Seth's stomach rumbled, reminding him that his first priority at the moment was to feed. The water beast agreed, anxious to hunt down a fat monk seal.

Nourished, he could regain his full strength quickly and rescue Jayden.

* * *

As Ozzi flew in another tight circle around the island, he let his anger bubble over to a full rage. He should have skewered Indar through the heart and dumped his body in the ocean. No one had ever escaped the nest — human or damien.

Irritating bitch. How did Jayden escape? Ozzi knew every inch of those tunnels. Someone must have helped her. When he found out who, he would pull their spine out with his bare hands.

His eyes constantly flicked to the harbor. He was certain that she would go for the boat, but it still bobbed empty at the end of the dock. Without Seth to whisk her off to some faraway location, she was limited in her mode of escape.

With her climbing experience, she would have no fear of the cliffs curving around the monastery side of the island. It was a risky choice, but he figured she had the guts for it.

His perseverance was finally rewarded during another pass over southwestern shoreline. He spotted her walking toward the water in a small inlet. Folding in his wings, he let gravity draw him down quickly. As he neared the ground, he opened his wings and slowed his quiet descent toward his prey.

His surprise arrival made her speechless. Of course, his dragon form was exceptional. He knew his silvery wings looked splendid against his dark brown skin.

As his feet touched ground, he shifted back to his human form. Not even wasting time to dress, he wrapped his fingers around Jayden's wrist, yanked her off balance, and enjoyed a delicious moment watching her eyes dilate with shock.

Her aggravatingly-shrill scream pierced his triumphant demeanor.

"Jayden, it's time to stop running around. You know there's nowhere you can go that I wouldn't find you."

"I will not be one of your birth mothers." She struggled and spit in his face.

He wiped it with the back of his hand. "Hush, dear. That is just a part of it." He just couldn't be bothered to work hard at keeping her still. There was another way. He smiled and reformed his fangs.

Ripping her shirt away from her shoulder, he buried his fangs into her flesh and injected a doubled dose of toxin that would immobilize her for hours. Satisfied with her limp cooperation, he suddenly remembered Seth's description of her blood — sweet, he'd said. No blood pooled at the puncture wounds.

He could find out for himself tonight at the Gathering. Time to take his wayward slave back where she belonged. Or at least where he could personally keep an eye on her.

He flashed them both to his bedroom.

CHAPTER ELEVEN

Jayden opened her eyes to a sea of red silk rippling above her. She could blink and swallow, but every other muscle in her body refused to obey her command to move.

So this was what paralysis felt like.

Frightening, but at least this was temporary. Ozzi had injected her with something that must have caused this. She couldn't feel the injection site at the moment, but her mind supplied the memories easily. Like hot acid infused every vein.

She closed her eyes and tried to sleep, knowing that her body needed rest. Seth had said he needed food. She prayed he found it. If the healing process required more time, would he be ready by tonight?

With nothing else to do, memories took turns in her mind. Jumps from bridges and mountains. Arguments with her father over treatments. Painful test procedures with thick needles. Long nights strapped to cold beds with only nightmares to keep her company.

Now she'd come face to face with the demons of her nightmares. They weren't hallucinations, but real flesh and blood creatures. They no longer scared her. She was just like them — trapped in a world they sought desperately to control.

Would she continue her quest for the adrenaline rush now that she wasn't losing control of her body? Seth might have something to say about her reckless stunts. An image of his stern face came to mind. But would he be there for her?

Warm tears puddled in the corners of her eyes. They dripped away when she squeezed her lids shut. What a stupid thing to get upset over. He was being honorable.

The memory still stung. She'd wanted to hear *I love you* — not *I'll keep my promise.*

Even if he never used the word love, she knew that he would remain devoted forever. It wasn't like she'd said it to him either. She'd only said it aloud when she'd needed to heal him. But it was true. She knew deep in her reckless soul that she'd fallen in love with the man who'd healed her, saved her, and died for her. Loyalty felt damn good, and she planned to show Seth how loyal she could be — until her dying breath.

* * *

She must have dozed. When Jayden awoke again, she lay on her side and curled up like she used to as a child. Her body tingled all over and her skin itched horribly. She hoped this meant the poison was wearing off.

She sat up, wobbling when a wave of lightheadedness threatened. She sat in the middle of a huge round bed. It looked like something out of a painting of Cleopatra. It was a bed made for many bodies.

Red silky fabric draped around the canopy and swirled around thin white columns anchored to the floor. At least a dozen pillows formed a mushy pyramid at one end of the bed. The seductive little corner of the room was marred by the sight of chains hooked to the columns, their cuffs open and ready for the next victim.

Jayden stiffened when she sensed movement in her peripheral vision. A large sunken Jacuzzi bubbled and steamed a few feet to her right, but she avoided looking at it — at the asshole she knew was sitting in it.

Instead, she inventoried her surroundings. The room could have been photographed for a home decor magazine. Pristine tiled floors gleamed. An immaculate white leather sectional angled through the middle. The far wall held a room-wide set of sliding doors leading to a large patio overlooking the Mediterranean Sea.

She recognized the patio. Every room on the north side of the castle, including her own, connected to it. She'd dined there last night with Ozzi — before her hike in the moonlight.

"Well, my dear. I'm pleased to see that you're awake."

She refused to look at him.

"It's almost time for your debut."

"I'm not some demon debutante and it's hardly a ball." She envisioned the black altar from the ballroom. Buffet table. *Right.* Okay, to whom was she going to be offered?

With snake-like grace, Ozzi slid from the steamy water of the hot tub.

She couldn't look away. He was a golden, sinewy god from head to toe. Water dripped in rivulets down his body, creating shiny trails across his skin. He definitely carried a heavier package than Indar, and he waved it boldly in her direction.

Lifting her eyes quickly to his face, she found him watching her assessment of him. He stood there naked, wearing only his fancy ring and a cocky grin. He obviously considered himself a prize.

"Do you like what you see, Jayden?" His amber eyes locked hers and held them without mercy. She bit her tongue, not allowing anything impulsive and stupid to fall from her lips. Ozzi flexed his muscles and licked his lips.

"No." She dropped her gaze back down to his package, lifting her brows in mock surprise. "But apparently you do. I thought you hated humans."

An evil smile slithered across his face. "I do, indeed." He held his arms up and away from his body.

At first, Jayden thought he wanted her to do something. Then, Indar appeared with three women. But not human women — damien.

As she had before, she marveled at how human-like these particular damien females were. They stood more erect, their limbs graceful and soft. Their facial structure featured high cheekbones and full lips. Their light brown skin seemed smooth except for small patches of opaque scales. Their nails were short, dark and rounded.

They were exotic beauties by any standards, and she couldn't stop watching them as they dried Ozzi and smoothed oils across his skin. They kneaded his muscles and cupped his privates, creating an erotic scene. He enjoyed it, evidenced by his half-lidded eyes and parted lips.

She realized hers were parted too, and her breath came in shorter gasps. Changing her view, she watched Indar. He too seemed mesmerized by the display, until she realized that his eyes tracked along the movement of the damiens' hands. He wasn't mooning over the women, he was longing for his master.

Ozzi preened from the attention. The bastard knew Indar was watching. She would bet that somehow he'd always known that Indar's loyalty was seated in longing. The display of female attention in front of Indar was intentional torture. Ozzi dangled himself in front of Indar like a treat, but she'd bet that he never awarded the sweet to his devoted follower.

"Maybe I should reconsider my abstinence with human women." Ozzi grinned in her direction and lifted one blond brow. "I could make an exception with you."

"You wouldn't like me, Ozzi."

"I already don't like you. You irritate me. I would have to sew your lips together and keep you chained to a wall that you couldn't climb."

"What a charming vision." Jayden didn't see the humor. "You've been here for all these centuries and you haven't once found a woman — of any species — enough to your liking that you wanted children?"

"The only things I hate more than humans are messy little brats running around."

"Yet you breed many damien every year on this small island."

"That's different. The younglings are cared for by their omega nannies until they are old enough to survive the nest." He nodded towards the damien women.

Jayden felt disgusted. They were slaves — part nanny and part prostitute. "Why do you waste all of this time and effort to create a species and then dump them in dark caves? What are they for?"

"My master plan, and enough of your questions. Now it's your turn." He swept his hand toward the steaming water.

"Ah, no thanks."

Silently, all three damien women surrounded her, wrapping vise-like grips around her wrists and tugging off every stitch of clothing.

Jayden rarely felt embarrassment, but in this moment she felt pure humiliation — and rage. The heat of her blood flushed across her chest and up her neck. The damien servants kept a firm grip on Jayden while dragging her into the hot water, washing her hair, and scrubbing every inch of her skin.

From directly behind her, one massaged Jayden's legs. Inching slowly inward, the damien boldly stroked between Jayden's legs. Her breath lodged in her throat. Shocked. Jayden felt the twin tips of a forked tongue slide up and down the back of her neck.

"Stop it!" Bile rose in her throat.

The damien ignored the command and continued. But when she began to tuck the sponge deeper between Jayden's legs, she'd had enough. If words didn't get through, actions would.

With brutal quickness, Jayden nodded her head forward and thrust it backward with all her strength. The back of her head connected with the damien's forehead. A guttural screech let Jayden know the message had been received.

Screaming with vengeance, the damien flashed her fingers in front of Jayden's face and flicked them until each one sported a two-inch, black claw. The damien swept her new weapons toward Jayden's throat, but something unseen held the sharp claws barely an inch from Jayden's jugular. The damien grunted from the effort of trying to force through.

"Away!" Ozzi issued a one-word command and all three — one very grudgingly — moved back into the shadowy corners of the room. They clicked cuffs onto their own wrists.

They'd willingly chained themselves to the wall at Ozzi's command? Jayden swore she wouldn't ever allow that to happen to her. She wouldn't be a willing victim. Yet, here she was standing completely naked in front of three damien creatures, an androgynous doctor, and a god-like alien. It was time to start formulating a new plan. Had she told Seth that patience was not one of her virtues?

Indar moved toward her with a large white towel in his hands. She shivered from the leer on his face and bloodthirsty look in his eyes.

"Oh, no. You stay away from me, you limp freak."

His face paled with shock, then quickly reddened with anger. Ozzi doubled over with laughter, which made Indar's face turn one shade shy of purple.

Indar dropped the towel to the floor just out of Jayden's reach. "I will go prepare for the ceremony."

"Yes, you do that." Ozzi flashed on a perfectly trimmed, shiny gray suit. Bending, he retrieved the towel from the floor and tossed it to Jayden. He sat elegantly on the edge of the bed while she dried herself. "You asked why I have no children. I simply wish to remain in power forever. I'm immortal here. Why bring a child into this world to usurp me and take my place? This is my dominion. It has been since the day I was sent here to fix my brother's mess. He turned a decent slave species into an ungrateful horde of spoiled, dirty creatures. They cried for mercy. They begged for freedom. They demanded power."

"Why not? *You* seek power."

He laughed. The sound bounced darkly off of the bright tile floors. "You humans have so little understanding of the true meaning of power."

"You obviously think lording over a weaker species is power."

He stood and advanced on her so fast she nearly stepped backwards into the tub. She wrapped the towel tighter around her body when he lifted a finger to stroke the bare skin of her arms. His eyes drew hers to look up at him, locking into a tense gaze.

"Humans think power comes from ownership of money and land. It doesn't. Power is in the blood — the blood of creation. The ability to create life and then control that life, that's true immortal power."

She envisioned the damien group coming back from hunting fish. It was very likely his prized creations were adapting faster than he would be able to control. "Immortality. You sound like an insane vampire."

Ozzi's fangs descended, reminding her that he'd used them to inject poison and not suck her blood. "Vampires. A creative but misguided human concept."

"Not so misguided. It's still all about the blood. Why is mine so special to you?"

He hesitated, as if considering how much to say.

"I know my blood contains more DNA of your kind than most humans have. So I have an Anunnaki relative a bit closer in my family tree. Why do you need that?"

"Your blood features the best of both species. Your Anunnaki blood contains the cells which control the elemental powers, and your woman's blood wields the power of creation."

"Stem cells with a kick." Jayden hated the way

his eyebrows lifted with an air of superiority. She tempered the urge to smack the smugness from his face. "Isn't there an Anunnaki woman available for the job?"

"Human women are a hundred times more fertile than Anunnaki women." He leaned closer to her ear, a secretive smile on his face. "Don't you see? *You* have the perfect blood and the perfect womb. And *I* will control it."

"If you see yourself in power, why would you align yourself with Apophis?"

He stepped away. A look of shock replaced his smile. "You know of my connection to Apophis?"

Seth had learned it from Zarick, but she couldn't reveal that to Ozzi. How else could she have learned of Apophis? "Indar's journal."

"Of course." His voice sounded distant. "You seem to have learned a lot from Indar's journal."

"Isn't Apophis some kind of overlord in your race? He doesn't sound like the type to share power."

"He's not. I have no intention of sharing power with him." Ozzi finally moved away from her. From a closet he withdrew a long-sleeved white robe. He laughed at her confusion. "Seth could never have known how everything fell into place when he trapped and imprisoned the mighty Apophis. It put me in a perfect bargaining position. Apophis' DNA in exchange for a few alphas."

"Sounds like he's building an army. Isn't there a prophecy of his escape?"

"I believe in making my own destiny, not in silly prophecies."

He brought the robe over, slipped it up her arms, and draped it gently over her shoulders. She could feel his breath on her neck. He licked a bead of water on her cheek that had dripped down from her hair. She shuddered from the warm slickness of his tongue.

He looked as if his excitement was barely contained inside his skin, like a child on Christmas Eve. "Your blood line will produce better damien."

"You don't need better damien to conquer weak, inferior humans." A slight tic appeared next to his right eye. She couldn't resist tweaking his composure further. "So that's your master plan? World domination? Oh, that's so lame."

The tics increased, but he didn't answer her. He pointed her toward a floor length mirror. Wrapping the robe around her, he tied the belt loosely around her waist. The doubled material covered up the dark triangle between her legs, but the thin fabric did little to hide the pink circles of her nipples.

"You'll be the belle of the ball." A sneer glittered in his eyes and curved gleefully across his face.

He left her, but just before he disappeared through the door, cold metal wrapped around her wrist. Damn him. He'd chained her to the bed column.

CHAPTER TWELVE

Seth slid easily through the dark depths of the ocean, his long dragon body made for speed. Although he'd been very weak, he'd found a group of seals and easily captured an old male. His belly full, he cruised through the water, gathering strength from the frenzied energy of the ocean.

He'd been right about the sword. It hadn't killed him, angling slightly away from his heart. He was certain that Ozzi counted on the poison to ensure the wound was fatal. It would have been, if Jayden hadn't found him when she did.

Sensing a large number of boats on the surface, he spread his wings to slow down. He kept enough distance to avoid any fish-finder sonar. But these boats didn't seem to be on a fishing trip. They travelled nearly the same path — towards Ozzi's island. Guests of the Gathering, no doubt.

Moving away from the procession of party-goers, Seth swam for the inlet. As he reached the shallow waters, he shifted into his human form and made for the privacy of the trees. He stood naked at first, savoring the cool breeze across his skin. His muscles twitched, anxious for battle. It was a feeling he missed.

He buried Jayden's bag, with the oracle safely nestled inside, in a tangle of roots. Gathering his clothes and sword, he moved over to the east side of the inlet and surveyed the harbor beyond.

The colors of dusk painted the sky. Boats took turns at the end of the dock. From the shadows of the harbor shoreline, Seth watched men disembark and line up along the beach. They stood for a long time until no sunlight remained.

The full moon provided enough light for Seth to see Indar appear in front of the group with a damien servant. The damien moved from man to man with a basket, collecting everything but their clothing. Each guest accepted a long dark robe, wrapping it around his body and pulling the cowl over his head.

Seth had encountered some of these men here before. Their auras held colors of confidence and power. Usually, Seth left before the festivities began. He never had an interest in mingling with men of commerce and politics.

Each man was given a lit torch. Slowly they filed halfway up the southeastern slope to a well-hidden entrance.

Seth flashed himself closer but didn't follow them into the tunnel. He wouldn't need a torch to see his way through a long dark passage. So he could wait and join them in the hall later. First, he needed to find out where Jayden was, and her energy would be easier to track from above ground.

Reaching out with his astral spirit, he found Jayden's energy signature on the upper level. Seth smiled. Her aura burned with anger and boldness. He also sensed Ozzi's presence in the same room, and it sparked an angry wave across Seth's tattoos. His beast wanted out — wanted to feel its teeth sinking into Ozzi's neck.

Guilt tempered Seth's anger. He could not rescue her now. He had to find out what his brother was up to. He must watch the ceremony.

Zarick said that a group of damien would be given to Apophis. Was the dark lord present in some form to witness the event? How did he accept this offering when he was securely imprisoned in the Underworld?

If Seth didn't stay and find out how this was happening, then the prophecy could very well come true. He could not allow that to happen. Not when it was his duty to ensure that Apophis remained in the prison that Seth himself had created.

Jayden. Her name whispered through his mind. He'd promised that he wouldn't allow her to be sacrificed — strapped to a bed again. Her greatest fear. He wouldn't break that promise, but he had to let this play out.

* * *

Through the open patio doors, Jayden watched the sky fade quickly from the rosy shades of dusk to the deep blue of night. The beautiful sunset taunted her, dangling an elusive vision of freedom. With renewed determination, she vowed not to sit here and wait to be dragged off to some damien ceremony. She would find a way to escape.

She remembered from last night that Ozzi's room was on the second floor, and the wall was at least five meters away from the edge of the cliff. Plenty of room on the ground for her to land.

Taking a quick inventory of the room, she formulated a mental checklist of the items that would aid in her escape. Long panels of silk hung in every corner. Some were cinched in the middle with thick gold rope. With the fabric all tied together and anchored by the heavy leather sectional, she could slide to the ground easily.

However, her first problem was getting out of the cuffs.

Not far from the bed, a desk held lots of potential lock picks. The perfect pen taunted her from the edge of the blotter. She pulled her chain to that side of the bed and reached. Her hands fell a little short of the mark. She changed positions and tried reaching with her legs. After repeated attempts, her toe managed to knock the pen onto the floor. It rolled along the tile and settled into a grout seam just beyond her reach.

"Damn."

The chain which held her to the bedpost just wasn't long enough for her to capture the pen. A rough giggle drew her attention to the sliding doors. The two damien women chained in the left corner were sniggering at her attempts. In the opposite corner, the bloodied damien sat glaring at Jayden with angry yellow eyes.

A familiar chatter reached Jayden's ears.

"Ushum?" Swiveling in all directions, she finally heard it again. From the service entrance, Ushum's little nose peeked around the door as he sniffed the air. "Ushum!"

She was elated to see him.

Ushum showed his happiness by crawling under her hair and wrapping his tail around her neck. He hugged her face, rubbing his nose across her cheek.

"I missed you too." She nuzzled back. "Help me, please." She pointed toward the pen. He scurried over and brought it back.

In seconds, the metal cuff fell away from her wrist. The damien who hated her started to shriek, swiping the air with her claws like she wanted to bury them in Jayden's flesh. Only the chains held the vengeful creature back.

The noise could attract unwanted attention. Jayden had to find a way to cover the creature's mouth. She ripped a panel of red silk from the canopy and twisted it into a thick rope.

The damien lunged until the chain reached its full length.

That was Jayden's advantage. With one arm shackled and pulled in the other direction, the damien only had one arm to fight with. That meant one arm and one set of claws to avoid.

It took a few moments to time it right. But after a handful of sharp nails swiped past Jayden's face, she jumped behind the enraged creature, encircled her neck with the silk, and twisted it viciously.

Jayden leaned in close to the damien's ear. "How do you like me now, bitch?"

The damien struggled to loosen the wrap with her one free hand. Like razors, her claws began to shred the outer layers of the twisted fabric. It wouldn't be long before she freed herself and turned her full fury on Jayden.

This idea was failing — fast. Jayden pressed her foot into the creature's back, forcing her to the end of the chain. Wrapping the ends of the silk tighter around both hands, Jayden gave one huge yank. The damien's neck cracked and her head hung limp to the side.

Jayden had never taken a life before. She wanted to feel regret, but her mind was too preoccupied with relief. She lifted a brow toward the other two damien women, a silent test to see if they would present a new challenge. But they sat quietly in their corner and lowered their eyes submissively.

Happy to step back into normal clothes, Jayden threw the white robe into the bubbling hot tub. As she walked the perimeter of the patio, she paused at the western end of it. Leaning over the railing, she could see the harbor. Moonlight shimmered on the water like a layer of ice crystals. The surface was dotted with many dark little shapes, which rocked and bobbed with the waves. Boats. Lots of them.

Ozzi's guests were here. Were they human or something else? She wasn't going to wait and find out. Seth wanted her to leave this island, and she was damned sure going to try now. Seth could still be in the inlet, healing and preparing to fight Ozzi. If she could get to him in time, they could leave together.

Not that she thought for a moment that Ozzi would defeat Seth a second time. But she knew she wouldn't be able to survive seeing Seth come close to dying again. Once was enough.

Quickly, Jayden fashioned a long rope from several silk panels. The slippery fabric was thin enough to hold a really tight knot. She used one of the gold decor ropes to anchor the makeshift line to the sectional's foot. The thick wood and the heavy couch would hold her weight just fine.

"Come on, Ushum." He scampered up and nestled in her hoodie.

Jayden threw the colorful line over the balcony rail and backed over the edge. In seconds, grasses crunched under her feet.

Her goal was the inlet on the far side of the harbor. To get there, she needed to cross a wide sloping pasture to get to the safety of the trees, and the moon lit up the area like a big celestial spotlight. She could take a quicker route to the harbor shoreline. But trying to sneak past the dock with Ozzi's guests in the area — that didn't seem like a great option.

Her decision made, she sprinted to the middle of the pasture, catching her breath while hiding behind a small group of cattle. The second sprint brought her safely into the pine forest. From there she could reach the harbor shoreline just past the dock.

She could hear that she was getting close. Waves lapped in a steady pattern. Turning towards the sound, she found her way blocked by a dense section of trees. Like a front line of infantry, evergreens and mastic shrubs formed a stubborn wall.

Finding no easy way through it, Jayden picked her way through the tangled weave of limbs and leaves. Something scratched across her forearm like a scalpel. She ignored it, pressing forward toward the freedom of the beach.

Soft sand gave under the weight of her feet. Jayden closed her eyes and inhaled the salty ocean breeze. Her arm throbbed from the cut, but a strange tingling sensation drew her attention to the injury. In the moonlight, she watched her skin reseal itself like a zipper. But there was no line in its wake. Just smooth, unblemished skin.

Ushum moved to her forearm and sniffed it curiously.

So this is what it's like? She remembered the beautiful lights that came to her and joined with her soul. Being part Anunnaki might be very useful. She smirked wryly. Her father would be so happy not to have to cover more medical bills from her stunts.

She wondered what other things about her would be different. She prayed that wasn't a jinx question. Better reserve those questions for when she got off this damned island.

Looking toward the west side of the harbor, she could see the corner, which curved away toward the familiar inlet. Toward Seth and the oracle. She was way past ready to leave this place.

The harbor seemed empty now. Not a soul around. Just the sound of water slapping against wooden hulls. The sound echoed across the water like an eerie chorus.

Jayden skirted the beach along the tree line, trying to stay in the shadows. She'd barely walked twenty yards when a scratchy voice called out her name.

"Jayden? Where the hell do you think you're going?"

Indar's voice skewered through her. She launched into a mad dash for the trees. Indar caught her hair with one hand and ripped Ushum from her hoodie with the other. He squeezed Ushum's neck briefly and threw him into the sand.

Yanking her hair, Indar pulled her hard against him. Terrible to find out now how much muscle his lab coat hid. She felt every ounce of his strength — and hatred — in the arms that held her.

His breath fanned hot against her cheek and his hip ground something painful into her leg. "There is nothing limp about me. Can you feel it?"

Indeed, she could feel a bulge growing under his lab coat. Small but firm enough.

"Can you feel it?" He jerked her hair painfully.

"Yes. Y-yes. I feel it." Her jaw ached from clenching her teeth.

"It's excited."

"For what?" She couldn't seem to stop herself.

"You're not interested in females."

His cackle brought silence to every creature. Even the crickets paused their nightly symphony.

"It grows hard because I'm envisioning your death at my hands. My hands, which have created new life, itch to cause your death. Human bitch."

"Don't you...need me..." He held her head back too far to catch enough breath. Her words came between choking gasps. "...to increase your damien spawn?"

He dug his erection even deeper into her thigh as if seeking something to appease the tension. His mind must be conflicted between his hatred of her and his loyalty to Ozzi.

"Ozzi has plans for you, yes. But I can find another to replace you. We have time." He breathed heavily in her ear. "But then again, it might be just as gratifying to see you strapped helplessly to the altar while your naked body is on display for all to see — and is invaded by the spirit of Apophis." His vision created even more excitement in his erection. Rock hard, it bruised her thigh muscle.

"What? Invaded?" Somehow she'd naively thought the process started in a Petri dish. Jayden struggled against his grip. She tried an old twisting technique she remembered from self-defense classes, and she almost gained a moment of freedom.

He regained his grip on her hair. "Then I am your only alternative. Your beloved hero Seth is gone. Ozzi is busy preparing for the ceremony. It's just you and me."

She tried to look around for something or someone. Poor Ushum lay unconscious in the sand. "What do you want from me?"

He sneered, spittle hovering on his lip. "I want

to paint my body with your blood. I want to feel your vain struggles and know that I am your executioner."

"Some choice. Live as a damien surrogate slave, or die with your putrid breath and weak erection as the last things I feel in life. You freak!"

He bellowed with anger that she would dare to insult him again. He withdrew a curved knife from inside his lab coat, and he held it to her throat, almost piercing the skin.

"Time to die, bitch."

"Indar?" Ozzi's voice sliced through the tension.

Jayden's emotions fumbled around as if she'd just jumped from a merry-go-round. She was grateful for Ozzi's arrival, but not. Neither outcome was to her liking.

"Ozzi." Indar kept her hair wrapped around his fist, but he relaxed the blade away from her skin.

"Should I be concerned about your loyalty to the cause?"

"No, my lord. I am just as anxious as you are to get this one chained and submissive."

Air rushed from her lungs in a strangled chuckle. "I will never be submissive."

Ozzi moved closer. She saw no anger in his eyes for Indar's near betrayal, only annoyance toward her. "You will be. The moment you give birth to your first damien litter, you will be begging for my mercy."

Like a ghost, the image of the woman they'd found haunted Jayden. The round jagged wound on the woman's arm, caused by a creature seeking sustenance from her body. When faced with such mindless creatures, would Jayden beg for death? Her body could heal itself now, but pain was still a very real factor.

"I am your lord now, Jayden, and you will obey

me from this moment forward."

Her father was wrong. Sometimes it was okay to feel fear.

CHAPTER THIRTEEN

Seth caught up with the procession of hooded men in the winding tunnel, which finally opened up into the massive underground hall. From the shadows behind a large vase, he watched them take seats at several long banquet tables lined on one side of the room.

The hall was ridiculously decorated with the grandeur of a king's court. False windows framed stained glass artwork. Flickering candlelight cast an eerie glow on the gruesome battle scenes depicted in them. Underneath each frame, polished weaponry hung as if proudly waiting for the next war to be waged. A gilded throne had been added to the dais behind the black stone altar. Beside it, red silk draped on both sides of the fountain.

He hadn't seen this level of pompousness since Napoleon, but at least Napoleon had put in time on the battlefield. As far as Seth knew, Ozzi had yet to step one foot onto a field of combat. He'd always preferred the political side of power.

Women entered the room carrying platters of food and pitchers of wine. It looked like a scene from ancient times, except the wenches were damien.

They were exotically beautiful with slanted eyes and smooth human-like skin. Some had patches of scales, which looked to be covered over with makeup to reduce them. They each wore wigs with long, curling tendrils to curve around their breasts. He'd bet they were here to serve in more ways than just food.

Amazingly, the men did not speak to each other. They ate in complete silence.

Seth flashed himself into the alcoves beyond the hall — the ones he'd walked through yesterday from the hidden staircase. But today he found the rooms divided by walls of black velvet curtains. Taking a peek through one narrow slit in the fabric, he found a room laid out for seduction: plush rugs, beds with fluffy pillows, and candles flickering anxiously. The chains still lay on the floor near the bed. Tonight, who would be chained, the damien women or their human lovers?

He ducked behind one of the curtains as he heard a new voice boom out from the dais. Indar had arrived. He looked official and professional, but Seth heard an edge of frustration in Indar's voice.

"Lord Ozimas will arrive shortly to begin the ceremony. As always, there are rules to be followed without exception. Your weapons and cell phones will be returned to you on the docks at the time of your departure. When the time is called to leave, you will do so immediately as instructed. Your arrival back on the mainland is specifically timed to maintain your secrecy."

Seth felt a presence in the stairwell. Inhaling the scent, he recognized Zarick and motioned for the damien to remain in the shadows.

Indar's voice dropped to a reverent level, much like the tone of a priest. "While you are here, decorum in your behavior is expected at all times. The Scarlet Women will be presented during the ceremony, and remember that you are forbidden to lay a hand on them. You may not contaminate the sanctity of these sacred vessels of life."

Scarlet women? Seth could not remember ever hearing of such a thing. It wasn't something from their world.

"The omegas are here to serve you in any manner you choose. There will be no fighting allowed for we have plenty to share." Indar disappeared into the hallway behind the dais.

Scarlet women. Damien sex slaves. What the hell was Ozzi doing? He seemed to be creating his own cult.

As the damien women finished clearing the tables, they filtered through the crowd of men and snuggled up to any who seemed ready for feminine company. The sounds of conversation filled the air.

As they savored fine liquor and cigars, the men discussed politics and made deals in a variety of languages. Then, they turned their attentions to the damien females. Carnal requests whispered throughout the room. Some couples tucked into shadowy corners, but others began to wander in the direction of the alcoves.

Seth slipped through the curtain and hurried down the arched hallway. Feeling a presence behind him, he ducked into the last alcove. Unlike the others, this one was loaded with bedding supplies, extra drapery, and stacks of the long brown robes.

A small damien female stepped into his alcove, her eyes sultry and suggestive. She tried to slip an arm around his waist, but he gripped her shoulder and sent a wave of energy into her. She sank to the floor, a look of sleepy serenity in her features.

The air in the hall grew stagnant and filled with the stench of sex and sweat. Seth cursed his brother's sadistic mind.

In a few strides, he joined Zarick in the stairwell, bringing a stack of robes with him. "Ushum?"

"I sent him to you."

Seth nodded. "He might have found Jayden first."

Zarick's eyes filled with concern. "This not be her..."

The damien struggled for a word, but Seth understood the meaning. "No, this will not be Jayden's fate. I promise."

The damien pointed towards the females. "*Bau* calls them omegas. Sends many away."

"Away to Apophis?"

Zarick shook his head and pointed to Ozzi's guests. Powerful men from all over the world.

Then *away* meant anywhere else on this planet. Since the omegas were more docile and human-like, they could easily assimilate into the human population. They could literally be anywhere. This was not a simple problem. These were slaves in a new land.

Seth swiped both hands down his face and wished that he could prevent life from repeating itself. Humans had once been slaves in their own land until they grew numerous enough and strong enough to take control of their world.

Six-thousand-year-old memories surfaced from the murky depths of his mind.

He'd led the first wave of Anunnaki to colonize the Earth. They had arrived in huge winged ships. To the simple nomadic humans of that time, the Anunnaki had seemed like magical gods from the heavens. Many of his kind, including Ozzi, had turned their faithful human followers into willing laborers who toiled on projects that had provided no benefit to the humans or their families.

Seth had preferred a more symbiotic approach, and he had appealed to the Anunnaki queen to intervene. But the queen had been more concerned with her mining operations, stripping the Earth of its most valuable resources. While she'd understood the rights of the indigenous peoples, she'd demonstrated little remorse for using the humans as slave labor.

He had eagerly joined the queen's own granddaughter — Shaila a'k'Hemet — to form a small secret group of warriors called the *medjai*. The *medjai* had sworn an oath to protect the human race and to teach the sacred knowledge to a select group of priests. He wished Shaila could be here now to see how the humans had changed their world. She would be proud. But she'd died protecting Nefertiti.

As the Lord of Command, Seth had fulfilled his duty to his queen. As a *medjai*, he'd fulfilled his soul's need for penance.

Like a wicked replay, Seth felt called upon again to clean up another mess created by one of his own kind. He knew this time would not be as easy. The problem the damien faced would be much harder to resolve.

He'd promised to support their fight for freedom, but how and where would they fit into this world? *Should* they fit into this world?

* * *

Once again Jayden stood chained to Ozzi's bed. At least she didn't have to deal with Indar for the moment. He'd been dismissed to begin his official ceremonial duties.

It didn't take long for Ozzi to discover the damien corpse, the silk panel still wrapped tight around her neck. He glared at Jayden. "You should have more appreciation for them. Especially since you will be carrying many of them in your womb."

"Over my dead body." It was easy to say, but not so easy to come to terms with. Just yesterday, she couldn't imagine how someone could prefer death. Now she understood, but she knew she didn't have it in her to kill herself. If Seth didn't get them out of this...

A loud sucking sound came from the Jacuzzi. The discarded white robe had lodged in the filter. Ozzi fished it out and threw the sopping mess on the floor.

This time the process of changing went much more quickly and less ceremoniously. He ripped the dirty clothes off her and angrily stuffed her into a new white robe, belting it tight around her waist.

From the closet, he brought out a new item — a heavy, floor-length cloak. Blood red. After cinching the tie at her throat and pulling the hood over her blond hair, he aimed her toward the mirror.

"What a beautiful Scarlet Woman you will make."

"Is that what you call your birth mothers — your surrogate slaves?"

"Precisely. But it sounds incredibly more elegant, don't you think?" Ozzi smoothed away the wrinkles from his metallic gray silk suit.

He pushed her toward the door and out into the hallway, keeping his hand on her back. He wasn't taking any chances this time.

"So, who's attending my coming-out party?" Barefoot, she curled her toes into the plush hall carpet.

She could feel his annoyance growing. She stole a quick glance at his face. The tic was back. "Do I need to sew your lips shut?"

"I just wanted to know who would be viewing my *display*." She let the last word drip icily from her lips.

"Men of power and influence. However, the only one you need to concern yourself with is Apophis. His particular attention will be most enlightening."

Her face flushed with heat. "Seth said he was locked away."

"He is. But there are ways to call upon his astral spirit. We will use it to awaken the Anunnaki cells in your blood and help them take control over your faulty human ones."

"I won't let your blood stud touch me." Her anger suddenly melded into concern. Would Apophis be able to tell that she'd already experienced the Awakening? Somehow, it wasn't the right moment to say *Aha, you're too late*. "If you're my new *lord and master*, why go through someone else?"

The tic next to his eye increased to a full blown spasm.

"Oh, I know. Maybe you have a limp one like Indar. So you can't awaken anything."

A choking sound came from somewhere in the hallway.

Ozzi came to an abrupt halt, growling viciously. He began to change to his beast form, but he seemed to get hold of himself before ruining his impeccable suit.

"Shut up! I can assure you that I am greatly gifted in that department. I simply cannot stand to stick it inside a dirty, inferior human." He gripped her arm so hard it made her eyes water. "Get this straight, woman. I can't wait to chain you to that damned altar and let Apophis' spirit have its way with you. I will enjoy his brutality on your body." He dragged her further down the hall and mumbled bitterly. "With my luck you'll probably enjoy it."

* * *

As Zarick left to gather his damien rebels, Seth flashed to the upper level, hoping to find Jayden. He knew he couldn't interfere yet, but he had to know that she was okay. He paused at a set of double doors, beyond which was Ozzi's private wing.

He felt Ozzi's energy approaching the doors from the other side, and his voice had a tremor of annoyance in it.

Seth tucked behind a huge drape, one of many throughout the castle. For once he appreciated Ozzi's overuse of the decor. Although Jayden was a hazy image through the fabric, Seth could see enough to know that she was okay. She looked like a really tall Red Riding Hood, and she had her wits about her. He nearly announced his location when he choked, just as shocked as Ozzi at her comparison to Indar's limp body part.

Seth sobered immediately as Ozzi gave up more information about the ceremony. So Apophis would indeed make an appearance in some form. Apophis' physical body was still imprisoned in the Underworld. His astral spirit had been stripped from him, kept away from his ability to use it. Thus divided, the astral spirit was trapped in its own way — trapped in the astral plane.

The important question was how Ozzi accessed Apophis and his astral spirit. Could this method possibly be a way for Apophis to escape? Seth would soon find out.

To remain under Ozzi's radar, Seth wanted to get back to the hall first and be in position. He flashed back to the shadows of the stairwell. Grabbing a brown robe from the last alcove, he slipped it on and pulled the hood low to cover his face. He moved along the wall and joined a group of guests to the right of the dais.

Jayden arrived with Ozzi, her profile hidden by the big red cloak. She seemed to be staring down every man in the room. Finally, her face panned around in Seth's direction. Her gaze seemed to center right on him.

Did she see him? Sense him? Could that change in her breathing be because of her excitement to know he was there? God, he hoped so. He hoped that her feelings for him gave her strength, because his feelings for her definitely bolstered his.

One corner of her lips curved upward very slightly before she turned to stoically face the gathered crowd of men.

Powerful men who'd just spent a great deal of time stuffing their faces and slaking their lust with damien slaves. Organized prostitution for wealthy clients would be very lucrative, and especially if you fully controlled the women and you didn't fear families coming to find their stolen daughters. But however lucrative this trade was, it could not be the main reason Ozzi has created a new species.

The ceremony began with Ozzi presiding over the Gathering from his opulent throne with Jayden forced to stand beside him. The fountain on the dais began to run red.

The water reminded Seth of some early Egyptian rituals. Water was often considered a conduit to the Underworld or other dimensions. That was partly true. Doorways generally required a key. What key unlocked Ozzi's connection to Apophis?

The damien women came forward and filled glasses with the blood-like liquid. Then they distributed the drinks to all of the men. As everyone else drank, Seth tossed his into the tall vase he stood next to.

A damien brought a glass to Jayden, who promptly declined. The damien looked frantically to Ozzi who nodded an approval. She whipped her palm across Jayden's cheek.

As her skin turned red, Seth felt his body shift. Scales began to raise defensively on his back. With great effort, he held his beast at bay.

Jayden stretched her jaw and spit blood in the damien's face. In a very low voice, she addressed Ozzi. "I am going through with your ceremony, but not with that. I will not be drugged."

Ozzi's brows lifted curiously, but he seemed to accept it as a non-issue. He waved the damien away. "Suit yourself, Jayden. I will enjoy watching your pain, knowing that you have full knowledge of every second of it."

Seth repeatedly clenched and relaxed his fists. He ached to wrap his fingers around his brother's throat. For a distraction, he fingered the patterns on the hilt of his sword underneath his robe.

Someone in the room began chanting an inane sequence of words and sounds. The men all joined in, chanting and swaying. A weird energy in the room played havoc with Seth's senses. It rose in a crescendo of noise and crashed into millions of energy orbs before finally fading away.

Ozzi used his smooth voice to create a level of hypnosis among the guests. "Men of commerce. Men of industry. Men of power. Feel the real power of enlightenment. Let the *star fire,* the ultimate gift of the Scarlet Women, infuse your spirit. Through their blood you will find immortality."

Ancient, fragmented memories unlocked from deep in Seth's mind in a chaotic rush: humans rebelled, populations exploded, new civilizations blossomed, and men declared kingship. The Anunnaki queen regained control of her human workforce with the promise of immortality. *Star fire* — a gift from the gods.

But gifts don't last forever.

In its primitive form, *star fire* was a solution of Anunnaki menstrual blood. A rare product since Anunnaki females have a blood cycle a hundred times longer than human females. *Star fire* was originally the base product in creating mannah, a supplement that was far more important to the Anunnaki than keeping human kings happy.

How did Ozzi have any access to something that didn't exist anymore? Birth blood.

Holy hell. Everything fell into place. That was why it was so important to find humans with stronger Anunnaki bloodlines as their birth mothers. They needed to tap into the blood for power. Power over humans. Power over the remaining Anunnaki. And feeding into Ozzi's quest for dominion — power over creation itself.

After all, even though their kind were like gods in the eyes of humans, they were not completely immortal. They had many of their own limitations.

He'd bet everything that Ozzi was looking for a way to become truly godlike.

With a posse of powerful humans at his beck and call, Ozzi had instant access to a world of followers and slaves. It wasn't enough to just create a damien army to destroy the rule of man. Humans had free will, and they would find a way to fight against the damien. *Star fire* would be mass-produced and distributed to the masses. The high-powered mannah would inhibit the humans' instincts of survival. They'd willingly accept his dominion in their drugged-up state.

And any Anunnaki who dared to challenge Ozzi would find their supply of mannah poisoned with a concentrated dose — large enough to kill.

Guess who's been the damned guinea pig for decades for that? He'd too easily accepted a false fate and exiled himself away from the truth.

* * *

Self-disgust was not going to help Seth get everyone out of this mess. It wasn't his usual battlefield, but it was still a war. Winning a war required a strategy, which he could develop once he found out how Apophis collected his semi-annual offering.

Seth didn't have to wait long.

The hooded men parted, opening a path from the alcoves all the way to the dais. A procession of more than a dozen large damiens — male and female — filed into the hall, each one chained to the one in front of it. While large, none of them hit the same height and thickness as Zarick.

A hush spread through the crowd as a cold

darkness seeped through every grain in the stone floor. The shadows in the alcove deepened and formed into something physical. Levitated and shrouded in perpetual fog, the evil forms cackled as they floated across the room.

Shadow walkers. Seth drew the cowl further over his face, hoping to keep his identity hidden from Apophis' personal guard. These were ancient demons — more ancient than the Anunnaki — with otherworldly connections. None knew exactly where they came from, only that they served Apophis exclusively.

Always there were five of them. If one was destroyed, a new one would appear in its place. Seemingly invincible.

A waspish voice came from one of the shadowy figures. "Is this your offering for Apophis?"

Ozzi bowed to the creatures. "It has been a hard season. Our birth mothers have endured a strange new virus, which dried up their wombs and brought on an early death."

Seth watched Jayden's face pale, and knew that she was thinking of the woman they had tried to save. The woman had asked for death, knowing that it would release her from her pain. Jayden's astral spirit would protect her from sickness, but not from pain. He could think of no worse prison than that.

"Our master does not care for excuses. He wants more soldiers."

"And he will have them." Ozzi grabbed Jayden and pushed her forward, but he held onto her shoulder to keep her in place.

Seth gripped his sword handle and whispered words to engage its power. He felt the energy within it grow warm against his palm.

"We have found a human woman with a strong link to the Anunnaki bloodline. Her womb will produce soldiers in numbers far greater than before. Assure your master that he will be pleased, but..."

Silence from the fog-shrouded creatures lasted several minutes before they responded. "Our master is pleased. What is your special request from him?"

"A new ritual. Her bloodline is dormant — it needs the Awakening."

Again, silence fell across the crowded room for several moments and then a cackle came from within the gray fog. "He is indeed pleased to assist in your ritual. When you summon the Great Master, she must remain in the pool."

Ozzi simply nodded. A gray, bony finger reached out from one foggy shroud and handed Indar a large vial of blood. Apophis' blood, no doubt. Then the demon grasped the chain. None too gently, the shadow walkers led the damien offering into a black swirling portal that appeared in the alcoves.

As the last damien entered the dark portal, it swirled shut.

Seth watched a new procession enter the hall. Damien females flanked a small group of human women dressed in long white robes, escorting them toward Ozzi. These had to be the birth mothers.

Ozzi smiled at them proudly and presented them to his guests. Seth noticed that the women were well-drugged, their eyes glazed and vacant, their movements slow and barely coordinated. Some of the damien had to hold their charges upright. Candlelight bathed the women in ethereal light. With their white robes and serene countenances, they looked like angels — at least in the way humans thought of angels.

The men applauded. Many had taken on a look of awe. One man was so moved he fell down to his knees before the women. Others followed suit quickly. Seth was the last one down as he struggled to keep his sword from scraping across the floor.

He kept his face aimed downward until he felt the others stand again.

As Ozzi waxed on about the tradition and sanctity of the birth mothers, his influential guests took turns pledging their faith and handing over a sizable financial donation. Each man was then promised a number of omegas appropriate to size of their donation.

Somewhere a clock chimed the eleventh hour. Ozzi abruptly ended his current speech. "It is time for the ritual of Awakening."

This was what Seth had been waiting for. *How are they summoning Apophis? Are they jeopardizing the security of the bonds that hold the dark lord in the Underworld?* Worse yet, what would Jayden have to suffer through before they got to that point in the ritual?

CHAPTER FOURTEEN

Jayden stared at the so-called scarlet women standing in a sickly row. Her heart rebelled at the idea that she was to be one of them, but her brain would not stop reviewing images of the dead woman. Wild eyes. Red suction bruises. Cold steel wrapped around her wrists. Begging — no, screaming for death.

The dribble of blood through the waterfall reminded Jayden that she was next. All of this — for blood. Her body shook violently, but not with fear. Anger. Her spirit nearly exploded with it. She refused to be a victim. There was no way in hell anybody was going to put her into that frigid water, let alone ignite her inner whatever.

Now would be a great time, Seth! She looked toward the shadows where she knew Seth waited, but her patience had run out. Well-honed survival instincts launched her into preemptive action. As Ozzi's back was turned, Jayden leaped from dais in Seth's direction. *I will stay in your cave forever, if only you would just take me out of here right now.*

None of the hooded men would touch her. Maybe they weren't allowed to. In fact, they rushed to move away from her. But the damien women descended on her like wolves on a kill. Gripping her arms and legs, they hoisted her off the ground and carried her back. As they set her on the ground at Ozzi's feet, Jayden kicked one of them in the jaw, sending her backwards into the crowd.

Another one retaliated with a swipe of her claws across Jayden's arm. Blood dripped from the wound and soaked through the white sleeve. Her skin already tingled with the sensation of healing. She pulled the edge of the red cloak tighter around her body to hide it.

Ozzi grabbed a handful of Jayden's hair and squeezed painfully, shoving her over to the waterfall. He pushed her into the pool.

Unlike before, the water was lukewarm and smelled of blood. Jayden's stomach retched violently when she surfaced. But Ozzi wasn't done with her yet. He held her head under for a long time before yanking her back up.

"Are we done with the protests, Jayden?"

Coughing up a great deal of bloody water, she nodded weakly. Indar appeared and jabbed his curved dagger into her side until she stood up again.

Jayden noticed that the men had all moved very close in around the dais, their eyes trained on her body. She didn't need to look down to know that the silky white fabric — now pink from the bloody water — hid absolutely nothing. She might as well be naked. She should be embarrassed. Instead, it pissed her the hell off.

Even though the water was warm, she began to shiver in the cold and stagnant air of the underground ballroom.

Ozzi led his guests into a strange chant with sharp, high-pitched vocalizations. An energy buzzed through the room like electricity. She could feel its vibration along her skin.

"*Ati me peta babka!*" Ozzi pointed his ornate ring toward the water beside her. "*Ati me peta babka!*

Gatekeeper, open your gate for me!"

The crowd continued to chant, bringing the electrical sound to a constant hum. Energy fingered out of Ozzi's ring in twin arcs. One moved in a jerky path toward the surface of the water.

The other leaped across and stabbed into Jayden's chest. She tried to brush it away. It didn't hurt, but she feared what was to come. A new current spread from her chest to connect with the one poking into the water, forming a jagged, buzzing triangle with Ozzi's ring at the apex.

In the center, a rush of water geysered up into the air and crashed back down again. Slowly, it rose once more to form a vague, watery profile of a large man.

His deep, smooth voice flowed over her like a river of oil, snaking its way into Jayden's mind. Watery arms reached toward her. She jerked away, but Indar and Ozzi held her in the pool. Liquid fingers splayed across her stomach, and then trailed up her body. She shivered as a cold, wet hand cupped her cheek.

She became aware of a presence within her body. Apophis demanded entrance into her mind. After she refused, he laughed and slid deeper into her soul.

He plucked at her emotions like they were guitar strings, each strum more painful than the last. The first note filled her with a sense of freedom, and she felt like she was flying. The second note brought physical pain searing across her skin. Then, next chord rang through her mind with the terrifying screams of the dead woman.

"Let me in, girl."

Jayden shook her head. "Get out!"

This time, Apophis skipped the single notes and brought a whole symphony of emotion in one painful chord.

As the sounds in her head finally faded, she heard only her breath coming in quick gasps. A fullness in her body told her that Apophis was still inside her, biding his time. Waiting for her to give in, which she eventually would as a weak, inferior human.

She didn't want him inside her mind. Hatred gave her the strength to fight a bit longer. She struggled to free herself from the invasion, arching away from the overlord's watery form.

A wet fog seeped into her consciousness, coating everything with darkness. A burning sensation of pure rage washed over her. This time it wasn't hers, and she knew that Apophis had discovered her secret.

"What is this?" The watery figure staggered back in outrage.

Ozzi seemed unsure of the question. "What is what, my lord?"

"You summoned me to awaken her blood?"

"Absolutely."

"Do not mock me, Ozimas."

"I do not understand." Ozzi looked at her in disbelief. "We tested her blood just yesterday. She has the cells."

"Idiot!" The liquid form turned bright red with anger. "She has already been awakened by another." Apophis' voice dripped with the unspoken accusation of Ozzi's deceit.

At first, Ozzi looked confused, and then his eyes pierced Jayden with malice. As if she cared. Suddenly, he took her arm and slid the material upward. The smoothly healed evidence did nothing to help Ozzi's temper.

He whispered through clenched teeth. "Fuck you, you little bitch."

"Go to hell."

Ozzi gripped the sides of his head and his lips pressed to a thin line. "We tested your blood. The cells were latent. You have been under watchful eyes since the moment you stepped into my home. Every moment. Every room. How — when could this have happened?"

Jayden refused to help him figure it out, but she couldn't stop a smug smile from spreading across her face.

Ozzi's eyes riveted on her lips, reading every nuance in her smile. With a hushed tone, he answered his own question. "When you escaped the damien nest."

Then he buckled over and ran his hands through his hair. His laughter began, low at first. It rose quickly to a screeching howl, which echoed through the hall. As he stood again, he unleashed a soul-deep growl with one name screamed on the end of it.

"SETH!" He swung around and eyed the crowd. "I know you're in here, damn you. I killed you! Can't you ever fucking stay dead?"

Rushing to the nearest wall, Ozzi removed a long, thin sword from one of the weaponry displays. The slim blade tinged against the floor as he whipped it in frustration. Jayden noted that the sword wasn't heavy or battle-worn like Seth's, but it sliced through the air in quick, clean arcs. No doubt it was just as deadly.

Ozzi waved the blade above the crowd and

pointed toward the exit. "Leave us now. The Gathering is over."

The omegas quickly obeyed and hustled the scarlet women from the room. Ozzi guests milled around in stunned aimlessness for a few moments, until one man dared to object. "What about our omegas? We've made our contributions to you."

Ozzi pinned the man with a lethal glare. Underneath his cowl, the man choked and gasped for air. "You can collect your whores later. Get out now!"

Released from the invisible grip, the man rushed to the door and led the processional through the long tunnel back to the harbor. But several dozen hooded figures remained, their cowls pulled low over their faces.

Indar left Jayden's side and resumed his official role. "What are you waiting for? You are in breach of the rules your lord has set. Leave now."

Instead, they all pulled back their hoods and removed their robes. Seth and a rebel band of damien moved forward to surround Ozzi. Zarick stood tall and proud next to Seth. Jayden felt a swell of pride for him.

As a watery Apophis gurgled in anger next to her, she finally understood Seth's delay. It had something to do with the imprisoned overlord whose deadly voice shimmered maliciously. "Seth. I have waited an eternity to fulfill my revenge upon you."

Seth's voice boomed strong and confident. "Sorry to disappoint you, but today is not that day."

Ozzi smirked at his rebellious damien. "What is this? A revolt? How very annoying." As he lifted his hand upward, every damien rose into the air and remained suspended. Ozzi waved his hand, slamming the creatures into the walls and dropping them harshly on the floor. "I am still your master," he said between clenched teeth.

Seth rushed the platform, swinging his sword in a wicked arc.

Ozzi's thin blade held little weight against a broader sword, but he made up for it in swiftness. Deftly, he sidestepped several swipes in his direction.

Seth had his own flair, although less elegant. From Jayden's perspective, his sword seemed totally in sync with his body, as if it were physically a part of him. He'd said he was bonded with it. There had to be an advantage in that.

Ozzi missed an opportunity to duck into Seth's personal space and instead became a perfect target. The broad sword swept across Ozzi's chest. As he stumbled backward, blood formed a fat line across his crisp white shirt.

Several damien seized the moment to descend upon their master. But Jayden was no longer interested in watching Ozzi's fate.

Seth strode toward her like a conquering hero.

Indar waved his dagger, but it was no match for the heavier sword, which easily knocked the little weapon across the room. Seth's foot sent Indar backward into the pool.

Jayden reached for Seth and wrapped her arms around his neck, releasing a breath she hadn't known she was holding

The darkness faded from his eyes, letting the candlelight in to make them shine like emeralds. He pressed a searing kiss as if to burn his brand on her lips. She wanted more but he pulled back. "Jayden, I..."

He looked like he wanted to say something important, but from over his shoulder she could see his brother approaching. "Ozzi."

Seth turned and met his brother halfway across the room to reengage their fight. Their swords clanged together repeatedly. One sword swooshed the air in graceful arcs. The other whipped back and forth. Each one took its measure of fabric and flesh.

Three damien lay dead on the floor. They'd been no match for Ozzi's blade. The others, including Zarick, seemed frozen against the walls. They hissed and struggled, but some unseen force held them fast.

Jayden chewed on her lip as Ozzi gained the upper hand briefly, but before he could take another slash at Seth, a great flash of pure white energy burst through the room like a nuclear pulse. The force of the energy blasted the brothers apart.

Apophis' watery spirit grunted in pain and shattered into a million droplets.

Jayden pulled herself to the edge of the pool. "What was that?"

"Someone sent a blast of pure energy across the astral plane — like an announcement to all Anunnaki." Seth looked heavenward. He seemed to be listening to something she couldn't hear. His smile indicated good news. "She's alive. Shaila's alive. We have a new queen. It seems the royal bloodline is intact, brother. We will no longer be leaderless. Kinda puts a wrinkle into your world domination plans, doesn't it?"

Ozzi's eyes glowed with bright yellow fury. He hurled his sword recklessly in Seth's direction. It missed the mark, but created enough of a distraction for him to rush to the fountain, jump into the water, and yank Jayden against him.

Indar lunged towards them, but his lab coat had hooked onto a jagged edge of the onyx tile. He fell to his knees, fumbling to free himself. "Take me with you."

Ozzi looked through him as if he wasn't there, and there was no mistaking the disillusionment in the freak's eyes. Jayden almost felt sorry for him.

She started to twist away from Ozzi, but everything felt thick. Seth ran toward her in slow motion. His eyes widened with fear. Then everything fell away into darkness, and the cosmic waves of the astral plane wrapped around her.

* * *

"NO!" Seth rushed to the pool but no trace of Ozzi's astral energy was left to follow.

Indar struggled to get out of the pool and away, but Seth grabbed the doctor by the throat and cast a holding spell around his aura.

"Where did he take her?" He suspected the answer, and he cursed himself for not seeing it before. Ozzi's ring was the key to opening the water portal. The opalescent brown moonstone was an oracle created to transcend and connect the various planes of Earth. It was only a small sliver of its previous form, but its power seemed undiminished. How had Ozzi obtained a piece of something Seth had destroyed thousands of years ago?

"You've ruined everything." Indar pulled on Seth's fingers. "Why can't I flash out of here?"

Zarick and his rebel damien moved in to corral the doctor in the pool. More damien gathered in the hall: alphas from the nest and omegas from the labs. All gathered around Seth and Indar. Their chant reverberated off of the stone walls. *"Bau. Bau. Bau."*

"I've blocked in your energy. You won't be

going anywhere, Dr. Hor'az." Seth held his free hand in the air again, conjuring a ball of blue flame to his palm. "I could burn your body from the inside out. Or you could tell me where Ozzi took Jayden."

Instead of shaking with fear, Indar cackled in between gasps. "That day...on the German battlefield...you should have died. We'd given you enough poisoned mannah to kill ten Anunnaki warriors."

"Yet I lived."

Indar laughed more. "You thought you had the Rage, and we went along with it. Would you like to know why?"

He knew that Indar was dying to tell him.

"You gave us the key. We had to know why you didn't die. We sampled your blood, and perfected the mannah until we had the ultimate drug. Humans and Anunnaki would come to crave it. Feel the rush from it. Become slaves for it."

Seth had all the pieces, but he hadn't completely understood the full picture until now. The alphas weren't the prize. The omegas were. The damien females that could pass so easily for human females with a little cosmetic help. The prostitution ring was the distribution method. Ozzi's human benefactors had no idea that they were slowly bringing home an army of beautiful assassins.

Ozzi hadn't been creating a species for the thrill of creation. He was creating his own army to dispense and protect his most prized creation — synthetic mannah. "This is all a drug war — or one in the making."

"And it's all *your* fault." Indar squealed the words gleefully.

Seth gripped Indar's throat tighter and lifted

him up above the water. He choked and gasped for air. Angling the idiot's head toward the room, Seth showed Indar the wonderful group of damien just waiting to get their talons into him.

Indar's eyes widened, showing a huge expanse of white.

"Their slave-like existence is all *your* fault. And they are dying to show you their gratitude. Now, tell me where Ozzi went."

"Save me." He rasped. "Save me and I'll tell you."

Seth shook him. "Tell me now and maybe you'll live through this."

"He used the Oracle of Xeshm to cross over into the Underworld. That's why there's no energy trail to follow."

"I figured that much out for myself." The Underworld was a very large place. Maybe Ozzi would go to where they kept the damien army they'd been sending to Apophis. "Where do the shadow walkers take the damien offering?"

"You have no power in the Underworld."

"Neither does Ozzi." Seth lowered the doctor to the ground again, but kept the pressure on his throat. "Why are you still so loyal to my brother? He left you behind. For thousands of years you've devoted yourself to him. Then, he discarded you so easily to make his own getaway. Didn't that make you angry?"

Indar fell silent, his eyes closed. "He would land along the ridge above the Valley of e'Den. I do not know where he would go from there."

Seth released the doctor and made room for Zarick and his group to surround Indar.

"Wait!" Terror exploded across his features. "Don't leave me alone with them."

Seth nodded to the damien, whose faces glistened with anticipation. "He's all yours for now, but don't kill him. I'm going to need him when I get back."

Zarick barked a series of commands to the others, and they carried a screaming Indar out of the great hall. The old alpha broke away from the group to bring an unconscious Ushum to Seth. The damien bent slightly in a pose Seth felt was meant to show honor.

Seth cradled the little guy, remembering how he liked to snuggle in Jayden's hood and twirl her blonde hair. "Your visions were right, Zarick. Her arrival brought freedom to you."

Zarick pointed towards Seth's chest. "To you?"

"Yes." Seth allowed a small smile. "She did indeed. I will find her."

"You go where the offerings live?"

Seth nodded.

"Must know. They will not be such as me."

"I am sure Apophis has poisoned their minds." Before Zarick could leave, Seth had a new promise for the damien seer. "When I return, we will figure out how to help you live in peace here."

Around his fangs, Zarick's lips curved into a weird version of a smile. Seth hoped it was a thankful one.

* * *

Peace comforted his soul as Seth arrived at the inlet. For a moment, he stood and soaked in the vague energy Jayden had left behind. He could almost feel the warm touch of her palm sliding up his arms. The ink of his ancient tattoos shimmered, telling him the beast inside also felt stirred by her memory.

Time worked against him now. Preparation would be critical for a return trip to the Underworld. He'd imprisoned the mighty Apophis on his last trip, saving the human race from annihilation. This time was far more personal, and his emotions could get in the way.

Grabbing the oracle and Jayden's bag, Seth flashed himself and Ushum to his cavern under the Sphinx. Gently, he settled the little damien's body on the pallet. He whispered the healing spell and his sword responded. Light infused Ushum's body, which swelled with a rush of fresh air into his lungs.

As the light faded, amber eyes flickered open and widened with happiness. He sniffed Seth's hand and nuzzled into it. Ushum's tail curled and flicked to express his joy, and he chattered in his primitive, broken speech. Seth scratched a soft spot under the ears.

"No, Ushum. She's not here." He heard the crack in his own voice and mentally buried the negative thoughts creeping in. "But we're going to go rescue her."

Ushum puffed his chest and growled in a quasi-threatening manner.

Seth picked the little damien up and held him eye to eye. "Ushum, this could be a one-way trip. She's in the place where they take the damien given to Apophis."

Ushum's yellow eyes nearly bugged and his body trembled. Then, he wrapped his tail around Seth's forearm and squeezed, confirming his desire to not be left behind.

"Okay then. We're going to need a few things."

He emptied Jayden's bag and placed the oracle inside. The straps needed to be loosened in order to secure the bag around Seth's wider waistline.

Armed with his sword, the oracle and Ushum, Seth was just about ready. In the Underworld, only Apophis could wield personal magic. Seth would only have his shape shifting abilities, though his sword would protect him, and the oracle would bring them home. But there was another item that could be of value in that dimension.

He waved a hand in front of the wall next to his pallet, and the stone disappeared. Beyond lay his private room, which contained all of his possessions. For centuries he'd fought beside great human warriors and generals. The room was a shrine to their history of war. He'd kept every suit of armor and every uniform as a badge of honor. For Seth, they represented his devotion to the cause of human freedom.

He waved his hand again, this time over a white stone. As its energy swirled to life, a warm light bathed the room. There was no need for torches. The stone would stay lit as long as Seth needed the light. Today, he just needed to collect one thing, and he couldn't remember where he'd put it.

Ushum cooed with delight when he found a pretty jeweled hair clip adorned with lapis lazuli beads.

Nefertiti. Seth now clearly pictured her face. He remembered the night she'd given him that comb. No, that wasn't quite the truth. He'd pulled it from her dark hair and held it teasingly beyond her reach. Normally, she would have jumped for it, but her belly was swollen with their child. Would he ever learn what happened to his child? His son? Maybe it was better that he didn't know.

He rubbed his fingers across the top of Ushum's head. "I think you're right. Jayden would love this." The beads were about the same shade of blue as her eyes and they would look pretty in Jayden's light hair. He tucked the comb into the bag next to the oracle.

Returning his attention to the task at hand, he finally found the small leather pouch he sought and slid a small mirror into his palm. He saw his dark reflection in the thin, polished layer of obsidian, which lay across a silver disk. The obsidian had come from Apophis' mountain in the Underworld, making this no ordinary mirror.

Armed and ready for his mission, he tossed Ushum onto his shoulder and moved to the edge of the water. He hadn't been totally honest with Jayden. The waters here didn't flow into the Nile. They flowed into the Underworld. Either way the outcome if she'd fallen in would have been death.

There was only one constant physical path into Apophis' domain and it lay hidden underneath the deceptively calm river within Seth's cavern. While he'd kept himself out of the human world, he'd never stopped guarding the entrance to the Underworld to prevent Apophis' escape.

This entrance would put them far away from where Jayden would be, but in his water dragon form he could close the distance quickly. Two rivers flowed around the Valley of e'Den, the Idigna and the Buranuna. Either river could help him catch up to Ozzi and Jayden, before they crossed over the mountains and into the Valley of Shadows. Even imprisoned, Apophis' power in this realm was strong.

Ushum leaned into Seth's neck, shivering. He

stroked the damien's tail reassuringly.

He removed the oracle and held it out over the water. Mentally, he levitated the ancient stone slowly to the center and waited for its energy to ignite. Even without Jayden here, it would know what to do. Its powers of protection were crafted for this very task of controlling the physical portal to the Underworld.

As its energy blazed to life, Seth felt his own powers flare. The oracle drew energy from him and gave it back in a new form.

He felt his eyes crystallize, and his sight colored with a greenish cast. He lifted his arms and the waters began to spin faster and faster. Wind whipped through the cave from the force of the whirlpool. He felt Ushum wrapping his little fingers around locks of hair to hang on.

As the waters swirled, the center disappeared into a deep void. The water vortex transcended dimensions, leaping past the living plane, the astral plane and into the Underworld dimension.

Seth held onto Ushum and dove toward the oracle. Snatching it from the air, he angled straight into the void as the waters slowly swirled shut.

The journey through the physical portal lasted much longer than one through the astral plane. He braced his body for the onslaught of cosmic pulses. Breaking through the veil of each dimension brought a sizzling pain to his skin. His astral spirit buzzed from disruptive power surges.

The winds of inter-dimensional travel halted, and Seth realized that they were underwater. Still clutching Ushum and the oracle, he desperately kicked in the direction he felt was the surface.

Finally feeling a warm breeze on his face, he lay back on the surface and filled his lungs with air.

Ushum collapsed on Seth's chest, exhausted. Seth could see the shore a few meters away and kicked over to it. Settled on the pebbled shoreline, he unzipped the waist bag and emptied it of the river water that had seeped in.

No more magic from this point, at least not his own. He couldn't flash them to the kingdom of Den.

"Can you swim?"

Ushum nodded and dove into the water. He used his little wings to glide through the currents. As he swam, his stunted body actually looked graceful, but awkwardness returned when he hauled himself on shore.

The water beast inside Seth demanded his turn, anxious to find the one woman who challenged and soothed both of them. It was time to swim — with great speed.

CHAPTER FIFTEEN

"Where are we?" Jayden hated to ask. She'd felt Ozzi's desperation when he drew her into the astral plane. The journey this time held no fascination for her as they'd been bombarded with waves of hot pulses. When ground formed under her feet again, the landscape confused her. Dread shuddered along her spine. "Ozzi, where have you brought me?"

The moon hung large in a deep orange sky, casting pale light over a very barren landscape. It reminded her of a painting of Mars. Underneath the moon, a supremely large mountain stood so tall its peak seemed to pierce the heavens. Close to her right, dark red rock formed a high cliff, dotted with black holes. Dry heat blasted across her body, making her wonder if this was day or night.

"We are in the Underworld." For once, Ozzi seemed uncaring of his appearance, running his hands through his blond hair nervously. "A very hospitable place, can't you tell?" Unknotting his tie, he slid it from his neck and wrapped it around her wrist.

She was no longer wet from the ceremonial pool, thanks to the cosmic winds of the astral plane, but sweat glistened on her skin from the oppressive heat. While he was preoccupied with getting the silk tie to stay in a tight knot, Jayden slammed her knee into his groin and twisted away.

He grabbed a handful of her hair before he

doubled over in pain.

"Let go of me, you coward."

"Shut your mouth." He emphasized his anger by yanking hard.

Tears sprung to her eyes. "Or what — you'll sew my mouth shut? I've heard that one already."

He put his hand across her mouth, pinching her jaw in a tight grip. "Listen closely, for this will be your only warning. We've arrived smack in the middle of the damien nest. This is where Apophis' damien live and train to kill. We need to get to higher ground right now."

"Can't you flash us somewhere else?"

"I have no power here. Only Apophis has power in the Underworld."

"Really? So that makes you as weak and lowly as a human."

Ozzi's eyes glittered with annoyance. "I can still shift into my beast form. Would you prefer that?"

Jayden chewed her lip. "Maybe. You can fly in that form, right?"

At first he looked like he wanted to strangle her, but then he accepted the idea and began to take his clothes off. He chuckled at her what-are-you-doing look. "If I transform now, the clothes will shred. At the other end, I won't be able to flash anything new on. Get the picture?"

She nodded and accepted his clothes, rolling them into a wrinkled ball. She hated this man, but she needed his help to get to a safer place. For now, her enemy was her lifeline. Without a protective Zarick around, she didn't count on making any new damien friends here.

Seth would be here soon. She knew he would find a way to get to her. He'd made a promise, and he'd never break it.

Ozzi transformed into his dragon form. She had to admit that he was every bit as impressive in this form as Seth. His skin was a dark earthy brown and held no scales, but his wings shimmered with a metallic silver shade. With his nose, he nudged her away slightly so he could hold his wings to their full length. As he lifted his great body into the air, he wrapped his talons around her waist.

They lifted higher above the cliff, giving Jayden a view of a flat plateau that seemed to stretch out far into the distance. Below her, the cliff face curved just as far in the opposite direction. It was lined with hundreds of holes. From this angle, the moonlight revealed the tiny dark shapes of damien as they crawled in and out of the caves. They looked like thousands of bees buzzing around a hive.

Ozzi turned and traveled along the plateau, which seemed to sit at the end of a large mountain range. Yesterday, she would have looked at these mountains and cliffs with a sense of anticipation. Adrenaline would have fueled a craving for adventure — for that welcome feeling of freedom.

Freedom. She sighed into the wind. In retrospect, she felt childish. Zarick and the others had spent a lifetime waiting for her arrival, waiting for true freedom. How could the feeling from jumping off a cliff compare to fighting for one's survival?

Maybe it was similar and maybe she was being too hard on herself. She'd fought her whole life for the right to live: to live without drugs, without doctors, without judgment. Her extreme lifestyle was just a function of that fight. And the skills she'd learned had definitely kept her alive on Ozzi's island.

They flew beyond the end of the plateau, and

on the other side, Jayden was shocked to see a lush landscape spread across a valley nestled between two rivers. Ozzi landed in the southern end of the valley where the two rivers joined.

As he shifted back to his human form, Jayden handed him the wad of clothing. "Where are we now? This is not what I would have expected of the Underworld."

"It's the Valley of e'Den. Den means light." He pointed back in the direction they came from. "We're in the eastern kingdom of Den."

Plucking an apple from a nearby tree, Jayden smelled the sweet fragrance of the fruit. "I feel like I'm standing in the Garden of Eden." She looked at him expecting a denial.

"This is still Earth. You are simply in another dimension of it. There was a time when it was much easier to cross into the Underworld, and for humans it was considered the ultimate goal to get here."

On the surface it seemed beautiful, but something here felt cold. There was no breeze to explain the new crispness in the still air. She shivered and dropped the fruit on the ground.

"This is not heaven, Jayden. This is a dimension that is and isn't. Time does not flow here. Life does not grow here. It is day, and yet it is also night. Perpetual existence. That is all I can say about this place." Ozzi pulled on his clothes and grimaced at the many rips and tears created by Seth's blade.

Jayden sat on the ground and rubbed her bare feet, trying to bring some warmth back into them. "What are we doing here? Do you have a plan?"

"You are my plan." Ozzi again pointed back in the direction they came from. Even on the other side of a mountain range, the peaks of that dark mountain towered over the horizon. "I'm taking you to Apophis. The Underworld is easy to get into, but very hard to get out of."

"Why did we fly away from the mountain if that's our destination?"

"It is easier — and safer — to cross over the Valley of Shadows on the north side."

Jayden rolled her eyes. He meant safer for his own damned hide. "So I get to be your bargaining chip."

He grinned, flashing a perfect set of white teeth. "Of course."

If her hands weren't wrapped with a silk tie, she would have slapped that grin from his face.

He held up his hand and pointed to his ring. "The oracle that brought us here does not have enough power to get me out. I will trade you for permission to leave."

"Why even come here in the first place, damn you?"

"Because Seth can't follow us here."

Jayden looked away to hide her face. She'd felt the blood drain away from it and she didn't want Ozzi to see her fear. "He'll find a way." She whispered, mostly in an effort to convince herself.

"You're right. I should not underestimate my brother," Ozzi snipped. "Let's say that he does find a way. But by the time he figures it out, he will be too late to stop my trade with Apophis."

"I thought he was in a prison."

"This realm exists through his energy. His power here is not diminished by his inability to move around in it."

Ozzi moved around the clearing, gathering wood to make a fire. "I suggest that you stay near me

— or the fire. There are things in the shadows that you wouldn't want to come face to face with."

"You're one of them." Her sarcasm only made him smile and lick his teeth.

"But I am very handy to have around." Slowly, he removed his clothes, folded them neatly, and shifted into his dragon form. He blew a stream of fire onto the wood, and warmth filled the area.

Unlike Seth, Ozzi didn't curl protectively around her. He chose a spot on the other side of the fire and stretched his long body across the grass. It didn't take long for the heavy breathing of slumber to rumble through the clearing.

Jayden found a soft spot and lay with her back against a fallen log. She watched the sky, but nothing changed to give her any idea if it was day or night. It seemed like perpetual dusk. The moon loomed large, and the sun blazed from a position far behind it. Stars dotted the sky like pale freckles. They didn't shine like they would in the deep of night, and yet they shouldn't show at all if it were day.

As Ozzi said, everything here seemed to represent perpetual existence. It felt like one big prison.

* * *

Jayden opened her eyes. She had no idea how long she'd slept, but her dreams lingered like sheer, wispy ghosts. She could still feel the tightness of fear in her chest. Being trapped featured heavily in her dreams.

"Jayden?"

She sat up and looked around for the source of the voice.

"Jayden?"

There was no mistaking Seth's deep, exotic tone. "Where are you?" She whispered so as not to awaken Ozzi.

"Come find me." She heard a touch of humor in his voice. She'd bet he was smiling.

"Keep talking then." Jayden tiptoed to the edge of the clearing, and realized that her hands were unbound. She wiggled her fingers in front of her face as proof. Looking back, she saw that her body lay in the same spot, with her wrists bound by Ozzi's silk tie. Ozzi's warnings came to mind. *Things here might not be as they seem.* "Seth?"

"Yes, my dear?"

"How do I know it's you? Ozzi said that you can't use magic here."

"I cannot, but your oracle is being very cooperative with me." Again, she heard the teasing tone. It warmed her heart.

"Tell me where you are?"

"By the river."

Slowly, he talked her through the path to the river. As she stood at the water's edge, she saw him striding her way. He moved with power and confidence, and her blood pulsed through her veins in a pattern matching his stride. By the time he stood inches away, her breath came in short gasps, her chest heaving from the effort to breathe. Every inch of her skin tingled with the desire to feel his touch.

He cupped her face with his hand and she thanked the heavens that her out-of-body spirit could feel it. She pressed her lips into his palm, kissing the warm skin. Hot, passionate energy undulated around her in waves. Was that her energy or his that she felt?

He started to speak. "Jayden, I —"

"Shhh." She placed a finger over his lips. She didn't want to hear him repeat his vow of commitment to her. She only wanted to feel. His body would show her what his mind could not tell her. And she was more than okay with that. She loved him, and she wanted to show him that love every second, for as long they had together.

Tugging him over to a tree, she leaned against the trunk and brought Seth's body against hers. Impatient, she lifted his shirt up and over his head. Her hands explored every muscle across his chest. Up and over his shoulders, she trailed the tips of her fingers along the watery patterns inked across his arms.

Pinned between tree and man, Jayden's body warmed quickly. Her heart beat a frantic tune and her breath hitched in a hectic pattern. Urgently, she kneaded her fingers through his hair and pulled his head toward hers. She watched his irises dilate wildly as her lips captured his.

The feel of his pulse through his lips mesmerized her. She closed her eyes to savor that single sensation. Tilting her head changed everything.

She tasted Seth's urgency as he deepened the kiss. He nibbled a path across her jaw and down her neck. She drew in a ragged breath when he found her sweet spot just under her earlobe. The sensations he created zinged through her body like bolts of electricity.

Like an addict, Jayden wanted more with a desperation she'd never felt before in her life. She craved something even more intoxicating than adrenaline. She craved Seth.

Her hands fumbled around his waist like a

teenager, but she finally managed to free him from his pants. She pushed them down to his thighs and pulled him hard against her. She could feel his smile on her neck.

His hands smoothed across every curve of her body, sliding down and over her hips. Pulling away slightly, he opened the red cloak and lifted the now-pinkish robe up by the handfuls.

She watched his dark brows lift when he discovered that she wore no panties. Only skin. As he cupped her bottom and urged her to lift her legs, she wrapped them firmly around his hips.

She felt every glorious inch of him as he buried himself deep inside her. Closing her eyes again, she hooked her arms over his shoulders and hung on. He rocked back and forth, and she slid up and down against the tree. She ignored the roughness against her back, and focused on the delicious smoothness of him.

Blood pulsed through her womb, adding to the erotic tempo. With each thrust inside, she moaned as her body enveloped him. With each withdrawal, she inhaled and memorized his musky scent. His tongue invaded her with the same eagerness and depth.

She tasted everything in his kiss: desire, loyalty, loneliness. His hands buried desperately into her hair and he moaned. His body shuddered with restraint, and she realized that he was waiting for her — giving her time to reach her ecstasy.

Like an approaching storm, the air grew heavier and her body sizzled with energy. Her need surged like a river overflowing its banks. Winding and speeding through the currents, she felt the end coming. She tumbled out of control, until finally Jayden crested the edge like a waterfall. She screamed as the force of her orgasm plunged her to the earth and her energy shattered into mist.

For a while, she remained as still as possible, just breathing. She feared that any movement would shatter the moment. He felt so good just where he was. She wanted to keep him within her body — keep him from leaving.

"Ozzi plans to hand me over to Apophis."

Seth nuzzled into her neck and drew in a deep, ragged breath. "I know. I interrupted the transaction. Ozzi still has to honor the deal he made, or his life will be forfeit to Apophis."

"But Apophis received the damien."

"He didn't receive *you*. I'm sure being denied it has made him want your astral spirit even more now. He will make you a slave to him." Seth's voice cracked on the last word.

Jayden tasted his lips again, and she whimpered a protest when she felt him slowly withdraw from her body. Cool air whispered across her flesh and she shivered as the sensation triggered an aftershock. His lips curved into a knowing smile, but he held her gently as she lowered her legs and tested her weight on them.

She shook the robe until it fell back down over her legs. "Where is my oracle? Could it help protect me from Apophis?"

"It's back at my camp."

"How far away is that? Can we get it?" The truth hit her as soon as the last word was out. Seth was here in the same out-of-body form as she was.

"Jayden, my camp is hours away from here. I entered the Underworld far to the south, but the river current flows in this direction. I made good time getting this close."

"Then what are you doing wasting time here with me? While our astral spirits are dallying, you could be here in the flesh by now." Her voice sounded bitter even to her own ears. She hadn't meant it to.

"So, we're dallying, are we?" Seth's smile only grew wider and his teasing tone returned. "Even a dragon needs to sleep and regain his strength. And so does Ushum."

"He's here too? Don't you dare let anything happen to him." Relief overpowered the bitterness.

"I will do my best, but *you* are my main priority." For emphasis, he leaned into her again, pressing her back against the tree.

She looked up and met his intense gaze. "I know. You promised me."

"It's more than that, and you know it. Why don't you trust me?" He whispered the question into her ear.

"If I didn't trust you, I wouldn't be here right now. I'd still be sleeping."

"No, I meant back during the ceremony. You knew I was there. You knew I would protect you, but you couldn't wait for me."

She had to look away then. He was right. "That wasn't lack of trust. That was impatience."

His hands cupped her cheeks and pointed her face towards his. She couldn't ignore the life-or-death look in his eyes. "Jayden, the Underworld is no joke. I can get us out of here, but if you don't trust me..."

He didn't have to finish his sentence. She understood the warning. If she didn't trust in him, then they might not make it home.

"Well, do you?"

"Of course, I —" Jayden's body jolted. "Ouch.

What was that?"

Whatever it was, it touched her again. Pain prickled across her arms. Something scratched her. No, something had scratched her body — her physical body.

Seth's image started to float away. She reached for his hand, but they no longer could touch. "Jayden, listen for me." He pointed to his head. "Listen!"

Then, he was gone, and she felt her spirit yank back through the pathway and slam back into her body. A handful of damien surrounded her, lifted her off the ground, and prepared to carry her off. They handled her roughly, pricking her skin with their claws. As she kicked and punched at their arms, they bared their teeth, hissing and snarling. She saw no hint of humanity to soften the yellow glow of their eyes. These were truly wild creatures.

They hadn't covered her mouth, so she screamed. "Ozzi! Wake up!"

The dragon hefted himself out of the shadows. He bared his fangs in a display of dominance, but these creatures had no fear of Ozzi's beast form. They clicked their claws together as if anxious to dig into a feast. Ozzi huffed a stream of fire at them.

Two damien screeched as their skin sizzled from the flame. Two others jumped on his back, burying their teeth in Ozzi's flesh. His scream sounded more of anger than pain. He shook them off easily and swiped them into the air with his tail. The remaining damien stood guard over Jayden, but the dragon's threatening approach sent him scurrying for the trees.

Jayden wasted no time in collecting Ozzi's clothes. As his talons wrapped carefully around her waist, he lifted them high into the air flying north along with the river.

Jayden?

Startled, she looked down toward the river. She couldn't see Seth, but his voice sounded very clearly in her head. She remembered the last thing he'd said before his wonderful body faded away. He'd said to listen for him.

Jayden, I can hear your thoughts when you direct them to me. Talk to me. What happened?

Seth?

She could hear his laughter in her head too. *Yes, my dear. Are you okay?*

It was a group of damien, but I'm fine now. We're traveling north. I can see the river below us.

When the mountain range thins, he will turn west to fly over the peaks. Tell me when he turns.

* * *

Jayden felt Ozzi's beast form trembling from exhaustion. A couple of hours ago she'd sent her mental message to Seth that they'd turned westward. Crossing through the mountains proved to be an extreme feat of endurance. Ozzi paused on several peaks to rest his wings and adjust to the thin air.

His breath wheezed through his nose, but she wasn't going to feel sorry for him. He brought them into this mess. She'd take some measure of joy from his pain.

Over the next rise, he dipped down toward the ground, the sudden motion leaving her stomach somewhere back up in the high altitude.

He landed heavily in a clearing that looked as inviting as a cemetery. Crumbled ruins lay scattered in pieces like ancient wreckage. She didn't recognize the stone at all. In fact, it didn't feel like stone either. It felt more like metal beyond oxidation.

She wanted to ask what it was, but Ozzi disappeared into the woods. She set about making a bed for herself, but grew tired of fighting against the bonds around her wrist.

Ozzi returned after a short time with some creature in his jaws. Jayden realized that Ozzi was looking at her expectantly.

"I don't cook — whatever that is."

The dragon shook his head and huffed in a sound that resembled aggravation. Disappearing into the woods again, he returned with several thick branches in his mouth. Dropping them to the ground, he blew a trail of fire across them until they held a flame. He carried the creature's carcass to the fire and dropped it right on top of the flames. Sparks fanned out in all directions before sizzling skyward.

Ozzi shifted to his human form and collapsed on the ground.

Jayden laughed when loud snores came from his naked, limp body.

Seth?

She waited, but no response came.

Seth? Can you hear me?

Still he didn't respond. She looked up at the mountain range they'd just crossed over. Maybe he wouldn't be able to hear her again until he'd crossed over too.

She waved away a trail of smoke that pushed out from under the creature's skin. Like a tea kettle, a high pitched squeal sounded from the force of the smoke escaping. As the skin blackened, juices dripped into the fire and popped like firecrackers.

Ozzi's body jerked awake from the sound.

Silently, he pulled away a large piece of meat and tasted it. Nodding approval, he ripped off another section and handed it to Jayden. Her mind said no, but her stomach said yes — loudly.

Jayden decided that if you could plug your nose and avoid the smell, the meat actually tasted pretty good. It was oily, like duck meat, so she used Ozzi's silk tie to wipe her face. She held her wrists towards him in a mock salute. He gave her a disapproving look but kept eating.

She watched him dispose of the bones by burying them. He'd finally pulled on his trousers, but the rest of him was bare. His build was so much like Seth's in height and muscle tone, but their coloring was like night and day. She had to admit that he wasn't a bad specimen of man at all.

"It's a shame you're an asshole."

He paused and turned his amber eyes on her. They were more brown now, probably from his state of exhaustion. "From you I'll consider that a compliment."

"I was just thinking that if you weren't some egomaniac bent on world domination, women would find you very appealing."

He shuddered, reminding her that he thought humans were dirty.

"How did you create a new species?"

He settled into a spot and leaned back, closing his eyes. She thought maybe he wouldn't answer her anymore when he finally spoke. "Apophis creates his followers by turning dead humans into demons. Their soulless forms get new life as vessels of his darkness. Demons are very strong, but they die quite easily. One prick of their skull and they turn to dust."

He tossed another branch into the fire.

"Plus, demons can be hard to control around humans. They crave human souls because they don't have one anymore."

"You thought you could create something better, a super demon."

"More or less. We experimented for years, suffering many failures until humans discovered modern *in vitro* fertilization techniques. That made it easier to experiment in larger numbers, but we still failed to bring a pregnancy to full term inside a damien female — not to mention that half the males carried blanks. And then we realized that surrogacy might help us bridge the time gap while their physiology continued to adapt."

"And then you started buying up blood companies."

He smiled wickedly. "Indar was already developing computer data collecting to analyze the flow of Anunnaki blood in the human population. We found that women with higher concentration of our bloodlines could more successfully carry a litter to term."

"I've seen the evidence of your failures — the mutations."

He shrugged and his matter-of-factness chilled her blood.

"So when you fully succeed, the damien will be able to produce and carry their own pregnancies?"

"That is the plan. The need for human surrogates would be gone, and we could focus on much more important things."

She lifted her eyebrows to urge him to reveal more, but he just smiled and remained mute.

"Ozzi, would you please untie me?"

He shook his head.

"Look, as much as I despise you, I'm not going anywhere." She nodded toward the mound of buried bones. "At least with you I know what to expect. Plus, nature calls."

With a chest-heaving sigh, he obliged. But he kept his eye on her as she moved around the ruins to find a private spot. Afterwards, she continued to explore the wreckage. That was what she felt it was now. An ancient *Titanic*. Some huge vessel whose destiny was cut tragically short.

A large section of it formed something like a small shed. She pulled back a curtain of moss and found that she could step inside. Something in the darkness hummed.

"I wouldn't go in there, Jayden."

"What is it?"

"Can you hear the buzzing? It's an energy surge left over from a collapsed void. At one time, someone used that old hull as a portal."

Portal? Could she use this to get home? Probably not without the oracle. She smiled as she thought of Seth. Last night he'd called it *her* oracle.

She stepped inside, but Ozzi voiced no further objection and he made no move to stop her. His lack of urgency made her decide that it wouldn't be deadly to go in. Curiosity, as usual, urged her to investigate.

Moving forward into the darkness, she felt the energy hum vibrate through her. Her blood seemed to shift its flow to match the tempo. A feeling of equalizing washed over her body. Then, a bright light burst forward, overtaking her and knocking her to the ground.

The room took shape around her. Bright lights. Air conditioning turned down too low. Sterile, white walls. Stiff and crunchy sheets. Leather stretched tight over her arms and legs.

Jayden realized that she was in her bed at the mental hospital. Nurses swung in and out of the room, bringing needles and little jars of medicine. Medicine that would only send her deeper into her hallucinations. But she knew better now. They weren't hallucinations. They were real. The demons were real. She tried to tell the nurses, but nobody heard her. She couldn't even hear herself.

A familiar voice drifted in from the hallway. *Father!* His smooth, commanding tone barked orders to the doctor to stop humoring his daughter. Then she heard the word that could still her blood. *Broken.* He'd called her broken.

Jayden tried to scream at him that she wasn't broken. She wasn't perfect, but she was alive and she loved him. Wasn't that enough? But he'd given up on her too long ago to care anymore. Too many doctors and not one with any definite answers. It was so unlike her father to give up on anything, but he'd given up on *her*.

Tears streamed like lava, searing a slow path of regret down her cheeks.

The scene melted away into darkness again. Clutching her chest, she heaved with sobs so powerful her whole body shook.

Eventually, she felt her body moving to sit by the fire, but her thoughts were too deep to absorb anything around her. Sitting, she stared into the flames and listened to the crackle.

Inside, her heart crackled too. Her whole life had brought her to this moment. She'd been accused of so many things. Her father thought she was suicidal. His circle of friends thought she was desperate for attention. The doctors thought she was crazy.

None of that was true. Jayden loved life. And even before she'd learned how not-crazy she really was, she'd never given up on herself.

Neither had Seth. But he'd asked her to trust him, when nobody else in her life had ever trusted her. *Can I trust you?*

She hadn't meant to send a message, but his voice calmly answered. *Yes, my dear, you know you can.*

CHAPTER SIXTEEN

Jayden's question entered his mind so suddenly that Seth nearly dropped Ushum, who was cradled in the curve of several talons as they flew over the mountains.

It was a short message, but he could hear a lifetime of pain through her tone. She hadn't meant to ask him directly. He almost didn't answer, until he realized she needed to know. And he wanted to know what happened to forge such desperation in her.

So he answered her honestly.

Her mind purged in a telepathic rush. As he descended slowly into the Valley of Shadows, he listened as she described her experience in the collapsed portal. If only he was there now to hold her and nuzzle into her hair like Ushum did.

Quickly, he set up camp very close to Jayden. He'd made good time going over the mountains since he'd decided to cross over a little further north than Ozzi did. There the range dipped lower, reducing the stress on the lungs in flight. He should be just shy of twenty kilometers north of them now.

He shared a meal of roots and berries with Ushum before tucking the little damien into a bed of grasses near the fire. Sliding Jayden's bag over to his lap, he withdrew the oracle and held it gently. He loved watching the soft blue-green glow expand and swirl. No, that wasn't quite it. He loved what the oracle had brought to him.

He lifted his gaze toward the hill above them and waited for the oracle to summon Jayden's astral spirit and bring her here. He didn't have to wait long.

Jayden shimmered to life in front of him. The blood red cloak still hung over her shoulders, elegantly framing her tall, slim form. As she stepped toward him, the white robe underneath parted to show incredibly long legs. Desire rooted him to his spot on the ground.

With great effort, he buried his desire for tonight. As the moonlight so aptly revealed across her face, tonight she needed something much more than physical touch. She needed the truth.

She leaned down to kiss him, and he tasted her tears. He tasted everything: desire and despair, freedom and restraint, trust and fear.

He pulled her down, cradled her on his lap, and held her as she cried.

But the heavens had more in store for him. As Jayden's aura exploded with uncontrolled energy, it merged with his in a way he'd never felt before. The beast inside him purred from the rush of power. Raw energy sizzled between them, weaving around them both like a spider's web.

In his long life, he had never felt so connected to another. He hugged her tighter and whispered the only thing left that hadn't been said. "I am in love with you, Jayden."

She tilted her face toward his. "You don't have to say that."

"Yes, I do." He nuzzled his nose in her hair. She'd been through hell but damned if he didn't still smell a hint of coconut. "And I will repeat it forever until one day you finally believe it."

She smiled then. It began softly and spread to her eyes. "I do believe you, Seth. I'm not so broken that I feel unworthy of being loved."

"You never were broken." And he would never allow her to use that word again. He chose his words very carefully, knowing that Jayden still loved her father. "Perhaps he'll be a better grandfather."

"That tenderness you hide so well — I'm in love with you too."

They sat for a long time, just wrapped together under Jayden's cloak. As the fire dwindled, Seth gathered more branches. It took a while since this area had few trees.

When he returned, Jayden was kneeling over Ushum and smiling. "I thought Indar might have killed him. He lay so still in the sand."

Seth stroked Ushum's back, but the little damien rolled over and sighed in his sleep, exhausted by their journey.

Seth led Jayden back over to their spot by the fire. "He's very resilient. He picked this out for you." Pulling the hair comb from the waist bag, he pressed it into her hand.

"It's beautiful." He watched her finger the lapis lazuli beads. She seemed lost in thought for several moments, and then her tongue slipped across her lower lip. "Did this belong to Nefertiti?"

"It did." He knew his smile was wistful. His passion for his former lover was now as vague as her memory, and somehow that didn't bother him anymore. Time healed all wounds. Wasn't that the old saying? "She was as fearless as you. She would have liked you very much."

He watched a myriad of emotions play across Jayden's face until she seemed to settle on pride.

Sitting up, she pushed the comb into her hair and angled for him to see. "Thank you." She pressed her lips to his.

"Ushum picked it out. I can't take the credit."

"Then I'll thank him in the morning."

She snuggled into the crook of his arm, and he buried his nose in her hair. He knew their time together was ending. "You need to return soon. Your spirit, as well as your body, needs rest. Tomorrow, we will face Ozzi together and pray that we can escape before Apophis finds a way to block us."

"Tell me about Apophis and how he came to be imprisoned in his own realm."

"There is nothing more ancient than energy. Our powers, which you think of as magic, are simply the manipulation of energy. Energy must always be in balance. When our queen's bloodline is intact, Apophis' dark power beyond the Underworld is limited, just as our light power is limited in his domain. That's the balance of energy."

"So things are thankfully in balance with your new queen. I can't help but wonder what the world would be like if you hadn't trapped Apophis back then."

"When our former queen died, Apophis could have easily taken over. He nearly did. Humans had their own battles going on for world domination. Alexander the Great conquered most of the known world at that time. He stumbled upon a treasure that contained an oracle."

"My oracle?"

"No, the one in Ozzi's ring. The Oracle of Xeshm was created in the Underworld to be a portal key between the Earth dimensions. It was seduced away from Alexander by one of my kind, a woman named

Lilith."

"You mentioned her to Ozzi."

"I did, and she kept that oracle for several hundred years. She was enjoying life as the queen of Egypt when she fell in love with an idiot named Marc Antony."

Jayden inhaled sharply. "She was Cleopatra?"

"One of her many incarnations. But this time, her romance affected me, because I was battling beside Caesar Octavian, successfully dismantling the traitorous Antony's army. But Antony abandoned his troops and disappeared. There was one last place to look for him."

"He'd gone running to Cleopatra."

"Yes." Seth pressed another kiss to her temple. "So in love with him, Lilith revealed what we are. Worse, she showed him the damned oracle. And desperate coward that he was — Antony used it to call forth Apophis to join him. Apophis, who would never submit to taking orders from a human, used the opportunity to come through with his whole demon army."

"I don't remember any of this in my history books."

He chuckled. "No, I wouldn't think so."

"Then what really happened?"

"Apophis killed Antony and paralyzed Lilith. He bit her, like Ozzi did to you, injecting a poison so strong she truly seemed to be dead."

"I guess asps sound more logical than a demon overlord. And what of you?"

"For me, it was time for duty — damage control. It was no longer good to be an Anunnaki in a human world. I sealed Lilith in a rock and buried it deep into the floor of the Caspian Sea. The problem of Apophis took a lot longer to solve. That was the last time Anunnaki and humans knowingly fought side by side. Many human and Anunnaki soldiers died, and those that survived spread stories of demons and monsters. Many legends began on those bloody fields. But we beat them back to the Underworld, and even Apophis had to go lick his wounds. I followed him there and trapped him in his own throne room. There he has stayed for thousands of years, waiting for the prophecy to begin. A prophecy that predicts his escape."

"You stopped him once. You could do it again."

He loved her confidence in him. "I hope it doesn't come to pass. The Earth is now the dominion of humankind, and the Anunnaki are strewn around the planet like nomads. Even if Shaila can find them, they might not be willing to come forward now."

The light from Jayden's oracle wobbled slightly and her body faded to a gauzy reflection. She reached for Seth's face but all he felt was a warm breeze as her hand passed through him.

"I don't want to go."

"I don't want you to go." His chest tightened. "Please remember, no matter what occurs you must trust me."

"I will." Her wispy form faded and was gone. Moments later, her voice came boldly into his head. *I will trust you.*

* * *

Jayden's body jerked awake. It felt like morning. Hard to tell in the dark orange that perpetually lit the sky, but the stars seemed fainter now. She found her new comb still tucked behind her ear and she used it to untangle several snarls in her hair. Never again would she doubt her oracle's power.

Ozzi hefted his beastly body on all fours and drew in a deep breath. He paced around her, snuffing the air repeatedly. An angry growl rumbled deep in his throat and he waved his fangs inches from her face.

She backed away from him when he snapped his jaws angrily. But he allowed her no room to flee, using the bulk of his body and his long tail to keep her cornered. He shook his head and body, ridding himself of the dew which glistened across his skin. Then grabbing her and his clothes with his claws, he lifted them up into the air and toward the immense black mountain that towered over the world like an overlord.

Looking back, she saw Seth in the distance flying toward them. Jayden's heart pounded blood through her body in a fierce tempo.

An eruption from the dark mountain forced all of them out of the air for a while. They took shelter under an outcropping of rock. Around them hot ash drifted from the sky like black snowflakes. Red lava oozed over the rim of the volcano and dripped down the mountainside like candle wax. Jayden covered her face to avoid the pungent smell of burning gases.

Both Seth and Ozzi had said that Apophis held power beyond his prison. So he probably knew everything that went on in his realm. She couldn't help but wonder if he'd caused the eruption. Was he toying with them? Or more likely he was toying with Seth, delaying any kind of rescue.

Seth had said that Apophis wanted her more now because he was denied her at the ceremony. She'd bet anything that Apophis' greater desire was revenge. What greater revenge than to torture Seth's woman in front of him? He'd endured enough pain in his life. Jayden vowed that she would not do anything to cause more of it for him.

As the ash storm subsided, Ozzi launched them back into the sky. Their destination quickly became clearer.

A large castle seemed embedded into the eastern face of the mountain. A long avenue jutted out from the castle like a landing platform. Dozens of small sphinxes lined both sides of the avenue. An eternity of ash had settled over them like gray icing, but she could still see the feline faces staring intently like a row of castle guards.

Ozzi landed near the castle, avoiding a long walk down the avenue. An immense doorway loomed before them, recessed within a pyramid-shaped frame. Cooling lava had formed stalagmites, which stood like tall sentries on either side of the doorway. Mentally removing the oppressive layers of ash, Jayden could almost see the grandeur of an ancient era.

She felt Ozzi next to her, reforming into his human body. He'd pulled on his suit. It was horribly wrinkled and torn, but he smoothed it out the best he could.

The doors remained closed. They were at least two stories tall and black as ebony.

They hadn't knocked, but the doors swung inward, squeaking heavily on their hinges.

"So he is expecting us." Jayden took one last look behind her, both happy and tense to see Seth approaching quickly in the air. He was too far away to see his face, but she felt his confident energy. It bolstered her own.

"Apophis knows everything here. He's known we were here since our arrival." Ozzi noticed the comb in her hair. "What is this? Where did you get it?" He ripped it from her hair and inspected it.

"It's just a comb." She snatched it back, sliding it firmly back into place above her right ear.

Ozzi looked back into the sky, his lips lifting into a sneer. "It's too late. He can't help you now." Grabbing her arm, he yanked her down a very long corridor. A thick layer of black soot or moss covered the stone walls. She couldn't quite tell by looking and she wasn't going to touch it.

Huge columns as wide as she was tall rose up into ceilings which were cloaked in darkness.

"This way." Ozzi took a left hallway when they reached the end.

Laughter cackled behind them. A scratchy, pithy sound.

"Indar?" Ozzi swiveled around quickly, almost knocking Jayden down.

Her heart sank to the floor. She didn't want to deal with that freakish doctor anymore. He made her skin crawl.

"My *lord*." Indar's voice dripped with bitterness. He bowed slightly, but somehow it looked more like an insult than a posture of deference.

"What are you doing here?" Ozzi seemed to gather his wits. "Shouldn't you be getting the rogue damien back into the nest?"

"You left me." Indar's demeanor shifted to fake disappointment. "You left me there at the mercy of your brother and the damien."

"Indar, I had every faith in your abilities to — "

The doctor held up his hand. "Silence! I gave you thousands of years of my loyalty, and then you left me to go with this *bitch*!" He screamed the last word, spittle slipping over his lower lip.

"Don't be stupid. I had to bring her to Apophis and complete the deal."

Indar's body shuddered, as if he was holding up a massive weight. Wildness settled into his dark brown eyes. He pulled a curved dagger from inside his lab coat.

Jayden's blood chilled as she watched his madness unfurl. He drew the blade tip across his own palm. Blood poured from the wound, dripping onto the floor. Cackling with excitement, he approached Ozzi, who watched Indar with morbid curiosity.

As blood oozed from the wound, Indar wiped his palm slowly across Ozzi's cheek.

Jayden shuddered at the fatal meaning of the gesture. Ozzi was a marked man — marked by blood.

"I gave you everything." Ozzi's arrogance remained intact. "What did you do? Did you cut a deal with Apophis behind my back?"

Indar wiped his bloody hand across his white lab coat. "I didn't need to cut a deal with the Great Master. I've been loyal to him for thousands of years."

Arrogance dripped slowly away from Ozzi's face. Shock paled his skin almost as white as Indar's coat.

The doctor stood taller, as if bolstered by angry confidence, and he grabbed Ozzi's face. Slowly, Indar licked his own blood from Ozzi's cheek.

Jayden felt the contents of her stomach bulging inside her throat, but Ozzi just stood there — staring, thinking, analyzing. If Seth didn't hurry it up, she'd damn sure rather be Ozzi's prisoner than Indar's.

Ozzi's normal color returned and he seemed to have come to some kind of conclusion. "He knew I would bring her here."

That's when it hit her. "And he knew Seth would follow." She hadn't meant to say it aloud, but it was true. And she was the lure. She turned back toward the entrance, hoping to stop him in time. *It's a trap! Seth, no!*

Destiny had wicked, eerie timing. The doors far back down the corridor slammed shut. In the darkness, things slithered and shifted. Torches burst to life, bathing Seth's form in flickering amber light. He looked every bit like a warrior god ready for battle.

But he wasn't a god. He bled like any other physical being.

In moments, he'd caught up to the party. Her waist bag hung around his hips, but where was Ushum? Seth had a slight uplift to the corner of his mouth, and his dimple appeared. But his determined green eyes fixed upon Ozzi and Indar ruthlessly.

"The Great Master will be happy to see you again, Seth."

"I'm sure he will, Indar. How did you get off the island?"

"Apophis sent the shadow walkers back to fetch me. They easily removed your puny spell." Indar swept his arm toward the hallway Ozzi had initially chosen to turn into. "It's time for you *all* to appear before the Great Master."

"I don't think so," Ozzi said.

Jayden felt dread shudder through every bone.

Indar seemed just as shocked. "But it's over for you. Apophis has been well aware of your deceit all these years."

"I'm sure you've been instrumental in passing along the information." Ozzi stepped boldly toward

Indar.

"He knows all about your plans for the damien and the synthetic mannah. He even knows of the alphas you've kept in order to build your own private army." Indar shifted his weight, uncertainty spreading across his face. "You must accept your fate now."

"You're a fucking prick. I do all the work, and you help Apophis waltz in and take over." Ozzi threw his head back and laughed. He looked at Jayden with a crooked smile. "Good luck. It's been absolutely fatal knowing you." To his brother, he simply nodded once.

Laughing again, Ozzi shifted into his dragon form. His clothes lay in tatters on the floor. He apparently wasn't planning to put them back on. As Ozzi bellowed what sounded like a war cry, Indar turned and stumbled away.

Ozzi vented a long stream of fire at the doctor's retreating back.

"Is he sacrificing himself for us?" Jayden couldn't decide if she should be horrified or thankful. Truthfully, she hoped to never see either of them ever again.

"That wouldn't be Ozzi. I think he knows his fate and decided that he's taking Indar down with him. Revenge for betrayal."

Something slithered in the darkest shadows of the ceiling.

Seth grabbed her hand. "We have to go."

"Where's Ushum?"

"He's fine, now *run!*"

Damien descended from the darkness and filled the hallways behind them, blocking their retreat. They sounded like a swarm of angry bees.

The only open path led deeper into the mountain. Jayden ran as fast as she could in long robes and bare feet.

CHAPTER SEVENTEEN

Ozzi half flew, half lumbered after Indar, until they stopped and squared off in the large banquet hall. Food had not been served in this hall in thousands of years. Now it was totally bare, with none of the grandeur left. No massive oak table stood in the middle. Dust and soot lay in a thick layer across the floor, which at one time had been kept polished to a high shine. The large windows facing the eastern mountain range still held a beautiful view, but the panes were covered in a layer of ash like gray snow.

As hundreds of candles suddenly flickered to life high up in the chandeliers, Ozzi heard the scuttle of dozens of damien as they shifted in the shadows. Their yellow eyes stared unblinking and watchful. Ozzi had no doubt that they would kill him if Indar failed.

So, this is how it ends. Apophis had won, damn it. Ozzi soaked in the eager energy within the room, even though it was all directed at him. It was energy, and he would need it.

How had he been so deceived for all these years? His beast craved blood, vengeance against the sniveling little traitor. Ozzi's talons clicked against the stone floors, leaving dark imprints in the dust as he stalked his prey.

He knew Indar would fight dirty, but Ozzi had an advantage in his ability to alter his shape. Indar, as the runt of his own family, had no shape shifting abilities. Only loyalty shifting.

As they faced each other from opposite sides of the hall, Ozzi was surprised to see Indar's form change — not much, just enough to give him more height, bulk and fangs.

Ozzi changed to his human form, but stayed wary enough to shift back quickly. "I see you've been indulging in Apophis' blood."

Indar's voice usually sounded scratchy. Now it was even more so as he tried to talk around long fangs. "Oh, he's given me so much more than that. Did you notice how many damien are here? The Valley of Shadows is filled with thousands of them."

Ozzi hadn't really noticed, but he remembered the view he'd had of the valley when he and Jayden arrived. Hundreds of caves had lined the cliffs. "You solved their reproductive issues?"

Indar nodded. "I gave that knowledge to Apophis — instead of to you."

"Why? I was the only Anunnaki to take you under his wing. When everyone else rejected you, called you sick names, I took you in. I gave you everything."

"No. Not everything." Shadows deepened Indar's eyes to nearly black.

Ozzi knew where the madman's mind was going. "I treated you like a brother."

"You treated me like a dog!" Indar waved his curved dagger back and forth, punctuating his words with anger. He pointed the weapon at Ozzi's naked body. "You flaunted yourself around me. You knew what I wanted most."

"So — your betrayal is *my* fault? That's rich." He watched Indar's features swing in and out of madness. That was a weakness Ozzi could exploit in order to defeat the bastard. "Who was there for you when the others threw stones at your head?"

Indar lowered the weapon, but remained silent.

"Who gave you the keys to the castle and access to all of the riches on Earth?"

Indar slowly rocked back and forth on his feet, and then mouthed, *You did.*

"And who let you play your sadistic games with the human slaves?"

Indar's face cracked with despair. He dropped the dagger, rubbed his temples, and whispered, "You did."

Ozzi patiently waited for the traitor to absorb a sense of guilt and remorse. He moved toward Indar with slow, measured steps. "Blood. You crave it far more than you crave sex with me. You love the feel of hot blood pouring over your skin. Don't you?"

"Y-yes. I do." Indar shrank back to his former size, but the fangs remained. "You do love me, don't you, Ozzi? You understand me. I'm sorry. I —"

"I don't love you. You're sick. But your sickness played into what I wanted to accomplish. It was so easy to manipulate you, Indar. So — very — easy."

Indar's eyes blazed with confusion. "You don't love me?"

Ozzi was ready with the barb that would draw the most blood and send Indar over the edge. "You're nothing more than a psychotic, small-balled freak."

It had the same blood-draining effect as when Jayden had used it. Indar screamed, the sound curdling with bitterness.

Ozzi shifted back to his dragon form and launched toward the traitor. He covered the long hall in seconds, tackling his prey. Dust sprayed into the air as they slid from the force of the impact.

Pain knifed into his side as he felt Indar's new fangs. Ozzi wrapped the end of his tail around Indar's neck and threw the body against the nearest wall. Damien scattered away from the spot.

Indar picked himself off the floor and stretched his arms and legs, which cracked as he realigned them. Taking an offensive move, he lunged back toward Ozzi.

Ozzi covered Indar with a blast of flame that set his lab coat on fire.

Indar screamed, his voice shrill from the pain. Quickly, he shook the coat off his body, but withdrew something out of an inner pocket. A syringe with a long, thick needle.

Ozzi spread a swath of flame to keep Indar away, but the lunatic leaped through the flames and landed on Ozzi's back. Before he could flick the mad doctor off with his tail, Indar sank the needle deep and depressed the plunger.

It was Ozzi's turn to scream as cold fire spread through his body. In a moment of euphoria, he mused about how it felt — the Rage. He briefly laughed at the irony before his body shifted in a painful transformation. It felt like he had no skin and every nerve ending amplified the pain. Again and again, his body shifted back and forth. Inside, a molten fire grew. He felt as if every organ was melting — as if he was boiling from the inside out.

He saw Indar move in closer, his eyes greedy with anticipation. With his eyes half closed and his chest panting in short rasps, he seemed almost orgasmic from excitement.

Ozzi refused to let that sick bastard escape unscathed. As he shifted once more into his dragon form, he exhaled all of the breath left in his lungs. The massive fireball engulfed the traitor, sizzling his skin.

The smell of charred flesh filled the air.

Damien slithered closer. Their hot breath fanned across Ozzi's skin. He knew they had waited long enough to feed. Several of the creatures tentatively sank their teeth into his legs. His body rocked as they tugged at the flesh.

Pain muddled his mind. He felt teeth everywhere now — sinking, ripping, tugging. Ozzi watched Indar, next to him on the cold floor, writhing and panting from excruciating pain.

Ozzi smiled in victory as his astral spirit slipped away into the deep, dark netherworld.

* * *

Jayden slipped on a mildewed rug when Seth pivoted suddenly to pull her down another hallway. "What is it with you people and hallways? Ever heard of open floor plans?"

They halted in a long room already filled with damien. Eerie rays of light angled in through large windows along one wall. Outside, white-capped mountains looked like teeth piercing the dark orange haze of the Underworld sky. The air was heavy with the smell of blood and burned flesh. In the middle of the room, damien fought for turns gorging on a mound of fresh meat.

Jayden gagged as she realized whom they fed on. She turned into Seth's shoulder, burying her nose in his shirt. She'd hated Ozzi, but he *was* Seth's brother.

More damien surged through the doorway behind them. They were trapped. She looked up into

Seth's face, but he didn't seem concerned about the damien at all. He just looked at his brother's corpse and shook his head.

"I'm sorry." Jayden barely gritted it out between clenched teeth as damien claws wrapped around her arms and legs.

"There is no escape from here, Jayden. We must face Apophis." Seth spoke to the damien in their language. He allowed the creatures to take his sword and remove the waist bag. But when they tried to grab and lift him off the ground, his eyes hardened into emerald crystals and he bared his long fangs at them. *"Nekelmu! Eli baltuti ima'idu mituti."*

Even Jayden took a step backward along with the damien. Seth radiated angry black energy. She'd once thought of him as being too dark to be divine. Now she wondered if maybe her idea of divinity was too tame.

As he turned to her, his eyes returned to their normal softness and color.

She put her hand back into his and they followed the damien from the room. "What did you say to them?"

A grin widened briefly across his face, and the dimple appeared. "An ancient warning. I told them to look upon my evil eye and know that I would leave more dead than alive."

She noted the body length of open space the damien maintained around Seth. "I'd say it worked."

The dimple faded and Jayden followed his intent gaze toward a small metal cage. A damien opened one end of the rectangular box and motioned for her to enter it. *"Quppo. Quppo."*

She climbed into it and felt Seth settle in behind her. As the door clicked shut, she heard the sound of a heavy chain being cranked. Then, the metal box lifted off of the ground. It lurched with each clank of the chain as it slowly ascended. Eventually, it settled about five yards up in the air.

Seth twisted around as if assessing their surroundings. "Too small for me to shift into my dragon form and too far away from a wall you could climb. Tell me he didn't know we were coming." Sighing, he leaned back and closed his eyes.

The damien seemed to leave the room. Even the dark shadows felt empty. How long would they be left suspended in this dark room?

"I realized too late that it was a trap. I would have warned you to stay away."

The dimple returned. "I would have come for you anyway."

Jayden crawled over to his side of the cage and tucked herself under his arm. Pressing her ear to his chest, she listened to the strong beat of his heart.

"Your eyes — they turned into bright crystals. I thought you had no powers here." Her breath misted in front of her face, alerting her to the severe drop in temperature.

"That wasn't power. That was physiology."

She sat up, curious as to why she hadn't thought about it before. "What about *my* new physiology? My body heals quickly, and I can communicate with you telepathically. What else can I do when we're not down here?"

"Time will reveal all the secrets in your blood." He cupped her face, and then pulled the cloak tighter over her bare legs.

"Will I transform into — something?"

He laughed as he shook his head. "Not all full-blooded Anunnaki shape shift. Many have only partial transformations. But I can teach you how to focus your mind and bend the energy around you."

"Did *she* have any skills? Was she..."

"Nefertiti?"

Jayden nodded. She felt a bit silly for avoiding his eyes, but ancient history was still history. There was a part of him that wasn't hers.

"No. She was all human, and she was every bit as fearless as you." His eyes turned vague and he seemed lost in a memory. "Chariot racing was the extreme sport in her time. She would take every opportunity to race across the plateau."

Jayden could almost picture the Egyptian queen flying across the desert, soaking in the feeling of freedom. "She does sound a bit like me."

"She also felt trapped. Trapped between doing what the priests wanted her to do and doing what was right for her people."

"I'm so sorry about what happened to her." Her teeth clacked. The chill air was seeping into her bones now. She snuggled deeper against his body, which felt very warm.

In the silence, she could hear her own heartbeat. It slowed and matched the pulse of blood through his.

Though his heartbeat was strong, his voice was not. It trembled with a guilt that must have festered inside him for thousands of years. "I wasn't there. I didn't protect her."

She knew better than to try to placate him with the usual it's-not-your-fault response. He wasn't really listening anyway. He sounded like he was purging. She knew from recent experience.

Thoughts of the ancient human queen led her to wonder about the Anunnaki queen. "How did your old queen die? Did Apophis kill her?"

"I don't really know. Some say Apophis killed her. Others said she had the Rage. And the wildest rumor said she was murdered by the *div'e sapid*, the white demon."

"Who's the white demon?"

"He was just a bedtime story to frighten little Anunnaki children into behaving."

"Really?" Jayden loved a good bedtime story. Her grandmother had so many that she'd rarely told the same one twice. "You have your own bogey man? Seriously, tell me the story."

"The White Demon of Mazandaran was said to be the only Anunnaki who gave his astral spirit to Apophis in exchange for revenge."

"Revenge for what?"

"Well, that's where mothers and fathers get creative in their storytelling. But there is one detail that never seems to change — that the demon's astral spirit resides in a little box. And if opened, it will release an evil plague that will blind all men."

"Just the m-men?" Although Seth's body was warm, hers began to shake with the first tremors of hypothermia. Yawning, she conjured up an image of a warm bivouac.

"Well, I'm sure that's up for interpretation. Is it literal or metaphorical, who knows?"

"I think he w-wanted revenge on a man, and probably over a w-woman. It s-sounds a bit like Pandora's box." Her blood felt thick in her veins, and her heart slowed its beat.

"Stories never die. They just evolve through many cultures and thousands of years."

"The queen has been d-dead and Apophis has been trapped for thousands of years. B-but you have a new queen n-now. Energy is in balance." She struggled to get the words from her brain to her mouth. "What does that do to Apophis?"

She sighed as Seth tightened his arms around her, drawing him into his warmth. But *his* body felt cooler now.

"Nothing, while he's imprisoned. But should the prophecy begin — should he escape his prison — her energy may be the only thing that keeps his full power confined to the Underworld."

Her shivers ceased, but it didn't feel like good news because she couldn't feel her legs. "Then *she* will be his main target."

"Y-yes." His jaw shivered against her cheek.

"It really sucks to be queen, doesn't it?"

She knew she shouldn't go to sleep right now, but her lids were too heavy to lift. Just a few moments of rest couldn't hurt.

* * *

Slowly, Jayden lifted one eyelid and then the other. Her head still lay on Seth's chest, but she felt no warmth. More frightening, she heard no thump-thumps of his heart.

She pushed herself up and a thin layer of ice cracked around them. She felt and looked like a Popsicle. A sparkly frosting of ice covered them both all the way down to their feet. It dusted the bars of the cage like dew on a spider's web.

Yet, the room didn't feel as cold as it had before. *Before?* How long ago was that?

"Seth?" She pushed at his body, rocking it with enough force to wake him up. "Come on. Wake up!"

Physiology, he'd said. Could his body be in a

state of hibernation? Jayden tried to find a pulse in his wrist and was rewarded with a slight flutter against her fingertips. His blood needed encouragement. She brushed the ice away from their bodies and moved to the opposite side of the cage. One limb at a time, she massaged warmth back into his muscles.

She worked her way up his body until his skin had returned to his natural olive color. As she traced the tattooed patterns across his arms, the ink began to shift. The watery image shimmered like sunlight glinting off of the ocean's surface. She trailed her fingers across it, and the pattern followed like a wake.

"If you keep that up, I won't be able to keep the beast inside. And we're cramped enough as it is."

Jayden squealed and threw herself into his arms. "Don't you ever scare me like that again."

"Like what?"

"When I woke up, we were covered in ice and you had no heartbeat."

"Apophis' version of cryogenic sleep."

"For how long?"

"Right now, I couldn't say. We might have slept for five minutes, five hours, or five days."

"Oh, right. I forgot. Time has little meaning here."

"Exactly."

Her next words merged into a scream as the cage suddenly dropped downward. The chains clacked into alignment, and the cage continued to descend at a much more agreeable pace. Metal scraped across stone as it came to rest on the ground.

The cage door swung open without visible assistance.

After they crawled out, they both spent a few

moments stretching tight muscles and cracking stiff joints.

"This way." Seth held a hand out toward a large oak door on the far wall.

"Where are we going?"

"The throne room. It's time to face Apophis."

Fear rooted her feet to the ground. Her legs refused to move, and her throat tightened. She'd been suspended in mid-air in a cage, and yet she hadn't felt the fear of being trapped. But the idea of facing Apophis — walking willingly into the presence of the dark overlord — felt worse than walking into the mental hospital.

Why was she thinking about that now? Why was her throat clogging up and her breath wheezing from her lungs?

Seth wrapped his arms around her and buried his nose into her hair. He whispered, "It's going to be okay."

Jayden hesitated, but finally nodded although her mind overflowed with doubts.

Her legs carried her, but they trembled all the way. It was an emotion she'd been taught to control. Fear hadn't held her back when she'd climbed up onto the roof of her home for the first time when she was seven. Fear hadn't held her back when she'd jumped off of mountains with little more than a square of fabric. Fear hadn't held her back when she'd encountered dragons and demons.

But as it seeped through her body now, it spread like a poison through her veins. She desperately needed adrenaline. She inhaled and exhaled deep breaths, but the fear was too powerful, dampening the effect. Confidence eluded her.

Then, she remembered the experience with

Apophis in the ceremonial pool, when his spirit had entered her body and played with her emotions. Was he doing that again now? Plucking at her fear like a bowstring?

As they approached the door, it swung toward them. No squeal from the hinges, but dust flew through the air in a shower of gray.

The throne room wasn't what she might have expected. There was no majesty to the room. No colorful rugs. No detailed wall reliefs. No stained glass windows.

Her feet trod on bare granite floors. Massive columns rose up into the shadows of the ceiling as if to hold the mountain at bay. Strange words shouted at her from the walls, haphazardly scratched into the plaster like alien graffiti. She couldn't read them, but the messages felt vengeful.

High on the back wall, something glittered. A golden, rectangular box sat inside a niche. From about twenty yards away, Jayden couldn't see the intricate details, but she could see the Egyptian goddess figures with their wings fanned protectively across the lid.

A gauzy mist shimmered, enclosing half of the room within its golden veil of light. It formed a pyramid with the golden box at its apex. A granite throne sat in the middle of it. Nothing fancy. No adornments of any kind. Simply a large, square-cut hunk of stone with the dark lord sitting in it.

He stood, but she knew the gesture was not welcoming. Intimidation seemed to be more his style. And was intimidating. Her eyes were barely level with his waist.

In a way, Apophis reminded her of fantasy paintings of the Devil. His skin was a dark reddish brown, and it rippled across his bare chest. A thick tail curled around his feet. He wore only a black Egyptian-style kilt and a set of golden handcuffs. Two large fangs descended from his upper jaw, and his nails formed long, black talons. He was a massive version of a damien alpha.

"Welcome, Jayden." Apophis' red irises dilated with anticipation. "Seth, did you enjoy your sleep?"

"Refreshing. But I thought you were impatient to see me again."

The dark overlord laughed, the sound vibrating Jayden's bones. "I wanted some time to have your things examined." He pointed to her waist bag and Seth's sword, which lay on the floor just outside the veil.

"Of course. I know how you hate surprises." Seth's voice lowered to something more sarcastic. "Especially after the last time."

CHAPTER EIGHTEEN

"Don't try to bait me, boy."

Seth was only a few thousand years younger than Apophis, but now wasn't the time to point that out. His time would be better spent in building a mental fortress around his mind to keep Apophis out of it. For emphasis, Seth plastered a mental *fuck you* sign on the gate.

"You can't manipulate me like you did your brother."

"There is no need to manipulate you — now." Seth moved away from Jayden to collect the bag and sword. Nobody jumped out of the shadows to stop him. That wasn't necessarily a good thing. More likely this was Apophis' way of toying with them — letting them think they had a chance to fight their way out. Seth swallowed a grin. Apophis was too confident of a victory. Ego was always a good weakness to exploit.

"What do you mean *now*?"

"*Now* that I've confirmed the bonds of your prison are as strong as the day I put you in them."

Apophis slammed his fists against the golden mist, which vibrated from the impact.

Jayden's body flinched and her gaze lowered to the ground.

An electrical charge arched from the veil to the wrist cuffs. Apophis' voice was tight, clenched from holding back the pain inflicted by the cuffs. "I will be free soon. You know it."

Seth unzipped the bag and slowly released a long breath. The mirror was still there, nestled in between Ushum's leftover nuts and berries from last night. His plan was working. Anyone looking through the bag would only think of its contents as basic supplies. "No, there is still time to prevent the prophecy."

"You can't stop it, Seth. The network has already been established. Your brother had a brilliant plan. A world-wide drug ring — the perfect network to enslave the human species with the perfect drug. Unfortunately for Ozzi, he didn't include me in his plans."

"He was smart enough not to trust you."

"He wasn't smart enough to see betrayal. Indar solved the reproductive issues a long time ago, and now I have my army. A massive army, and they are far stronger than even Ozzi could have anticipated."

As if on cue, damien streamed into the room and filled the shadows.

"But they are an army without a battlefield." Seth tested his sword with a few wide swings on either side of his body. One damien moved forward, clicking his claws. Seth ignored the challenge, but kept part of his senses trained on the creature.

Beyond the organic smell of the damien, something new had entered the room. Swiveling around, Seth tried to find the source of the burnt smell. His eyes paused over Jayden.

Under the cloak, her shoulders sloped forward and her arms were crossed over her chest. She would not meet his eyes.

Indar stepped into view beside her, holding the tip of his curved blade against her throat. Half of the skin on his body was wrinkled with black scorch marks. Ozzi had left his mark on the traitor. He had probably intended to kill Indar, but the freak doctor seemed to have many lives like a cat. But he would suffer great pain now through all of his lives. Third-degree burns were the one injury that Anunnaki skin could not heal. Too much cellular destruction to repair.

"Just like your brother. No imagination." Even Indar's voice sounded burnt as it crackled instead of his usual rasp.

"What should I be imagining?"

Indar wore Ozzi's oracle ring, twisting it around and around his finger. "Your vision is clouded by what you think you know as fact. True vision is seeing beyond what we know. We don't need to bring the damien to the Earth. We will bring the Earth to the Underworld, and then the damien army will spread across the planet like a global plague. The new Black Death."

"You can't merge dimensions. The astral plane holds them apart."

"When the shadow walkers brought me here, they showed me the weakness of the astral plane," Indar rasped excitedly.

"There is no weakness." Seth struggled to visualize their plan. There was no way of eliminating the astral plane, unless... "You create a vacuum. But how is that possible?"

"Dimensions?" Jayden's voice sounded soft and thin. He almost didn't recognize that she had spoken at all.

Seth continued to put the pieces together aloud. "Redistribution of energy. Like two bubbles bumping into each other and merging into a bigger bubble."

"Bubbles burst." Jayden giggled like a child and her finger pointed into the air, poking imaginary bubbles.

"Good point." *What the hell is going on with her?*

Suddenly, she straightened and her voice deepened to its normal tone. "What would happen to the Earth?"

"It would cease to exist." Indar licked his lips, wincing with pain when his tongue slid over a raw blister. "Like an instant portal, the humans would find themselves in our world. Eternal slaves to the Great Master."

Jayden shook her head as if trying to clear it. "We can't let that happen."

"We can't let that happen." Apophis imitated Jayden's shocked tone. Then he jeered at Seth. "Human devotion. So misplaced. I bet that you haven't told her the full truth yet?"

Seth ignored the jibe. He had to figure out how they intended to eliminate the plane.

"Told me what?" The strange wobble in her voice returned.

"Girl, I feel your contempt for me. You hate me for being a slave lord. Ironic, since you are in love with the very first slave master to step foot on your planet."

"No." Her blonde hair shimmered around her neck as she shook her head.

The dark lord moved to the side of the prison closest to her. "No? Ask him his name. His astral name." His lips lifted in a coy smile.

"What is your name?"

Seth watched Jayden's aura burn red with frustration — and fear. Why so much fear in her? She'd already been through so much, and yet...

He set aside the mental analysis of the dimension issue. The puzzle had distracted him from recognizing Jayden's suffering. "Ea. Seth Ea'nki."

Silence lay like a suffocating blanket as Jayden rocked back and forth, confused.

Indar gleefully filled her in."Ea, as in Earth. Lord of the Earth. He named the planet after his astral spirit. That's how highly he thought of himself."

Seth probed deeply into her beautiful blue eyes, which now held a dark ocean of pain. He'd been a fool to take his focus off her. She'd had the same look on her face in the ceremonial pool when the dark lord's spirit had probed into hers. Apophis was inside her again, amping up her fears and feeding off them. *You know me.*

Do I? Her telepathic voice pitched high like a child filled with fear and confusion.

For a moment, he feared that his plan would fail. He'd come to the Underworld to save Jayden, but he'd learned that far more was at stake. Apophis planned to collapse the astral plane and bring the two dimensions together. And there was no way to reach the new queen from here.

Seth mentally shook himself. His plan would work. He and Jayden would escape back to the Earth dimension.

He hadn't consciously kept his strategy from her, but now he was thankful that he'd not shared it with her. Apophis wasn't a mind reader, but he gained energy from fear. As he fed on the dark emotions, he could pick up on the thoughts attached to those fears. Jayden hadn't yet learned to build a protective wall around her mind. Had she known the details, she could have unwittingly alerted him to Seth's plan.

Destiny had so far worked in his favor, but for how much longer? The next step was now much harder. How was he going to convince Jayden to give herself up to Apophis — to give up her freedom? He'd counted on her love to make the hardest choice of her life — to go against her nature. But would she, now that doubt had crept into her mind?

How could he challenge that?

* * *

Jayden?

She heard a familiar voice inside her mind, but her brain felt too heavy to think straight. It was like her thoughts were covered in thick honey. She licked her lips, suddenly dying for a spoonful of honey. It sounded delicious.

Jayden?

No, it wasn't her thoughts that sounded so sweet. It was his voice. Sinfully sweet. Dangerous. *No, go away. I'm not supposed to talk to strangers.*

Can't do that. I have to stay.

Why?

Because I promised you I would never leave you.

I'm scared.

What are you scared of?

The straps. The needles. The doctor — he likes to peek under my hospital gown when he thinks I'm asleep.

Did you tell your father?

He doesn't believe me. He thinks I'm broken.

I don't think you're broken.

You don't? Why?

You are the most fearless woman I have ever known, and I love you.

Why do you love me?

Because you taught me how to live again.

Images fanned across her mind like a scrapbook ripped apart. A scrapbook of her childhood. But she wasn't a child. She was a woman now, and she was in love with a man named Seth. The man who'd healed her, who'd died for her, and who'd followed her to Hell to rescue her.

How long had they been standing there? Her last clear memory was her first view of Apophis. From there, her memories were as sheer as the mist that surrounded the overlord's prison. Words scattered across her mind like the alien graffiti across the walls.

She'd love a recap, but now was obviously not the time. She could hear the shuffle of many damien in the room, and worse yet — she could feel Indar's presence beside her. His body was horribly burned, and his charred clothes hung in tatters around him. His eyes burned with pure hatred.

"Apophis will take your astral spirit now." Indar prodded her hip with the tip of his dagger. He leaned into her ear and whispered. "He has promised your body to me to do with as I wish."

She shrank away from the freak's tongue, which flicked suggestively near her cheek. *Seth, help me. You have a plan, right?*

Yes. Do exactly as he says. Give yourself to Apophis.

What? How could he possibly ask her to give up her freedom? She looked at Apophis, whose smiled curved with wicked anticipation. How could she willingly submit to him as her eternal master?

You have to trust me.

The dark lord lunged toward the veil nearest Seth. "Stop! I feel your interference."

Indar's blade against her side kept her from

rushing to Seth's defense as damien attacked him from all sides. They buried their claws in his legs. Light glimmered from his broadsword as he it whipped through the air in a wide arc. The wicked edge of the blade sliced easily through damien bodies.

Seth fought valiantly, but the sheer number of damien finally weighed him down to the ground. The creatures released him and moved back into the shadows. Blood dripped from many wounds, joining together in a red pool on the floor. He lifted his body up until he sat back on his heels. Seth's body heaved as he took in lungfuls of air, but his eyes blazed with relentless determination.

And that was all Jayden needed to see. He would never leave her. He'd asked her to submit to Apophis, and somehow she knew that Seth wouldn't ask that of her without a good reason. She believed in him. She trusted him. She would give up her freedom — for Seth.

"Bring her to me now!" Apophis screamed, pacing along his prison walls.

Indar pushed her toward the misty veil, but her feet dug into the ground. She would go, but she wasn't going to make it easy.

Seth's telepathic voice calmed her nerves. *Jayden, you must repeat this phrase over and over again. Do not stop repeating it. Do you understand?*

Yes.

Siwah, me peta babka. Now, repeat it.

Siwah, me peta babka.

No, say it aloud.

"*Siwah, me peta babka.*" Jayden whispered it in the tone she'd heard Seth use when speaking in his ancient language. She repeated the phrase as Indar shoved her toward the prison veil. As she reached for it with her hands, the golden mist coated her skin. It was so cold. She shivered as memories of hospitals surged forward in her mind.

She held strong against the fear and continued repeating the phrase a little louder.

Apophis licked his lips, his anticipation of new astral energy obvious. But his grin faded a bit. "You are repeating something. What is it?"

The veil turned out to be much thicker than it looked from the outside. It was a narrow four-foot wide space tinted with a yellow gold mist. Apophis rushed to the veil wall in front of Jayden's path. He held his hands ready to grab her when she emerged on his side.

She stared into the dark lord's angry face and felt the confidence-boosting swell of adrenaline course through her body. She put on her most daring face, exited on his side of the veil, and answered him. "*Siwah, me peta babka.*"

Keep going, Jayden. You are asking your oracle to open up your gate.

Jayden wasn't sure what the gate was, but she knew she wanted it open. She screamed the phrase at Apophis.

"What oracle?" He grabbed her arms and pulled her close to his face. Her gaze locked onto his large fangs. She closed her lips as she watched a new wicked pair of teeth slide upward from his lower jaw.

"This one." All eyes swiveled silently toward Seth. He unzipped the waist bag, withdrew a very old-looking mirror, and smashed it against the hilt of his sword.

The shattered pieces froze in midair. A bright light burned in the center of it, drawing in and fusing all of the pieces into a ball of white glowing mist. As the glow settled onto the floor and ebbed away, Ushum sat in its place. He cradled the aquamarine stone gently in his precious little hands. Her oracle.

Boldly, she screamed the phrase once more in Apophis' face. "*Siwah, me peta babka!*"

Light swirled around her body and hot energy burned across her skin.

"No!" Apophis squeezed her shoulders tighter. "Your spirit is mine. Give it to me!"

A thin blue arc of energy leapt high into the air above Jayden. It spun around and around until it looked like a ball of glowing yarn.

Apophis shook her body but spoke to her astral spirit. "Stop. Come to me! You must obey me."

The blue light shuddered, as if fighting against a great force. Slowly it sank toward the dark lord's outstretched hand.

Movement outside the veil drew Jayden's attention. Calmly, Seth picked up Ushum and accepted the oracle stone. He held it out toward the golden mist.

Energy swirled to life inside the stone, spinning and flickering wildly as if generating a great power. White light pulsed through the room, and the damien slithered deeper into the shadows to get away from it. A single eerie note rang from the oracle like a siren's call.

Jayden's astral spirit paused its descent, hovered for just a moment, and then speared through the veil.

"No, no, no, no, NO!" Apophis roared furiously, but he held onto Jayden's body like a war prize, taunting Seth with it. "She's still mine."

Seth just smiled back.

Her astral spirit was safe, but she was still trapped. Why was he so happy to have her chained to the dark lord?

As her spirit merged with the oracle, the lights burned brighter until the stone was a ball of pure white energy. It pulsed, sending vibrations through the room like waves on the ocean.

Indar screamed in pain, holding his ears. He tried to run away, but Seth threw his sword, impaling the freak to the wall.

The pulse of energy outside the veil quickened until power shimmered everywhere. On impulse, Jayden reached toward her oracle – and noticed her arm was fading.

"Seth, what's happening to me?" She could hear the terror in her voice. She didn't want to disappear. She wanted to live.

"No, you can't have her. You can't win this time!" Apophis lost his grip on Jayden as her body lost substance. She could see his thick arms swooping through the air where her stomach used to be.

With a loud crackle, the oracle shattered into a cloud of tiny energy sparkles like the ones that trailed her fingers in water. It was the most beautiful thing she'd ever seen. *Can I touch it?*

Seth motioned for her. "Yes, Jayden. You can touch it."

She slipped away from Apophis' side and ran through the veil. She could hear the overlord pounding on his prison walls, but he no longer held any power over her. She felt free, and yet she felt incomplete — until she held her faded hands inside the glittering cloud.

Ushum chattered excitedly, but Seth restrained the little damien. "She'll be all right. Patience."

"I can hear her." Jayden felt like a child on Christmas morning. "My spirit. Her name is Enir."

"It means *the shining one.*"

"She's beautiful."

"She's you. Let her in, Jayden."

Like being possessed? Panic spread like acid through her mind. The fear might have ruined everything, but then she heard Apophis chuckling gleefully from inside his prison. She knew that the dark lord was trying to trick her. Jayden would have no more of him. She glared at both Apophis and Indar, saluting them both with her middle fingers. "Stay in hell, you freaks!"

Taking two deep breaths, she stepped into the energy cloud. At first, warmth swelled around her like a whirlpool. Then, her skin burned as millions of energy shards knifed into her body at once. She screamed and collapsed to her hands and knees.

The light in the room faded back to only that of the golden veil and the ark it descended from. She heard only the sound of her own breath as she panted for air.

Ushum appeared under her, his yellow eyes looking up into hers with joy.

Jayden scooped him into her arms and hugged him tight. "I missed you." She nearly crushed him, but he didn't seem to mind. He made a new home for himself in the roomy hood of her cloak.

She was alive, and she'd never felt such a rush before. It was all because of him. She stood and faced the man who'd never given up on her. He'd saved her, trusted her, and loved her.

Jayden rushed into his open arms and pressed every inch of her body against his. Pulling his lips down to hers, she commanded her energy to surround his, staking her absolute claim over man and beast.

CHAPTER NINETEEN

Seth smiled against her lips. Her aura enveloped his with such possessive energy that even his beast purred with fierce pride.

Callous laughter came from Indar, whose ruined body still hung from the wall. "You are still stuck in the Underworld, Seth. There are more than thirty thousand damien crawling around the Valley. You cannot escape."

Seth stood in front of the traitor. The sword had impaled the doctor through his right shoulder, leaving the arm to dangle uselessly. Seth removed the oracle ring from Indar's finger and stared into his pain-filled brown eyes. "It hurts, doesn't it? The pain from a dragon's fire."

Indar shrieked and collapsed to the ground as Seth wrenched the sword from the wall. Blood and tears pooled around his knees. In a tight, raspy voice, he swore, "I will have vengeance on you, Seth — and on your woman. Someday." He slid through a parted section along the wall before Seth could grab him.

"Seth?"

He heard a quiver in Jayden's voice again and swiveled back to her, praying that Apophis hadn't found a way into her again.

She held her palms toward him. "What are they?"

He moved forward to inspect the strange new markings on her hands. He traced a finger around the beautiful blue ink patterns on her skin. He gave her a big smile to help her relax. "It is the oracle."

"No. The oracle is a stone." She twirled around looking for it on the floor.

"The oracle is inside you now. This mark is the oracle's brand." He put her hands palm up and side-by-side so that they formed a cup. Each palm was inked with half of a circle. Joined, they formed a full one. "Remember when I said that you were like a key?"

She nodded.

"Now you *are* the oracle."

He cocked his ear toward a new buzzing sound. More damien were coming. Lots of them.

Seth swore they would not be their next meal. He made sure they had gathered everything they came with. "Jayden, it's time for your first lesson, and I'm sorry I don't have time to explain it better." He brought her hands together again to form the ink circle. "Focus. Close your eyes and search for the path of light. Find the path home. Lock onto it."

She was doing it. The evidence rose from her palm in a warm sphere of light energy.

Inside, he was screaming for her to hurry up. Damien slithered around them, closing in. He held his impatience in check. It would distract her. "That's it. Keep focusing."

"I think I found it."

"Great. Now, take us home."

"How?"

He could smell putrid breath around him. "Picture home. Now!"

The last thing Seth saw before the ground fell away from their feet and the world darkened around them was Apophis. The dark lord had collapsed back onto his lackluster throne, seething with hatred.

Seth couldn't hear what he said, but he read the movement of Apophis's lips. "I will kill you."

But not today! Thankfully not today, because he'd kept his promise. Now, he had a future with a beautiful, fearless woman. His mind swirled with images of what his life would be like with Jayden.

* * *

Jayden laughed at Seth's shocked expression. Her vision of home had brought them back to Ozzi's castle. This time it wasn't an accident or wayward oracle. She chose to return here.

With Ozzi and Indar's departure, the damien had trashed and pillaged the place like little gremlins. Claws had ripped and poked everything within sight. Curtains sagged across exploded cushions. Paintings sported holes and slices. Candles looked chewed up and spit out. Jagged fragments of light bulbs and vases lay across the floor like puzzle pieces waiting to be put together again.

"What the hell happened here?" Seth moved to the window to see where the sun was in the sky. The direction of the shadows indicated it was late morning.

Ushum caught on quickly. He leapt from Jayden's hood and sped off in the direction of Ozzi's office. He came back in moments with his little teeth buried in a fat cigar. Settling on the back of a chair, he stroked his prize adoringly. He alternated between nibbling and sniffing.

"Seth, how long do you think we've been gone?"

He took her hand and pulled her to the front door. "Let's go find out."

They entered the underground complex cautiously in case any damien mistook them as an enemy. They found Zarick in the labs, and he looked genuinely happy to see them. He confirmed that they'd been gone for almost two weeks.

Jayden knew a lot could happen in two weeks. She addressed Zarick, relying on Seth to translate for her. "Where are the others?"

"Life is same. They sleep now. Fish tonight." Zarick motioned toward the sea. "Humans come at night. They watch from out there."

Seth nodded. "It could be Ozzi's clients, trying to work up the nerve to come on the island and collect the omegas they paid for."

"What about the birth mothers?" They were Jayden's main reason for coming right back to the island. "Are they well?"

Zarick brought them through the wings that once held Ozzi's human surrogates. Only one had survived the strange illness Indar had mentioned. She still lay unconscious, dark rings around her eyes and sweat beading on her forehead.

"We did not know what to do. The omegas watched. Brought water. But this one suffers." Zarick smoothed his hands across her forehead.

Jayden admired how careful Zarick was not to scratch the woman with his claws.

Seth held his palms over her body and analyzed her vitals. "You did a fine job. She is doing well. Her body is in a protective sleep while it finishes her healing time."

The alpha released a long breath and nodded gratefully.

It took a full week to clean the mess the damien had made throughout the castle.

Jayden threw the last bag of trash onto the huge pile in the front room and flashed herself to the upstairs patio. She still giggled every time she arrived in the location she intended to. There were just so many wonderful possibilities with this new skill. Although some of them Seth would disapprove of.

Seth had his nose buried in another one of Indar's journals.

She removed her scarf and wrapped it around his neck as she slid onto his lap. "The house is clean. You know what that means?"

He let out a huge sigh. "It means you are ready to go jump off a huge cliff."

"It's not just any cliff, Seth. It's the Troll Wall. The last thing on my bucket list."

"But you are not dying, Jayden."

"Which is fabulous, but I have to finish the list." She looked at the stack of books on the table. She stopped counting at fourteen. "More of Indar's journals? What did you learn?"

"Everything except what really matters. I can't find any references to how Indar solved the reproductive issue. I have no idea what will happen to the damien here."

The sun was setting beyond the western side of the island, casting long shadows across the patio.

"I am impressed with their capacity to learn." Jayden poured them each a glass of spicy red wine. "They are picking up English very quickly."

"My dear, they do have Anunnaki in their blood." His tone was deliberately teasing.

"You know I hate it when you act superior like that."

He drew her back onto his lap and captured her lips in a deep kiss. "Climb in bed with me right now and you can show me who's superior."

"Later." But she licked her lips suggestively.

His green eyes dilated. "Gods, you can tease."

She tucked her head against his chest and listened to his heartbeat. For the thousandth time she sent a mental thank-you to her grandmother, whose wish to have her ashes spread across the pyramids ultimately brought Jayden and Seth together. Jayden knew now that her grandmother had been one of the remaining Anunnaki left on Earth.

Jayden thought of Seth's earlier description of his kind — leaderless nomads. It had been easy for Anunnaki to blend in with the human world. The damien would not be able to do that. "We have to help them, Seth. I believe the oracle brought us here to help them."

"I agree."

She loved how the colors of the setting sun reflected in Seth's eyes.

He smiled when he realized she was inspecting him so closely. "Are you suggesting that we live here on the island?"

She nodded. "If they adapt and outgrow this island, they could spread to several along this area that are uninhabited."

"But if they go beyond that the humans will find out and become very nervous about them." Seth swallowed the last of his wine. "I think we're going to need help."

A female voice interjected from behind them, and Jayden knew it wasn't one of the omegas. "Maybe we could help?"

* * *

Seth helped Jayden out of his lap, and together

they turned to greet their guest.

"Hello, Shaila." He suddenly felt at a loss for words. What did one say to someone he thought had died over three thousand years ago?

"Hello, Seth." Shaila's eyes travelled up and down his body. "Great goddess, you look thin."

He analyzed the new fashion of an ancient warrior goddess: black boots, pants and vest. "All leather. You never change."

Laughing, Shaila stepped forward with her hands out, and Seth drew her in for a hug. As their astral energies merged, he felt her genuine affection.

When they pulled apart, he realized that she wasn't alone. A lean but muscular bald man stood near her. His stance was protective, but the look in his hazel eyes was possessive. There was definitely something between Shaila and her bodyguard.

"They told me you were dead — that you died protecting Nefertiti." He didn't even try to hide the hint of bitterness in his voice. He'd learned through recent events that at least some of what he'd been told back then had been lies. Did he want to know which parts?

He was completely happy with his new life. Old wounds had no place in his heart.

Yet, as he looked into Shaila's green eyes, he clearly read her guilt and it put a large crack into the joy of their reunion.

Jayden didn't wait for introductions. "I'm Jayden. Are you the new queen?"

Shaila's features brightened too quickly. Oh yeah. She definitely had something to get off her chest.

"Yes. I am Shaila a'k'Hemet." She held up her hand to halt Jayden mid-bow. "Please do not do that."

Shaila's man intervened with a deep, confident voice. "She's not comfortable having people treat her like royalty. She says she hasn't earned it yet."

A hint of humor glimmered in the man's eyes. But there was something else about his them — something familiar. Seth's beast demanded to be released. It took supreme effort to keep him inside.

Shaila's eyes swiveled back to Seth and glowed with calming energy. He'd never seen that from her, but his beast settled. "There is so much to tell you, but you must keep your beast inside — for now."

"Meaning I can let him out later if I keep him on a short leash?"

"Something like that." Her eyes softened back to emerald green.

"Then let's get right to the point. Typically, people come with good news and bad news. I think I'll start with door number two, please."

The mysterious man leaned close to Shaila. "He means the bad news first, honey."

Shaila gave him a pointed look. "I understood that reference just fine." He backed off, but kept half a smile on his face.

The connection between the two clearly pointed to them being a couple. That piqued Seth's curiosity. He couldn't remember Shaila ever being in love. Maybe her news wasn't going to be so bad.

"Seth, we lied to you — back then."

He knew the time frame she meant. "Unless you were resurrected from the dead, it is clear that your death was a lie. I was also told that Nefertiti was killed in an uprising of her priests, but Ozzi admitted to killing her."

Shaila looked stunned with that information. "Ozzi? I too thought the priests..." She nibbled on her lower lip. "She was in so much danger."

"He also mentioned something about my..." He fought through a choking sensation. Strangely, his beast stirred again. "Something about my son."

Shaila stole a glance at the man beside her and then she looked down at her own feet. "That is the subject."

If he wasn't feeling so aggravated at the moment, he would be fascinated with her discomfort. So out of character for her. "Well, give it to me straight. What's the bad news about my son?"

"No, that is not the bad news. The bad news was about Nefertiti. More directly, about how I was not there to protect her. I am so sorry, Seth. I had promised you that I would look after her, but Nefertiti knew that Lilith was too determined to eliminate the child of the prophecy."

"I am aware of the prophecy."

Seth's beast grew more insistent. He wanted to inspect the man with Shaila. Why was he so focused on that man?

Jayden's hand settled on Seth's shoulder, and a wave of calming energy spread through his body. He wanted to stop her, but instead he soaked it in. "Seth, she said that Nefertiti was the bad news."

"Yes. I know."

"I think the good news is about your son."

Jayden, stay out of this.

Fine, but first take a damned long look at him. She nodded toward the man.

The ink on Seth's arms shimmered insistently. The beast, like Jayden, sensed something he couldn't quite connect with. "Shaila, what happened to my son?"

"Nefertiti knew that they would never stop

trying to kill your son. She gave him to me to hide and protect. Which I did for over three thousand sun cycles." Shaila's voice cracked.

The man stepped forward and stood just about eye-to-eye with Seth. They both had the same lean physical build. Up close, the man's eyes were the color of Egyptian sand.

"My name is Darius Alexander." He barely blinked, staring intently into Seth's eyes as if gauging his worth. "I've been told that you are my father."

The beast demanded and this time Seth set him free. Shifting quickly, he stretched to his full height and length, posturing dominantly.

Shaila stepped back, but her aura held no defensive or submissive energy. She was simply giving Seth space to inspect the man. Impressively, Darius held firmly to his place and refused to posture submissively. Or didn't know that he was supposed to.

Seth sniffed the air around Darius and took in every speck of information he could. He nuzzled closer and inhaled the man's scent. Thousands of years could not hide it. Nefertiti's essence was there. Faint, but enough to satisfy the beast.

Shifting back to his human form, Seth collapsed into his chair with his head in his hands. For a moment, he sent a silent thank you to the woman who'd given all she could to protect the men she loved.

"Why keep it from me?" He rubbed his face. "I blamed myself."

Shaila moved forward to kneel in front of him. Tears streamed down her face, and he knew that she shared in the pain of guilt. "It was so hard, but we could not tell you that she gave birth before she died."

He looked at the man his son had grown into. All those life moments missed. "I would have moved the heavens and every dimension of this planet to find you."

"That was why we kept it from you."

Seth knew the pain was clearly written across his face. He felt Jayden's lips against his temple and her warm hand on his cheek. He cupped his hand over hers and brought it to his lips. He drew strength from her.

"Your son was the child of the prophecy. His destiny lay far, far into the future. If you had kept him in the ancient world, this world — right now — would be lost to Apophis."

"There is still that chance, Shaila."

"True, but we have bought time to find and gather the *medjai* warriors."

Seth stood and drew Shaila up with him. He hugged her tight. "I don't feel like talking prophecies right now." He let her go and stood once more in front of Darius.

Darius rubbed the back of his head in a sudden, nervous gesture. "You look too young to be my father."

"You obviously didn't inherit my wonderful head of hair." Seth felt a big stupid grin spread across his face. He threw his arms around his son for the first time, and when Darius returned the hug, all was very right with his world.

EPILOGUE

Seth tucked a satiny comforter tightly around Jayden's naked body. Yawning, she snuggled deeper into the newly stuffed mattress. It was only their second time away from the island in a month. She refused the idea of staying anywhere else but his cave under the Sphinx.

He kissed her lips and nearly climbed back in. "I won't be long."

"Come back soon." She rolled over and disappeared under the blanket.

He flashed away from the cave and appeared on the top floor of the cafe. Shaila had already cleared the patio of other guests. They settled on either side of a table with a perfect view of the Great Pyramid. Looking into the broken face of the Sphinx, he found it hard to bring back the image of what it was like when it was first carved.

"Do you think we should ever tell the humans that the Sphinx was originally carved in Ozzi's image?" Seth always thought it ironic that his cavern was hidden below his brother's statue.

"That was so long ago, Seth." Shaila's lips curved in a knowing smile. "I remember that Ozzi hated it. He wanted to kill the entire crew of stone carvers. We had to relocate them for their safety."

A man silently brought a tray of food and Turkish coffee.

"You're really getting the hang of this modern

age." Seth pointed towards her leather outfit.

She grinned. "Fashion, yes. But I do not always understand their sense of humor. They have odd expressions."

"Shaila, you have to know that I remain bound to my commitment to protect the humans."

She shifted in her seat, as if hesitant to bring up something he likely didn't want to hear. "We may be facing a new threat beyond the war with Apophis. One that was not accounted for in the prophecy."

"What kind of threat?" Seth could think of no greater threat than Apophis' desire to dominate the human world.

"The *medjai* will fulfill their ancient pledge, but we may end up fighting against those we are sworn to protect."

"When we freed the humans, we suspected that one day they would forget." Seth looked down at the street below, crowded with humans. "We've been outsiders since the fall of the Roman Empire."

"Darius has been helping me find surviving Anunnaki, but it is a very slow process. I fear we may run out of time."

"I can help there. Ozzi had been tracking Anunnaki bloodlines around the world. His database will help us find them faster."

"Goddess, I needed to hear that good news." Shaila sat back against the colorful cushions of her seat. Her finger trailed around the rim of her coffee cup repeatedly. "The few I have found shared stories with me about humans who follow them. Just watching. The stories are too similar to be coincidence. These watchers sound organized. They must have a database too. A way of tracking us."

"You make them sound paranoid."

"They might be. Their fear of us may destroy our ability to protect them."

"*If* we end up at war with the humans, it won't be over fear. It will be a war over *star fire,* the drug that Ozzi was distributing through his damien prostitution ring. His associates are worldwide — men of power, men of money. Apophis will capitalize on it. I'm certain that Indar will continue to create more of the drug from the safety of the Underworld."

"Could it be part of Apophis' plan? Have the humans keep us occupied while he maneuvers a way out. We cannot possibly fight two wars at the same time."

"Apophis has a bigger plan, Shaila. Indar is working on a way to destroy the astral plane and merge the dimensions."

She leaned forward too quickly. Coffee dribbled down the side of her hand, but she didn't seem to notice. "Merge the dimensions? Is that even possible without destroying one or both?"

Seth shrugged. "It's the universe. Anything is possible."

"I am certain the shadow walkers are a key to how Apophis' power reaches into the astral plane and the Earth dimension. Everything has a weakness. If we can destroy them, we may weaken all of Apophis' plans."

"Thank you for saving my son." His voice faltered, but he didn't care.

"You are most welcome." A smile spread wide across Shaila's face, the kind that hinted of a longer story. "Darius is aggravating and wonderful at the same time."

"I know exactly what you mean." He chuckled, picturing his own interesting start with Jayden.

"Remember, you promised never to lie to me again."

"I will repeat my promise, if you want me to."

"This could be the beginning of a new age for the Anunnaki."

Her aura clouded with concern. "I fear for what lies in our destiny."

Seth knew her fears were justified. Apophis would target the queen and those she loved.

Shaila nodded toward the horizon. "I never grow tired of watching the pyramids as the sun sets. Even now, with their grandeur stripped away by time, they still glow."

"They do indeed." He pictured Jayden taking her leap of faith from the top of the Great Pyramid. If she hadn't been so bold, she would never have fallen into his cave. If she hadn't been so fearless, he might never have lived to meet his son.

Shaila smiled as if she knew where his thoughts had turned.

"He's definitely my son. He knows when he's found a good woman." He smiled back, kissed her on the forehead, and flashed away from the cafe.

As he slipped under the blanket, he curved around Jayden's body and nuzzled his lips against her neck. She'd saved his soul, and for that he would prove his love for her for eternity.

~ The End ~

ABOUT THE AUTHOR

Lynda Haviland is a USA Today Bestselling Author of paranormal fantasy romance. She is addicted to coffee, caramel, and ancient alien conspiracy theories. She will read anything about ancient Egyptian gods and goddesses, and she is constantly planning her next trip to Egypt. *Immortal Dominion* is the second novel in her debut series, *Age of Awakening*.

Visit her anytime online at **LyndaHaviland.com**

Photo courtesy of Kevin Kolczynski

ABOUT THE AUTHOR